D0090225

STILL WATERS

STILL WATERS

Nigel McCrery

Quercus

Quercus
21 Bloomsbury Square
London
WC1A 2NS

A CIP catalogue record for this book is available
from the British Library.

ISBN (HB) 1 84724 074 7
ISBN-13 978 1 84724 074 3
ISBN (TPB) 1 84724 075 5
ISBN-13 978 1 84724 075 0

10 9 8 7 6 5 4 3 2 1

Printed and bound in Great Britain
by Clays Ltd, St Ives plc.

For Nelly with all my love

ACKNOWLEDGEMENTS

With grateful thanks to: Andrew Lane, for help and assistance; John Catherall, for allowing me to borrow some of his physical characteristics; Robert Kirby, for brokering a deal so tirelessly; Nic Cheetham, for having faith in me; and the irrepressible Gillian Holmes, my long-suffering editor. Sylvia Clarke, Eve Wilson and Iris Cannon, who taught me in various ways how to write and, more importantly, how not to write.

PROLOGUE

'Granny, what are these?' shouted Kate.

Iris Poel sighed. The sun was a white-hot eye in the centre of a bright blue sky, staring at the back of her neck. Her head felt leaden, and it hurt when she moved. The prickling of sweat on her arms and back made her feel as if ants were crawling all over her skin.

'What are what, darling?' she said for the hundredth time that morning. Putting her secateurs down, she turned away from the rose bush that she was pruning and looked over to where her granddaughter was supposed to be playing with her brothers and sisters.

'These.' Kate was standing over by a shrub on the other side of the garden. It was covered in glossy leaves and small red berries. Kate was cradling a cluster of the berries in her hand.

'Leave those berries alone,' Iris said sharply. 'They're poisonous.'

'I know that, but what *is* it?' Kate repeated.

'It's called a daphne,' Iris snapped, feeling spikes of pain lance through her temples with each word. 'Now leave the berries alone and go back to your game.'

'That game is boring,' Kate proclaimed with the weariness that only a six-year-old child can manage. She turned away and ran across the garden to where Iris had set out a low table for the children, covered with a white cloth. An entire toy tea set was arranged on the table, along with plates of cakes and biscuits.

I

Nobody was sitting at the table. Three of them were kneeling on the grass playing with Kate's dolls. Two more were running around a small tree that Iris had planted in the middle of the garden the previous spring. The rest were probably in the house – Iris's daughter-in-law's house. Or rather, her son's house, but Frank was in Africa, fighting for his King and his country, and Judith went to work in a factory every day, making parts for aircraft. And Iris was left to look after the children. Every day. Every single day that God sent to try her.

Iris sighed, and turned back to the rose bush. There were dark splodges on a couple of the leaves. She snipped them off. It looked like blackspot, and there was no point taking chances.

'Are these blackberries?'

Iris jerked her head around. 'Kate, I thought you were supposed to be having a tea party with your friends?'

'That tea tastes funny,' Kate said. 'Are these blackberries, Granny?' She was closer to Iris now, gazing up at a yew tree that cast a little shade across the lawn.

'No, they're not. Leave them alone.' The pain in her head intensified. 'That tea, as you call it, is sarsaparilla. You *like* sarsaparilla.'

'I don't like *that* sarsaparilla.'

Iris's hand was shaking, holding the secateurs. She closed her eyes. She had spent all morning making those cakes and biscuits. She had put the best tablecloth on the table as well, just to make it look nice, and the girl was ruining it.

Iris looked over at the table, and the food that was going to waste. Wasps were crawling on the jam tarts.

Iris closed her eyes, but she could still feel the sun glaring down on her. The pounding in her head was making her sick. It felt as if something was coiling and uncoiling in her stomach. She couldn't keep still; her fingers were twitching and her head kept flicking left or right, like she had seen something out of the corner of her eye.

She took a deep breath, and opened her eyes again. The garden was too bright; the incandescently blazing sunshine made her eyes ache.

She reached out with the secateurs for another leaf that was showing signs of blackspot.

'Granny!' Kate yelled.

Iris's hand jerked, and the secateurs cut through the stem of the rose. The plant toppled into Iris's face. A thorn caught her cheek as she turned her head, catching the skin just below her eye and ripping a long graze.

The pain seemed to rip through her soul.

'You stupid child!' Iris shouted. Kate stepped backwards in shock. 'Look what you've done!'

Iris lashed out and caught Kate's shoulder with her hand, dragging her closer. 'Do you know how long I spent making those cakes, you ungrateful little bitch? I'll teach you to wander around the garden touching stuff you shouldn't when you ought to be having a tea party with your sisters and brothers.'

The words were spilling uncontrollably from her mouth like a stream of vomit, and she couldn't stop herself. She didn't know where it was all coming from. All of the boys and girls were staring solemnly at her. Her head was pounding, and the shimmering heat in the garden was making her disoriented and nauseous.

'You want to disobey me? I'll show you what happens when you disobey me.'

Before she knew what was happening, Iris had closed the secateurs on the thumb of Kate's right hand. The child screamed, eyes distended with horror. She tried to pull herself away, but Iris's grip was too strong.

The handles of the secateurs were held apart by a powerful spring, and Iris had to put all her effort into forcing them together. The blades sliced through Kate's thumb like they had through the rose stem. The thumb fell away. Bright blood spurted across the glossy green leaves.

3

The pitch of Kate's screams went up and up. Her eyes rolled back in her head and she started jerking.

Iris closed the secateurs on the girl's index finger, and brought the sharp blades together. The finger swung down, but a flap of skin still held it on to the palm. Iris cut again and the finger vanished.

The next three fingers were easier. Kate's hand looked so small when she had finished.

Iris turned around. The other children were rooted to the spot. Their gaze was fixed on Iris as if they couldn't believe what they had seen, and they were waiting to see how the trick had been done.

Iris straightened up and concentrated on the nearest girl. Her name was Madeline.

'Come here, Madeline,' she said calmly, although the inside of her head was a raging torrent of incoherent thoughts. 'Come here now, or I will come and get you ...'

CHAPTER ONE

The sky above the rooftops was a misty grey-blue, a wash of unbroken colour from one end of the street to the other. Hidden behind the half-cloud, the sun was just a brighter patch in an already bright sky. No shadows darkened the pavement or the road. Something about the diffuse light made the cars, houses and lamp posts seem as if they had been cut out and placed onto a perfect picture of the street, barely connected to reality, able to be repositioned at will.

The delicate, almost translucent quality of the sky put Violet in mind of the duck eggs she used to collect as a child: a colour so unusual, so textured, that it almost seemed like the product of a deliberate act, rather than the randomness of nature.

Now where had that thought come from? She remembered the duck eggs perfectly – the weight of them in her hand, heavier than chicken eggs, and she also recalled the way tiny scraps of feather would still be stuck to their shells – but she couldn't quite place when or where. The detail was there, but the background was absent.

She tucked the thought away. There were more important things to worry about today. She had a job to do.

As she toiled along the street from where she had parked her car, pushing her wheeled shopping bag ahead of her, she kept casting glances up into the sky. No aeroplanes, no helicopters – just a deep, translucent blue. For a moment the world was timeless. With a small effort she felt as if she could be six again, or sixteen, rather than sixty.

But the effort would have been too much. That's what

happened when you got old. Things that were easy were suddenly hard. Energy that had once seemed boundless was something to conserve in miserly fashion.

With relief she realised that she had arrived at the front door of number 26. She stopped for a moment to gather her breath. There was a chill in the air, but the long walk from where she had parked her car had left her feeling hot and flustered.

She glanced at the front of the house. The paint was cracked in a pattern of small scales across the top half of the door, where the sun caught it every morning. Scratches marred the surface around the keyhole. The letterbox had been repaired with sticky tape on more than one occasion. The bricks were a faded red, pitted with small holes and scabbed areas, and the mortar holding them together was powdery.

Her gaze wandered to the small front garden, barely large enough to accommodate the dustbin and a few tired geraniums in pots. Weeds had found their way through the paving slabs and around the circular metal cover that led down to the coal cellar. The bottom few bricks of the garden wall were half-hidden by dusty cobwebs and old snail shells layered one upon another like an outbreak of boils.

It really was time to move on.

The seaside, perhaps. She could do with some fresh air, and a change of scenery.

One of the geraniums was badly overgrown and dehydrated. A few of its leaves were brown and wilted, giving up their life so that the other leaves could soldier on. Violet reached into her shopping bag and removed the small pair of secateurs she always carried with her. Taking one of the dying leaves, dry and papery, in her hand, she snipped it off close to the stem, then repeated the pruning with the others. There, wasn't that better?

Making a mental note to bring a jug of water out later to moisten the soil, she pushed the shopping bag up to the front door and delved into her handbag for the key to the door.

Slotting it into the lock she forced the stiff mechanism round and pushed the door open.

Darkness, and the smell of old lavender and boiled vegetables reached out to embrace her.

'Dear – I'm back!' she called.

No answer. She moved into the house and shut the door behind her. 'Daisy? I said I'm back!'

The small hall was carpeted in linoleum patterned with small diamonds. Stairs to the left led up to the bathroom and the bedrooms, while the walls were papered in a floral pattern that looked almost as tired as the geraniums outside. A barometer hung opposite the stairs, massive and pendulous. According to the indicator there was a change ahead.

The house had an air of neglect, of something that was sagging into dust and decay. Violet could tell the first time she walked in that nobody visited any more. That nobody cared any more.

She pushed the shopping bag ahead of her, past the parlour and the dining room, and pushed open the door to the kitchen. Bordered by slide-door cupboards and melamine-covered work surfaces, it was more like a split-off section of the hall than a room in its own right. Tucked to one side by the cooker, just next to a china teapot, was the kitchen's sole concession to the modern age – a cordless electric kettle. A small refrigerator wheezed asthmatically in one corner, next to the door that led out into the conservatory. It gave the impression that it was about to fall over and die at any moment, but it had been working away for the nine months that she had been visiting the house, and for many years beforehand. It would almost certainly outlast Daisy Wilson.

Placing her handbag on the corner of the kitchen counter, she folded the handle of the shopping bag down and unzipped it. She hadn't picked up much shopping – the important items she had collected from her own flat that morning – but Daisy didn't seem to need much to keep going.

In her experience, older people could subsist perfectly well on cups of tea, slices of bread, boiled carrots and the occasional biscuit.

Slipping on a pair of thin cotton gloves that she always kept in her coat pocket, she unpacked the bag. Bread, butter, bleach, rubber gloves, tea towels and a caddy of tea leaves that rustled as she put it down on the counter.

She reached across, switched the kettle on at the mains and clicked the button down to boil the water. The initial *whoosh* settled down into a steady murmuring as the water heated up. She opened the top of the tea caddy and let the smell of the leaves drift up to her nose. She closed her eyes and mouth, and breathed in. Dry, slightly spicy, and overlaid with the delicate floral notes of the Christmas rose petals and leaves that had been mixed in with the Darjeeling. Perfect.

The fragrance was mesmerising. For a long moment, she wasn't in the kitchen at all. She was standing in her own garden – her private, secret garden, not the one belonging to the ground-floor flat she rented – breathing in the mixed scents of the foxgloves, the delphiniums and the corn cockles.

No. That thought needed to be tucked away as well. She had a job to do. Once today was over, she could relax for a while. Go away. Move away. By the sea. A change was as good as a rest, they said.

While the kettle was talking to itself she walked back into the hall and took her coat off. Before placing it on one of the hooks just behind the door – so reminiscent, she always thought, of a row of butchers' hooks waiting for the meat to be hung from them – she took a look around the hall, committing it to memory. The lino. The wallpaper. The stairs. The whole thing so rooted in the 1950s, when the street had been built to replace ones lost to Hitler's bombs, that it was almost possible to hear the laughing voices of *Children's Hour* drifting on a wave of static from the speaker of a bakelite radio set.

She shook herself. Stay in the present, Violet, she told herself. Stay focussed.

She pushed open the door of the parlour. The curtains were half-closed, and in the turquoise light of that strange sky the room could have been underwater. The fireplace dominated the room on one side: cold now, as it had been for some years, and flanked by two metal andirons. A massive bureau dominated the other side of the room: the marquetry almost invisible in the dim, aquatic light. Over in the window recess a television set stood mute.

Daisy was sitting in the armchair with the curved wings, grey hair still curled from her last visit to her hairdresser. Her eyes, nestled in puffy, criss-crossed flesh, were closed. She didn't seem to be breathing.

'Daisy?' Violet reached forward to shake her parchment hand. 'Daisy?'

Daisy jerked awake with a cry. She flinched away from Violet like a dog expecting to be struck.

'It's only me. I'm back from the shops.'

Daisy was still twisted in her chair. She gazed suspiciously up at Violet. Slowly the suspicion receded, and she smiled. 'I was only resting my eyes,' she muttered.

'You dropped off,' Violet said, moving across to the window, beside the television, and pushing the curtains open.

'I was thinking. Remembering.'

'I'm making a cup of tea.' Violet turned and smiled at Daisy. 'I was remembering too, walking up the road. Duck eggs. Do you remember duck eggs?'

Daisy laughed. 'I haven't had a duck egg in an age. Not since the War. Used to have them all the time, then. Blue, they were. Tasty as well.'

'They're coming back in the shops now,' Violet said. 'Speciality items, they're called. Did you want a cup of tea?'

'Speciality items,' Daisy said scornfully. 'That's supermarkets for you. Make you pay more for food that tastes the way food is meant to taste anyway. I remember when ordinary eggs weren't just eggs, they were Norfolk Greys, or German Longshanks, or Dorkings. All different sizes and colours. Some of them with freckles and some plain, some rough and some smooth. Not like now. They're all plain and brown and the same size now.' She suddenly caught up with what Violet had been saying. 'Tea would be nice, ta.'

Violet went out into the kitchen. The kettle had just boiled, and the air was tropical. She poured a little water into the teapot and sloshed it around, warming the china, then she poured it out in the sink and scooped two spoonfuls of tea from the caddy into the pot. She poured water from the kettle carefully, watching it froth as it hit the leaves. The smell wafted up to her nose again: that wonderful aroma of age and spice and roses. She closed her eyes and luxuriated in it, feeling the steam turning to moisture on her cheeks and forehead.

'I'll tell you another thing I remember,' Daisy called from the parlour. 'The coal man, making deliveries, wearing that cap with the leather back on it, reaching down his neck. Black with the coal dust, he was. Three sacks of anthracite every Tuesday fortnight, poured right down into the cellar.' She paused. 'He always had a smile for me, he did. Called me his little flower.'

Violet slid open one of the cupboards and retrieved two cups and two saucers. Placing them on the counter, she turned to the wheezing fridge and got the milk from the shelf in the door. A splash in each cup, and she returned the bottle to its place.

'Did you ever get the scissor-man coming around?' she called.

'The scissor-man? With his bicycle and his grindstone attached to the back?' She chuckled. 'Haven't thought about him in a while. Whatever happened to the scissor-men? Don't scissors or knives need sharpening any more?'

'I think people just buy new ones nowadays,' Violet said absently as she poured the tea into the cups, one after the other.

'Wasteful,' muttered Daisy. 'That's why there's so much clutter. Too much stuff being made, not enough stuff being kept.'

Violet reached down to where a tray was resting on its edge against the side of the fridge. She carefully lifted the cups and saucers onto the tray and carried it into the parlour.

'Here's your tea,' she said as she placed the tray carefully on the side table beside Daisy. The elderly woman glanced down at it, then up at Violet.

'Thank you, dear,' she said with sudden hesitation.

Violet crossed to the window again and gazed out. The skin on her cheeks and forehead was prickling from the steam, and she could feel a slight pressure in her throat. No matter. Every road had its potholes. Hadn't someone told her that once?

The street outside was peaceful. Most of the houses were unoccupied during the day. Husbands worked and wives worked too: Violet still found that a little disturbing, but she supposed the world changed and people changed with it. Wives so rarely stayed at home, these days. It was term-time, as well, and the children were still safely at school. The best thing about the street as far as Violet was concerned was that it didn't lead anywhere. People or cars never cut through on their way to somewhere else. If you were in the street then you were visiting one of the houses, and during weekdays that was rare.

From behind she heard a slurp as Daisy drank her tea. She smiled.

'I picked up your pension from the bank,' she said, the thought just popping randomly into her head. When Daisy failed to reply, she turned around. Daisy was staring at her, eyes defensive, teacup poised in her hand.

'You don't have to do that for me,' Daisy said. 'I used to be able to pop down to the post office myself, when I still had a pension book. The bank's not that much further.' She paused, judging Violet's reaction. 'In fact, I was thinking a walk wouldn't do me any harm. Might be nice to get out into the fresh air ...'

Violet let Daisy's words hang for a moment. She deliberately kept her face impassive. They'd had this discussion about once a week for the past two months, and there was no point getting angry. The decision was made and the river that was life was already flowing on, except that Daisy hadn't quite realised yet. Or still had some hope of reversing the current and taking back some small measure of independence.

'Not with your leg,' Violet said. She knew Daisy couldn't see her expression, with the light from the window behind her, but she kept her expression neutral. 'Those ulcers still need dressing every day. You don't want to make them any worse.'

'Maybe I should make an appointment down the doctor's,' Daisy wheedled. 'The ulcers don't seem to be clearing up, and Doctor Ganz was always so good about looking after me.' She sighed. 'I used to be a dancer, you know? Now look at me. Can't even walk down the shops.'

'I told you,' Violet said, 'I talked to the chemist. The cream will clear up the ulcers if we keep using it. What you need is rest. I can get all your shopping and your prescriptions, and now you've written to the bank I can make sure your pension is drawn out on time as well. Now, don't let your tea get cold.'

'I'm very grateful to you, m'dear.' Daisy took a noisy sip of tea, spilling some into her saucer. 'You look after me properly. Don't know what I'd do without you.'

'Everyone should look after their friends and neighbours.' Violet grimaced. The skin on her forehead was feeling tight and warm. 'There's not enough of that around, these days.'

'You know what I really miss?'

Violet wasn't sure whether Daisy was going to keep on about her lost independence or go back to duck eggs and anthracite, so she just said: 'What's that, then?'

'Whist drives down at the church hall. Once a week, Friday mornings. Used to see all me friends, have a chat and a cup of tea and some biscuits. Used to look forward to it, I did.'

'I'm not sure they do whist drives any more.'

'They do – I'm sure I saw it in the local paper.'

'Well, you don't want to strain your eyes. You've got to be careful at your age.'

'I can read the paper all right.'

'Daisy!' Violet let a tart edge slide into her voice. She was getting tired of this bickering. 'I'm only trying to help out. If you don't want me to do things for you – if you don't want me to get your shopping, and your prescriptions, and whatever else – then just say so and I'll leave you to it. I'm sure there are lots of other ladies your age who'd be grateful for the help.'

'I'm sorry, Violet, I didn't mean—'

'That's okay.' Soothing. 'Least said, soonest mended. Now did you want a refill?'

Daisy looked down into the dregs of her cup. 'Don't mind if I do,' she said. 'That was a nice cup of tea.' She swilled the cup around in her hand, staring intently at the tea leaves as if she was trying to see the shape of her future in them. 'What's these white bits?'

Violet took the cup from her hand and walked back into the kitchen. 'I took some Christmas rose petals from my garden and sprinkled them in with the tea,' she replied as she sloshed the remaining tea into the sink. 'I always think it gives it a nice, flowery taste. And it's meant to be good for you.' She paused for a moment. 'Who knows – if you drink enough of it, maybe you'll be able to *run* down to the shops and the bank!'

Daisy laughed, and Violet felt herself relax slightly. Crisis over.

She poured another cup for Daisy, and brought it back into the parlour, placing it carefully down on the tray next to her own cup. Daisy had drifted off again, and Violet sat quietly watching her breathe and thinking about her garden. Her beautiful, bountiful garden, filled with the most marvellous flowers. She didn't visit it as often as she should, but she knew she would be making another trip very soon.

After a while, Daisy stirred. She blinked a few times, then smiled hesitantly at Violet.

'Your tea's still warm,' Violet prompted.

Daisy smiled her appreciation, and reached for the cup. As she glanced down to see where it was, she noticed Violet's still full cup beside her own. 'Don't you want your tea, dear?'

'I'll wait for a while. I'm still out of breath from going to the shops. The pot's still hot: I can get another cup if that one goes cold.'

Daisy nodded, and sipped at her tea.

'Can you play whist?' she asked eventually. 'I really fancy a game, right now. Make a change from the telly, and the local paper.'

The question caught Violet by surprise. 'I'm … not sure,' she said eventually. 'I *think* I can.' She tried to remember. There were flashes of memory, like images cut from photographs, of her hands holding cards, but there was no context, no background. The memories were isolated, barely connected to reality and able to be moved around at will throughout what little she could recall of her life.

And there was another memory, another image. A table. A long table, set for tea in a darkened room.

Push that memory away. Push it away *fast*.

'I'm sure there's a pack of cards somewhere,' Daisy said, gesturing vaguely to the bureau. 'Perhaps we could have a game later. Just a short one.' She smiled hesitantly.

'Perhaps,' Violet said, still feeling unsteady after the intrusion of that unwelcome memory.

'And then I could—'

Daisy stopped, her words gurgling into incoherence. Spittle flew from her lips, spraying the air. Her lower lip suddenly glistened as saliva spilled across her dentures and down her chin. 'Violet—!!' Another explosion of spittle as she coughed. 'What's happening to me?'

Violet backed away, her heart fluttering lightly but rapidly. The world seemed suddenly bright and pin-sharp. She could see red streaks in the saliva as a thick glistening string of it dribbled out of Daisy's mouth.

'Not to worry,' she heard herself saying. 'It'll all be over soon.'

Daisy's hands clutched at her throat, clawing the sagging parchment skin. Her lips were crimson, puffy. A deep flush spread across her throat and thick, guttural noises emerged from her mouth with every burst of spittle. 'Gra – geh – helgh—!'

'You know, I'm amazed how quickly the blistering has come on,' Violet said, taking a deep breath to calm herself down. She backed away from Daisy and perched herself on the edge of the sofa. 'I had expected it to take a lot longer. I wasn't sure of the dose, of course, so I probably erred on the side of extravagance.'

She leaned forward and looked into Daisy's eyes. Normally the whites were yellowed and the irises were a faded porcelain blue, but now they were heavily bloodshot and weeping profusely, the tears rolling down her cheeks to join the red river of saliva streaming from the gaping cave of her mouth.

'I realise it must be alarming,' Violet murmured as Daisy fell back into her armchair and her eyes rolled up in her head, 'but it will all be over soon, I promise.' She leaned forward and patted Daisy's hand, which was clawing at the arm of the chair. One of Daisy's eyes fixed on Violet with desperation. The other seemed to have taken on an independent life, and was pointed away toward the ceiling. She broke wind: a long, wet sound that seemed to last forever.

'You're probably wondering what has caused this,' Violet went on, chatting to block out her reaction to what was happening. 'Christmas rose sounds so charming, doesn't it? Or winter rose, which it's also referred to as in the gardening books. Black hellebore sounds much more forbidding, but I don't suppose you would have drunk so much of the tea if I told you that it had black hellebore in it. Not just the flowers, but powdered root and bark as well. Funny, the different names that people give to the same things.'

Rolling over the lavender and boiled vegetable smell of the house came a darker, nastier smell. A smell of faecal matter, cloying with foul sickness. Violet winced and turned away on the sofa. It'll all be over soon, she told herself. All over soon.

Daisy was sitting in a spreading pool of her own watery, bloody-soaked faeces now, squirming in it, convulsing in it, grinding it into her dress and the fabric of the armchair. Violet was going to have to burn that chair in the back garden later, along with Daisy's clothes and a lot of garden waste to cover the smell. And the remaining tea leaves, of course. She couldn't leave those lying around. What if she forgot, and made herself another cup of tea while she was cleaning up!

Violet giggled to herself, covering her mouth politely with a delicate hand. Despite the mess, she really did enjoy this part of the game.

'There are all kinds of horrible things in the Christmas rose,' she said, watching to see whether Daisy could still hear her. 'Helleborin and hellebrin are both like digitalis, which I've also used before, but there's saporin and protoanemonin as well. It's a very nasty cocktail.'

Daisy's hands were both clutching at the armchair now, levering her body forward as if she was going to stagger upright and totter over to where Violet was sitting. Violet raised a hand to ward her off, but Daisy convulsed, falling backwards into the chair again as a thin waterfall of muddy vomit cascaded from her mouth and into her lap. Some of it splattered onto the floor. That, Violet thought ruefully, would be difficult to get out.

She decided not to use the Christmas rose again. It was certainly quick, and definitely easy to prepare, but it was too messy for her purposes. Cleaning up was bad enough at the best of times, without all those bodily fluids to worry about. Foxglove, perhaps, or bryony. Or perhaps oleander. She liked the smell of oleander.

Daisy's arms were flapping around now. The end was very close. Very close indeed.

'Your throat will have closed up almost completely by now,' Violet murmured, 'and your heart will have slowed down quite dramatically. I don't know whether you will suffocate before your heart actually stops beating of its own accord, but either way you will be dead within a minute or two. I don't even know if you can still hear me, but if you can I'd like to tell you that you are a selfish, stupid old woman, and I've hated every single moment of the time I've spent with you. Apart, of course, from the last few minutes. Those I have enjoyed very much.'

Daisy was silent and motionless. Her eyes were dull and sunken, and the saliva dripped slowly from her slack mouth.

Violet leaned forward, trying to see whether her heart still fluttered in her chest, whether the blood still pumped sluggishly around her veins, but she couldn't tell. She would come back later and check Daisy's pulse, she decided. After she tidied up. And if Daisy wasn't dead now, well, she would be within the hour.

It was going to be a long afternoon, and Violet found that she couldn't immediately raise the energy to get off the sofa. The light streaming through the window seemed to have a weight all its own. It held her down, sapping her strength and sending waves of languor flowing over her body. From where she sat she could see a slice of the smoky blue-grey sky imprisoned between the top of the window frame and the roofs of the terraced houses across the street. The sight didn't quite provoke an image in her mind of a slate-grey sea eternally lapping at a stone causeway, but it provided an avenue through which the image could creep into her thoughts. Wave after wave after wave, battering against the stone, wearing it down a minuscule amount at a time.

Violet shook herself. If she wasn't careful she would fall asleep, and she might lose half the afternoon that way. The seaside could wait: tidying came first.

Despite the fact that she had been visiting the house – often every day – for months now, Violet had a very good idea of what she had touched over the course of that time. The kitchen and bathroom would have to be scrubbed with bleach, of course, to remove any fingerprints or whatever else might give her presence away. The parlour and the dining room were less problematic: Violet had been careful about what she touched, and had often wiped down a handle or a surface while Daisy wasn't paying attention. If she had noticed at all, she had just thought that Violet was helping keep the house tidy. Daisy's bedroom and the spare bedroom – used for storage for the past thirty-odd years – had nothing of Violet in them. No, removing traces of her passage through the house would be easy.

Cleaning up after Daisy's messy death would take longer, and would be less pleasant, but there Violet didn't have to be perfect. Old people were often incontinent, in her experience, and as long as all the obvious signs of diarrhoea and sickness were removed then the odd stain and the odd lingering smell would not be too disastrous. And besides, modern cleaning technology was marvellous.

Violet stood up and made her way into the hall. Her legs were unsteady – the relief of having got Daisy's death out of the way, she assumed – and she leaned against the wall for a moment before pushing open the door to the dining room.

Daisy had always kept the dining room immaculate, in case

she ever had to entertain, which meant that it had been used perhaps twice in the past ten years. The centrepiece of the room was a solid mahogany table with legs turned in spirals. Three silver candlesticks sat on the table, and prints of hunting scenes were spaced around the walls.

A folded wheelchair leaned incongruously against the far chimney breast. Behind it, a large sheet of grey plastic was folded on the carpet.

Violet had brought the wheelchair and the plastic sheet into the house a few days ago, whilst Daisy was snuffling and murmuring in her sleep. Now she carried the sheet back into the parlour and looked around. Not the floor – she was going to have to scrub and hoover that pretty thoroughly. Perhaps the sofa.

Yes. She unfolded the plastic and draped it over the sofa until it was just a grey lump, like a shiny outcrop of stone. She could lift Daisy's body – light as it was – onto the sofa, then take the chair out to the garden and clean the carpet thoroughly. Once she had done that she could undress Daisy, wash her down with flannels and towels which she could also take out into the garden, and then re-dress Daisy in some of her other clothes from upstairs. Then Daisy could be lifted into the wheelchair, covered with a blanket and wheeled out of the house and down the street: just another old lady out for a breath of fresh air, fast asleep and dreaming of the past.

Violet glanced over at Daisy. In the time since she had last looked, something mysterious and irrevocable had happened to the woman she had once called 'dear'. What had once been loose flesh and jowls was now just a covering laid on top of an ancient skull. What had once been eyes that had looked out on eighty-odd years of history were now just dull buttons upon which dust was already beginning to settle. There was nothing there any more. The miracle had occurred once again: what had once been a woman named Daisy who had loved and lost and lived was now just ... just nothing. Skin and bone and a hank of hair. And everything that she had owned now belonged to Violet. Soon it would just be money.

It would have to be done carefully, of course. One step at a time. Nothing to cause suspicion. But given a few months, it would all be hers.

Once she had cleaned the house.

Because every journey started with a first step.

CHAPTER TWO

When Mark Lapslie's mobile phone bleeped, the sound tasted to him like chocolate. Dark chocolate, bitter on his tongue and gritty between his teeth and on the inside of his cheeks.

It was still dark outside his bedroom window, but birds were beginning to chirp and there was a freshness to the air that told him it was almost dawn. He had been drifting for some time, dreaming of the days when his house had been full of life and laughter, so the shock of the sudden noise – and the sudden flood of flavour in his mouth – hadn't disturbed him too much. Part of him had been expecting a call. He'd been tasting strawberries very faintly all day – a sign that something unplanned was about to happen.

The bleep was telling him that he had a message, rather than an actual incoming call. If it was a call the ring tone was an extract from Bruch's 1st violin concerto and tasted more like mocha coffee. He gave himself a few minutes to wake up fully before he reached across and picked the mobile up from the bedside table.

Pls call DS Bradbury, it said, followed by a mobile number.

Before dialling Detective Sergeant Bradbury, whoever he was, Lapslie padded into the bathroom and turned the shower on full. Catching sight of himself in the mirror above the sink, he winced. In his mind, he was twenty-five years younger, his hair wasn't grey and his stomach didn't bulge. Reflections kept catching him by surprise; the only reason he didn't take a screwdriver to the mirror and remove it for good was that shaving would be almost impossible.

'Hello?' The voice was female, tainted with lemon and lime, the accent pure Estuary.

'DS Bradbury? This is DCI Lapslie.' He walked back into the bedroom so the cauliflower hiss of the shower didn't drown out her voice. 'What can I do for you?'

'Car crash, sir,' she said succinctly.

'Car crash?' He took a breath. 'Sergeant, I'm on indefinite sick leave. I don't get called out on investigations any more.'

The voice was wary. 'Understood, sir, but there's something about the scene of the crash that, when it got called in, made your name jump up on the computer. When I tried to get a number for you I was told that you were on gardening leave, but it didn't say why, and when I put a call in to Chief Superintendent Rouse, he gave me permission to ring you.'

'Okay, what was it about the crash that made my name jump up on the computer?'

'I'd rather not say, sir. It's just … special.'

'Give me a clue, at least.'

'There was one person in the car, sir – the driver – and there was no other vehicle involved, but when the first responders got to the scene they found two bodies. One of them was the driver's. The other had been there for some time.'

Interesting. That was almost worth being woken up for. 'And?'

'And there's something about the state of the second body that apparently links to some old case you were involved in.'

'An old case of mine?' He cast his mind back quickly, thinking of anything odd, anything out of the ordinary in his career, but he could come up with nothing. No serial killers still on the loose, no bizarre cults, nothing. 'What was strange?'

'Sir, I'd really rather not say. It would be easier if you came on down.'

'Where are you?'

There was a pause. Steam was drifting in from the bathroom, and Lapslie imagined the DS looking around her in the dark, trying to work out the local geography.

'Out along the B1018, heading from Witham to Braintree, there's a side road that cuts across to Faulkbourne – you know it?'

'Cuts across the river?' He cast his mind back to the last time he'd driven up that way, for a dinner date that had ended in an argument and yet another night sleeping alone, longer ago than he really cared to remember. 'Near the Moorhen pub?'

'That's the one. We're about five miles down the road from the pub.'

'I'll be there within the hour,' he said.

'You won't have any problem spotting us,' she replied. 'Look for the chunk of metal that used to be a Porsche.' And, Lapslie thought, there was genuine sadness in her voice at the thought of a deceased high-performance car.

He showered quickly, his brain picking over the bones of his career, but finding nothing of any relevance. By the time he was dressed the sky was tinged with pink and the birds had gained confidence. He was in his car and pulling out of his drive barely twenty-five minutes from the time the message arrived.

His car was almost silent as it slipped through the narrow country lanes that led away from his isolated cottage near Saffron Walden, guided by the satnav system toward Witham and an event that was already over apart from the inevitable clean-up. He didn't bother putting on the radio, or a CD. He could never listen to music when he drove: there was no knowing what tastes and, occasionally, smells might suddenly distract him if a particular track was played. Before his medical condition had been diagnosed, back in the time when he thought *everyone* could taste sounds rather than just him and a handful of others in the entire world, he had once been almost fatally distracted whilst driving when a Beatles song suddenly flooded his mouth with rotting meat.

Life was just a rollercoaster of unexpected sensations when you had synaesthesia.

The sun rose above the horizon, casting long shadows across the fields. He drove fast but carefully, pacing himself on the long stretches of road that cut through town so that the traffic lights were all green when he reached them, then accelerating on the bypasses and ring roads to make up time. The minutes slid away, one after the other, as the houses fell away behind him and were replaced with woodland. He drifted into a trance as he drove, deliberately trying not to speculate about what awaited him at the scene of the crash.

The fact that he'd been called in the first place was strange. Lapslie had been on special medical leave from the Essex Police for the past six months – ever since his synaesthesia had suddenly escalated and his wife and children had been forced to move out of the house because the constant noise was driving him insane. They still kept in contact, but Lapslie was becoming slowly used to the fact that they would never be a proper family again. He was between posts, in a kind of limbo, reading reports and keeping himself current on the ever-changing world of police practice, writing the occasional report or think-piece for the police hierarchy, popping into the Headquarters in Chelmsford every now and then but never actually attending a crime scene or leading an investigation. Until now.

The case – whatever it was – obviously had something to do with his previous career, but what it was he couldn't tell. It wasn't as if he'd ever worked on anything particularly high-profile. After joining the police, with a degree in Psychology, he'd spent some time in the Met. in North London before moving on promotion up to Liverpool and then down again to Essex. He'd spent a few years assigned to the Association of Chief Police Officers, using his background to look at better ways of profiling major criminals, then taken two years out to complete a Masters Degree in Criminal Psychology. Looking back, there was nothing that particularly stood out. Nothing that might have tied him in with any unsolved case more important than assault and battery, or low-level burglary.

Shortly after crossing the Brain, and about an hour after leaving his cottage, Lapslie turned onto the road where the crash had apparently occurred. Trees laced their fingers together above the car, and the rising sun behind him cast a deep shadow along the road.

Striped barriers blocked his way a hundred yards or so before a lazy curve in the road. Bright white light spilled through the trees. A uniformed constable with a clipboard self-consciously straightened up and walked towards him, silhouetted by the false white dawn, already shaking his head. Lapslie brought his car to a halt and rolled his window down.

'DCI Lapslie,' he said, holding his warrant card out.

The policeman looked at the card and then back at Lapslie. He frowned. 'You might want to get this renewed, sir,' he said. 'The photograph's a bit ... out of date.'

Lapslie glanced down at the card in his hand. Okay, his hair wasn't brown any more, and there was a little more of it in the photo than in real life, but apart from the size of the collar on his shirt he didn't think he looked *that* different.

But it had probably been taken while the policeman standing beside his car was running happily around a playground somewhere.

'Happy the way it is,' he said tersely.

The policeman noted his name and car registration on the clipboard as he spoke. 'Shall I move the barrier for you?'

'Don't bother. I'll leave the car off the road and walk.'

It wasn't difficult to spot the crash site, just around the curve. The Crime Scene Investigators had set up arc-lamps on poles which bathed the scene with a harsh, unforgiving light, despite the encroaching day. Lapslie paused for a moment, taking in the sight.

The smell of petrol and burnt rubber still hung in the air. Twin skid marks intertwined with each other along the road surface, showing where the car had braked, skidded and spun like some demented fairground ride. He could only imagine the horror in the driver's mind, twisting the wheel back and forth in the sure and certain knowledge that it wasn't going to do any good and he was probably going to die. Judging by the marks, the car had been hurtling along the country road before suddenly seeing the curve ahead. What had happened? Had the driver's attention been distracted by a boiled sweet or a phone call? Had his headlights been dipped so that he couldn't see the curve until it was too late? Or had he just been drunk? That was for forensics to determine, but Lapslie couldn't help speculating. Alive one moment, dead the next. The facts could be explained, but the driver's state of mind? That could only ever be guessed at.

He'd made the mistake of saying to a colleague at another crash scene some time ago, 'I wonder what the last thing that went through the driver's mind was.' The man had just looked at him blankly. 'The windscreen,' he had muttered, and walked off.

The melted rubber marks ended at the point where the road curved away. A stone kerb marked the point where tarmac gave way to uneven ground covered in leaves, tiny fretted ferns and bushes. The car had obviously hit the kerb side-on and the impact had flipped it into the air, spinning again but now around its longest axis so that when it struck the trees it was almost exactly upside down. Two trunks had been splintered at a point some ten feet off the ground. The car – or what remained of it – sat beneath them, crumpled like a discarded chocolate wrapper.

Another barrier had been set up fifty or so yards down the

road. An ambulance was parked by it, beside a police Peugeot 406 – painted in the yellow and blue squares that had jokingly become known to police across the country as the Battenburg colour scheme – a dusty Mondeo and a van which had probably brought the CSI team to the area. Two paramedics were chatting to a uniformed policeman, their casual demeanour indicating that their work was done, if indeed they'd had any work in the first place apart from pronouncing the driver of the car dead at the scene.

A plastic marquee had been set up just off the road, a few feet from the remains of the car. The arc-lamps behind it made it glow. Grotesque shadows of the people inside it were cast against its walls: bent figures with distended hands, moving together and apart again in some strange ritual dance.

It was all so familiar and yet, after his time away from work, so alien. So strange.

He pulled his mobile from his jacket pocket and, after a moment's thought, dialled a number that for a moment he didn't think he would remember.

'Essex Constabulary, can I help you?'

'Superintendent Rouse, please,' he said.

'Putting you through now.'

Moments later, a new voice said: 'Detective Chief Superintendent Rouse's office.'

'This is DCI Lapslie. Would it be possible to speak to the Superintendent?'

'He's not arrived yet. Can I ask what it's about?'

'I've apparently been pulled off leave of absence on the Superintendent's orders. I was wondering why.'

The voice on the other end of the line went muffled for a moment, as if Rouse's PA had put her hand over the receiver while she sought instructions. After a few seconds, she was back. 'I can get the Superintendent to call you later. Does he have your number?'

'I wouldn't be surprised,' Lapslie said grumpily, and broke the connection.

Slipping the mobile back into his jacket, Lapslie headed for the marquee and pulled the entrance flap open. The interior was large enough to host a wedding reception or a giant vegetable competition. The CSI team – figures clad in papery yellow coveralls – were gathered in two groups, taking photographs and examining the ground for evidence. A woman was with them, chatting. Her hair was short and spiky; her make-up highlighted her sharp cheekbones. Her breath gusted like cigarette smoke in the cold morning air. When she saw Lapslie she broke away and walked towards him.

'DS Bradbury?' he asked.

'Morning, sir,' she said. Lemon, as on the mobile, but with a hint of grapefruit now. Her suit was a designer special, but it looked like she'd been sleeping in it when the call came in about the crash. 'Sorry to get you out of bed this early.'

'Not a problem. I'm just glad to be back in the saddle. Gardening leave gets very tedious after a while.'

Bradbury was obviously dying to ask him why he was on gardening leave – that wonderful catch-all term that meant someone was being paid to sit around the house all day, without actually specifying why – but she was too polite, or too political, to try. Covering the momentary lapse in conversation, and remembering Bradbury's comment on the mobile about the wreck of the performance car, Lapslie nodded back to where the car was located, outside the tent. 'Sorry to hear about your loss,' he joked.

She sighed. 'Porsche. Lovely machine. Complete bloody write-off. What a tosser.'

'I presume from the tyre tracks that he lost control coming into the curve. Hitting the kerb knocked the car into the air and hitting the trees totalled the car.'

'That's the way I read it. Nothing to indicate that any other vehicles were involved. The car'll be checked out, of course, but there's no reason yet to assume mechanical failure.' She shook her head sadly. 'Some people just don't deserve to have nice cars.'

Lapslie glanced across to where the CSIs were gathered in their two groups. 'What happened to the driver?'

'Pulled himself out of the near-side window and crawled into the trees, which is where we found him.'

'Dead?'

'As a Dover sole on a fishmonger's slab.'

'What happened?'

Emma Bradbury smiled, revealing small white teeth. 'He must be the unluckiest sod in history. Even at the speed he was going, his seatbelt and airbag should have saved his life, but a short branch on one of the trees punched through the driver's-side window and went right through his neck. He bled out while he was crawling.' She indicated the left-hand group of CSIs. 'That's him over there. We're waiting for the forensic pathologist to turn up. Apparently she's been delayed.'

'Do we know who he was?'

Emma fished in her pockets and pulled out a transparent evidence bag with a wallet inside. 'Name of Sutherland. Businessman, apparently. Mid-forties, lives just outside Chelmsford. Looks like he might have been on his way home after a late meeting, or something. I've sent someone to notify his wife.'

A late meeting. A snatched dinner at a Little Chef or a Beefeater before the long drive home, dazzled by oncoming headlights. Lapslie remembered it well. Once upon a time, there had been someone curled up in front of the TV in their dressing gown, waiting for him to turn up. Someone who would have cared if he'd been involved in a car accident. Once upon a time.

He shook himself, and looked around. 'If there was no other car involved, who called the police?'

Emma grinned. 'A couple who were parked up and at it like rabbits just down the road heard the impact and the sound of glass breaking.'

'So the earth really did move for them,' Lapslie murmured.

'They motored down – after adjusting their clothing, of course – and when they saw what had happened they called it in. Uniform took statements and let them get back to their respective partners.'

Lapslie turned his attention to the other group of CSIs, clustered around something on the ground. 'And the real reason you woke me up and dragged me all the way here? The reason my name flagged up on the computer?'

'The other body Uniform found near the driver when they were checking to see whether he was still alive.'

'You said on the phone that there was something about the state of it?'

'I think we're dealing with *Dawn of the Living Dead*.'

He nodded. 'Well, let's see.'

The two of them moved towards the group. Small twigs and branches snapped underfoot, and Lapslie wasn't sure whether the sour smell in his nostrils was due to the sounds or the crash or both. Dawn had shaded across into morning now, and the scrap of sky that he could see through the tent flap was clear and blue. All around him he could taste birds and animals moving around.

They walked past the first group of CSIs, and Lapslie couldn't help glancing across at the figure on the ground: a man, crumpled up like his car, wearing a dark suit that was glossy with congealing fluid. A bloody write-off, to use Emma's phrase.

The second group was clustered around something on the ground, no more than ten feet or so away from the first body. As Lapslie approached they seemed to tense, possessive of their find.

'DCI Lapslie,' he said firmly. 'What have you got?'

The Crime Scene Manager stood, brushing his gloved hands on his coveralls. Lapslie had seen him at other crime scenes, years ago: a small man, mid-fifties, with a paunch pushing out the fabric of his coveralls and a quiff of white hair standing straight up from his head.

'We appear to have a dead body,' he said in a disconcertingly thick Irish accent, the final words sounding to Lapslie almost like 'deed baady'. His voice tasted the way Lapslie imagined blackberry wine would taste: musty and thin.

'Not connected to the crash?'

'Connected, but not in the way you mean. Take a look.'

There, rearing up from a pile of earth, ferns and leaves, was a corpse. And this *was* a corpse, more like a skeleton to which things had been added rather than a body from which things had been subtracted. The face was all sharp cheekbones and hollow eye sockets, the head twisted to one side and the jawbone gaping open as if in some terrible, silent agony. Whatever skin remained was as dull and as grey as the hair that was spread out around the skull. Its arms were stretched out behind it, as thin and as dry as the twigs that surrounded them. What Lapslie could see of the fingers clutched in vain at the loam of the forest.

And most bizarrely of all, the body was surrounded by dirt-encrusted plastic sheeting, bunched to form two huge wings, one at each shoulder.

Half-aware of the banter between the CSI team members, Lapslie knelt down by the body, checking first that he wasn't disturbing anything that hadn't already been disturbed. All corpses looked old, of course, but this one looked like it was actually the corpse of someone old. The bottom half was still buried in the ground, the plastic tightly wrapped around hips and legs, but the torso was slanted up at an angle of about thirty degrees. The arms looked as if they were supporting the weight of the body, but that was just an illusion caused by the fact that they were hanging down, the bony knuckles resting on the ground. Although the material of the clothes had been stiffened and faded by the passing of the seasons, it seemed as if the corpse had been wearing a blouse, a cardigan and a pair of slacks in some dark material.

He leant forward to check around the back of the skull. Difficult to be sure without touching it, but there looked to be some evidence of damage. It might have been caused by predators, but it might also have been caused by an act of violence. Whatever the cause, this was certainly a suspicious death. People, in Lapslie's experience, did not wrap themselves in plastic before calmly lying down to die.

Without disturbing the twigs or the dirty plastic sheeting around the body, Lapslie made a close examination of the area around where the hands rested. The body was actually half-buried in a trench of some kind. Somehow, the trench had been disturbed – the ground around it was churned up and the ferns partially ripped out – and the body had been pushed up and out like a moth from a chrysalis. The fingers were half-buried in the loam, and—

Wait. The ground beneath the fingers was covered with a layer of detritus – leaves as skeletal as the body – and some of them appeared to pass entirely under the fingers, almost as if ...

Lapslie leant closer. The scent of damp and decay filled his nostrils, but bizarrely he could taste something decadently fragrant in his mouth, like lychees.

He was right. The fingers weren't complete. The ends were missing from about the second knuckle onwards. Although it looked at first sight as if the rest of the fingers were embedded in the earth, he could see that the ends rested *on* the leaves, rather than poking *through* them.

Somewhere in the back of his mind a memory that had been asleep for a long time began to stir. Hadn't he talked to someone about a case like this once? Hadn't he written something about it? Not a case he was working on as a policeman, he was sure, but something else. Something that was almost a sideline.

'Is this why you called me?' he asked DS Bradbury, who was standing behind him. 'The fingers? They look as if they've been removed.'

'I noticed them when I first saw the body,' she said. 'When I radioed the details in, the Duty Officer typed them into the computer system. As soon as he typed the stuff in, a message flashed up with your name attached. Apparently you've seen this kind of thing before – a body with missing fingers.'

'Not as far as I can remember. Not a body, at any rate ...' And yet, there was something. The taste of lychees, and a vague memory of someone telling him about missing fingers.

He deliberately moved the memory to one side. He could worry about that later. For now he was back at work, for the first time in a long time, and he had a body in the here-and-now to worry about, not something vague in the past. A body that was pushing itself out of the ground as if possessed by some restless spirit.

But what had disturbed it? What had forced the earth to give birth to its dead?

Lapslie's head was turning toward where the wreck of the car sat, outside the marquee, before his mind had even formulated the obvious conclusion.

He rocked back on his heels. 'You've got to be joking,' he muttered to himself.

'We never joke,' the Crime Scene Manager said, coming over towards him.

'Are you seriously telling me that the body was buried here in plastic sheets for some ungodly length of time, undisturbed by anything, before that car came along and just scooped it up out of the ground?'

'I'm not telling you anything, serious or otherwise, until we've collated all the evidence, photographed the entire scene and assessed it all back at the lab.' He shook his head, lips twisted into a grimace. 'But if I were a betting man, which I am, I'd put a pony on that being the final conclusion. Bizarre as it may seem, I think that car crash managed to excavate a murder victim.'

Which might, Lapslie thought, explain the damage he thought he'd spotted to the back of the skull.

He glanced over his shoulder to where the other group of CSIs were attempting to slide the dead businessman into a large vinyl body bag without disturbing it too much. 'We owe you a vote of thanks,' he said to the body, a kind of final valediction as 'he' turned to 'it', a person becoming a thing to be moved around, cut up and pored over. 'If it hadn't been for you, we might never have found her. Whoever she is.'

He straightened up and turned to the CSM. 'And you are?'

'Burrows,' he said. 'Sean Burrows.'

'Well, Sean, I think you've got a busy day ahead of you. I'll make sure to get a supply of bacon rolls and coffee sent up.'

'That,' the CSM said with a heartfelt sigh, 'would be most welcome.'

Emma Bradbury was standing over to one side. Glancing between Lapslie and Burrows, she smiled. 'What now?' she asked.

'Now we talk to the first responders,' he replied.

The two of them exited the marquee and walked back towards the road in silence. As they emerged from the tree line, Emma glanced down at the skid marks left by the car.

'Look at that,' she said, pointing. 'See the darker and lighter stripes in the rubber?'

Lapslie looked closer. She was right, there were indeed streaks where the rubber appeared to be embossed into the road's surface, and areas between them where the fine structure of the road could be seen. 'What's the cause of that?'

'ABS,' she said gloomily. 'Anti-lock Brake System – pulses the brakes automatically to maintain grip on the road. That car had everything, and the bastard trashed it.'

Walking on, they found the uniformed policeman still talking to the paramedics. 'Excuse me, sir,' he said as the paramedics melted backwards, 'but can we shift the car and open up the road yet? It doesn't get particularly busy, this time of day, but there's no easy alternative route.'

Lapslie considered for a moment. The crash was just a red herring as far as he was concerned. The old woman's body intrigued him more. 'Get the car out of here and shipped back to the garage so they can test the brakes and whatever. When it's gone, get the local authority to cordon off about fifty feet of one side of the road next to the trees and set up temporary traffic lights for traffic on the other side.'

'You sure that's necessary, sir?' Emma said from beside him.

'No,' he replied firmly. 'As my old Superintendent said, when in doubt – cover it.' He turned his attention to the policeman: a young man in a cap that kept threatening to slide forward over his head. 'You are?'

'Henson,' muttered Emma from beside him. 'I've already talked to him.'

'Were you first on the scene, Henson?' he said, ignoring Emma.

'I was,' he said. 'Me and PC Rhodes. He's manning the other barrier. The one you came in through.'

'What about this road, then? Does it see many accidents?'

He shrugged. 'It's not a blackspot, but the corner can come up on you fast if you're not paying attention. We get called out here a couple of times a year.' He thought for a moment. 'Last time was probably before Christmas – maybe five or six months back. Maybe a little bit more.'

'When you were here last, did you see any churned-up areas of earth? Anything that looked as if something had been buried?'

Henson shook his head. 'Nothing like that, I'm sure.'

'Thanks,' Lapslie said. 'We may be in touch later.'

The PC turned away to rejoin the paramedics. Lapslie looked up and down the road. From where he stood, in the centre of the curve, he could see in both directions: long stretches of trees on either side forming a tunnel with their interlaced branches.

Not a bad sight, if it was your last.

Emma glanced down the road towards where he had left her car. 'Well, if that's all, boss …'

'We need to establish who she is, as a matter of priority,' Lapslie mused, only half-hearing his sergeant. 'We can come at it from two directions. A search of the body might throw up a purse, a receipt, a scrap of paper, a bus pass or something with her name and address on it. I didn't see a handbag anywhere around the body, but the search might turn it up somewhere in the long grass. I'll keep in touch with the CSIs and the pathologist, but you can cover the other direction. Once we've got an approximate age and a likely range of dates for the death, I want you to check through the missing persons records and pull out anything that fits. With luck, we can narrow it down. And then, when we know how she died, we can start pulling everything together.'

'Wouldn't it be nice,' Emma muttered. 'Look, sir, I'd like to make a move, if you don't mind. I've been here since about three a.m., and I could do with a shower and a change of clothes.'

'Okay,' Lapslie conceded, 'you crack on. I'll hang around and wait for the pathologist to turn up. He should have been here by now.'

' "She", sir. Apparently the local pathologist is a Doctor Jane Catherall. I've called her twice, but no response. CSI claim she's always turning up late to crime scenes.'

'I'll get the number off them and try again. You can go. Check in with me later.'

Emma nodded gratefully, and walked off. Lapslie watched her go, the material across the seat of her designer trousers pulling diagonally in one direction and then the other as she walked. Women in the police force had a rough time of it: most of the time they were forced to come across as more laddish than the lads, protective coloration in the tight-knit boys' club of the police. Emma was no exception, but Lapslie suspected that underneath was a schoolgirl vulnerability. Perhaps he ought to reach out: make sure she understood that he was not taking her at face value. And he probably owed her an explanation of his time away from the police; a period that had so abruptly come to an end with her call.

He found himself following Emma before he had even made a conscious decision to move. Perhaps now was a good time to start building bridges.

She reached her Mondeo a few seconds before he did. As he approached, formulating the words of praise in his mind, he could hear her talking. He assumed for a moment that she was making a call on her mobile, but then she moved to one side and he realised that she was speaking to someone sitting in the passenger seat of the car, someone who was rubbing their eyes as if they'd just woken up.

'I can have you back in—' she was saying, and then she saw Lapslie. The skin around her eyes tightened, and her gaze flickered from side to side as if she was automatically looking for a way out.

'Sir – was there something else?' she asked, sliding sideways to block Lapslie's view of her passenger.

Lapslie stepped sideways, but Emma's companion had turned his head away so that all Lapslie could see through the open passenger window was an ear with a small gold earring and a tousled mane of hair.

'Can I have a word?' Lapslie snapped, all the praise he had been about to deliver sliding out of his mind like rain off a windowpane.

Emma stepped away from the car, walking around Lapslie so he had no choice but to turn away from the car.

'You brought someone with you tonight,' he said, stating rather than asking.

'Sir.' Not giving anything away.

'This is a crime scene. We're professionals, doing a job. You don't just bring spectators along. What's going on?'

'Difficult to explain, sir.' Her gaze slipped away from him. 'Although not as difficult as explaining it to his wife,' she muttered. 'I'm sorry, sir. It won't happen again.'

'Emma—' He used her first name, trying to break through the barriers she had thrown up. 'Talk to me. Tell me what's going on.'

She sighed, and looked away. 'I was ... with a friend when the call came in about the body. The extra body. We were in a hotel. His car was back in a car park near the club where we met. I wanted him to take a cab, but he wanted to ... well, to come along with me. I honestly thought there wouldn't be much to see, just a pile of clothes or a tramp who'd had a heart attack. I thought we'd be clear inside an hour. Didn't plan on this turning into a crime scene.' Her gaze switched back to meet Lapslie's. 'He never got out of the car, boss. I promise you that.'

Lapslie took a deep breath. These things happened. Sometimes it was difficult to disentangle personal from professional. God knew, he'd had enough experience of that himself over the years.

'Okay. We'll leave it there. Get your boyfriend home, get a bacon sandwich and a cup of coffee inside you and I'll see you back at the office later.'

'Thanks, boss.' She nodded, waiting until Lapslie had started to move away before she moved back towards her car. Lapslie took a few steps more, until he heard the *clunk* of her car door closing, then he turned and watched as she gunned the car to life and pulled away. He stood for a couple of seconds, watching it go, wondering whether to take things any further or just forget about it.

And just as he realised that there was another car, a black Lexus with a tinted windscreen, parked in the trees a hundred yards or so down the road, it too gunned its engine to life, quietly pulled out of the tree line and drove away after DS Bradbury.

CHAPTER THREE

It was dark by the time Violet returned to the house that had once belonged to Daisy but now belonged to her. The thin wash of cloud that had given the sky its texture and depth during the day now gave the night an oppressive closeness, like sheets of sackcloth pinned from one side of the street to the other and sagging in the middle under their own weight.

She turned the ignition key and let the Volvo's engine die away. Something inside the bonnet whirred for a few seconds more, then it, too, gave way to the silence of the night. Violet just sat there, sinking back into the seat and letting the nervous tension drain out of her body.

Lights were on all the way down the street. Behind those lit windows, families were boiling pasta and heating up sauce, watching TV, telling stories to excitable children or sitting quietly and reading a book. Life went on – if repeating the same old routine, night after night, was life.

Tiredness had wormed its way into Violet's joints. Every time she turned her head slightly she could feel the tendons and muscles pulling tight across her neck. Sometimes, when she felt like this, she had the worrying thought that all she had to do was keep turning her head further and further and the tendons would snap, one by one, like the horsehair on an old violin bow.

She shook herself. *Come on, Violet*, she thought, *focus. You still have a job to do. This was only the first step.*

She climbed out of the car, locked the door and took a look around her. Nobody was watching. No curtains were twitching. She was safe.

Violet had parked a few hundred yards down the street from her new house, of course – just opposite a patch of waste ground where children played football at the weekends – and now she walked slowly along the pavement to that familiar front door, with its crazy-paving paint and its tape-bandaged letter box. She paused for a moment, gazing at the drooping geraniums. Those would have to go, she thought. Too dreary. Too drab. Too meaningless.

Perhaps she could plant a nice Christmas rose before she left. In memory of Daisy.

Smiling, she inserted her key into her lock and walked into her house.

The smell hit her as soon as she entered. Older now, and fouler, undercut by the acridity of bleach and overlaid by Daisy's favourite lavender perfume, but still lurking there like some old, mangy dog in the undergrowth. Air fresheners and pot-pourri could only do so much, but there was obviously more cleaning required. Quickly, Violet walked along the hall – slipping her thin cotton gloves on as she did so – then through the tiny kitchen and out into the conservatory. She flicked the latches on the back door, top and bottom, and opened it as far as it would go.

The fresh air was a sudden relief, and she took a couple of deep breaths, gazing out into the dark, shadowy back garden as she did so. From a patio of pebbled concrete, criss-crossed with silvery snail tracks, a tongue of paving stones wound its way through big, unkempt bushes of various kinds. Tall fences on either side separated the house from its neighbours, and the far end of the garden gave on to a ten-foot brick wall, almost invisible in the murk at the bottom of the garden. Daisy had never been sure what was beyond that wall, even though she had lived there for over fifty years.

A metal dustbin sat in the centre of the concrete patio, its sides streaked red with rust that had leaked from the rivets and welds of its construction. Inside the bin were Daisy's stained clothes, along with the cushion that she had been sitting on and the doilies that had been draped over the arms of her chair. The chair itself stood next to the bin, looking smaller in the open air than it had done in the dark parlour.

Tomorrow she would set the clothes in the bin on fire, accelerated by a splash of lighter fluid. The chair she would have to think about. She could either burn it where it stood, and risk leaving scorch marks on the concrete, or she could attempt to take it apart with a screwdriver and a small saw to a point where she could get the various parts into the burning bin. That might work.

The deliciously cool, fresh air reminded her that she needed a through draught to get the house to a state where she could work in it, so she turned around and walked back through the house and into the parlour. The smell was worse there, and Violet held her breath until she could undo the catch on the central sash window and push it up six inches or so. The sudden breeze through the house, from back to front, quickly cleared the air, and for a moment Violet had a strong image of the house itself slumping with relief as it exhaled a stale, rank breath and inhaled clean air again.

Turning away from the window, Violet's gaze was caught, as it often had been while listening to Daisy's interminable rambling stories, by the bureau opposite the fireplace. She had carried an image of that bureau around in her mind for months. Whenever she got the chance she had checked books on antiques in the local library, or browsed through them while standing by the shelves in the nearest bookshop. She was fairly sure it was mid-eighteenth century, and in very good condition. If she was careful, it could perhaps realise ten thousand pounds at auction. The barometer in the hall was almost certainly French, dating from the early nineteenth century. That could net something approaching two thousand pounds. The andirons on either side of the fire could fetch between three and five thousand pounds, depending on whether they were originals or merely good reproductions. And there was other stuff in the house, such as the dining room table, the silver candlesticks and a complete set of pristine Spode china that Daisy had shown her once, wrapped in newspaper and kept in a Queen Anne chest upstairs 'for best', as Daisy had put it.

All in all, Violet thought that there was about twenty-five thousand pounds' worth of furniture and nick-nacks in this house. They had all been in the family since before Daisy was born, bought by her father, her grandfather, his father and so on when they weren't antiques but just ordinary items. Daisy had been widowed young, with no children, and so there was nowhere for them to go. And here they had stayed. To Daisy they were just a part of the house, but to Violet they were something else entirely. They were assets to be realised as cash as soon as possible.

And that was before she stripped Daisy's estate of the small amount of pension that had accrued over the years, the various bonds and shares that she might have collected and, most important of all, the house. That wonderful unmortgaged 1950s house, in a quiet part of the city, ideal for commuters who wanted to be near work and yet isolated from it. Worth, according to an estate agent with whom Violet had once had an interesting chat, something in excess of a quarter of a million pounds.

Not that she would sell it straight away. No, that would raise too many questions. Although it had only taken a couple of glasses of brandy to persuade Daisy to sign power of attorney over to her, some months ago now, Violet was a little wary of exerting too much authority too soon. More haste, less speed, as they said. Best to wait until the dust had settled a bit.

Although it was late, she had one important job to do before she could slide between the sheets of her bed and gaze up at the ceiling of her room with the calm satisfaction that comes of a job well done. She had to clean the parlour.

Violet went into the kitchen and retrieved the plastic bag of cleaning utensils from the counter. Looking along the shelves in the shop, she had been bewildered by the sheer range of things that people used to clean their houses. How could anyone use that many products? And how was it that houses these days were so much dirtier and dustier than they were when Violet was a child, when all they had was beeswax polish and soapstone and coal tar soap?

And, of course, soda crystals.

She pulled the blue, rather plain box proudly from the bag. At least someone still made soda crystals.

Using hot water from the tap, she made up a strong solution of washing soda in a bucket from the conservatory, and set to work with a pair of rubber gloves and a brush, working the liquid into the parlour carpet and soaking up the brown residue – the remnants of Daisy's blood and faeces – with a series of tea towels. The area where the chair had sat was almost unaffected, apart from splashes and drips that had found their way down through the upholstery. After half an hour the carpet around the edges was almost indistinguishable from the carpet in the centre, and the smell had transferred itself to the growing pile of tea towels. Carefully, she carried the towels out into the garden, threw them into the metal bin and sprinkled bleach over the top. Then she threw the rubber gloves in after them. They almost certainly wouldn't melt properly in the fire, but at least any last trace of Daisy would be burned off them.

According to the clock in the parlour – reproduction ormolu, unfortunately, dating from the 1950s and worth less than ten pounds – it was almost midnight. The muffled sounds of the TV set from next door had vanished some time before. There was no sound now, apart from the slow creaks that resulted from any old house settling itself down for the night. Violet desperately craved sleep, but there was one more thing she had to do before she could surrender herself to the darkness. One last act to make the house hers.

Methodically, room by room, Violet collected up all the photographs of Daisy. There was one in a frame in the dining room, set high on the bookshelf: an old black and white picture with creased corners of a young woman with a beehive hairdo posing against a railing with a beach behind her. On the back, in spidery brown writing, were the words 'Camber Sands, July, 1953'. It didn't look much like the shrunken woman with the liver-spotted arms and baggy medical stockings that she had become, but then, it looked even less like Violet, so it couldn't stay.

Violet held it for a moment, reluctant to let go. Camber Sands, July, 1953. The photograph had been taken by the young man Daisy had been seeing at the time. He had worked in a bank. They had seen each other for two years – 'walked out', Daisy had called it – until he was called up for National Service. He had promised to write, but he never did.

Another photograph rested on a small table in the hall: a colour picture of a group of four middle-aged ladies laughing in front of a hotel entrance. It had been taken in Mallorca some time in the 1980s; Daisy hadn't been too sure of the year. Susan, Janice and Patricia. They'd worked together on the checkouts in a supermarket on the edge of town for a while, and all decided to go on holiday together. Patricia had met a widower and ended up spending most of her days and all of her nights with him. Daisy had been bitterly jealous.

And there was the wedding photograph, set on the white melamine bedside table where it would have been the first thing Daisy saw when she woke up and the last thing she saw at night. Black and white again, two people, formally posed. Daisy in a huge white Bo Peep dress foaming with lace, a wide-brimmed hat on her head, and beside her a taller man with short hair and a moustache, stiff in a formal morning suit. His name had been Peter, and Daisy hadn't been able to talk about him without a tremor in her voice and tears forming in her watery eyes. He had been the love of her life, and he had died of an aneurysm in 1979 after twenty-one years of marriage.

They were all that was left of Daisy's life, and so, despite the memories that sprang up whenever Violet looked at them – memories that weren't hers but were *becoming* hers – the photographs went in the bin in the back garden. For burning.

The frames she kept, of course. They might bring in a few extra pounds.

After a quick bath to wash the remains of the day from her body, Violet changed Daisy's bedding for a fresh set of sheets and blankets and slid naked into the bed. She lay there, staring at the ceiling, allowing the pillows and the mattress to gradually adjust themselves to the shape of her body. Or perhaps to allow her body to adjust itself to the indentation left by Daisy Wilson after however many years she had slept there.

The street lamp outside cast an orange glow across the ceiling. The alarm clock on the bedside table tocked loudly, regularly. Somewhere outside, a cat yowled, and then it was quiet apart from the normal background rumble of distant traffic that nobody in the city could ever get away from.

As Violet felt her body gradually grow limp, and as her thoughts flitted from image to image, never settling for long enough to feed, she realised that she could hear the soft hiss of blood in her ears, a susurration like waves lapping gently against a shingle beach. The cat yowled again, but this time it sounded more to her like the cry of a seagull as it floated above the waves the way she was floating *on* them. The room itself grew dim around her, and the cold orange glow of the street lamp became the warm light of the sun setting behind a watery horizon, casting a glittering path across the sea towards her floating body. She drifted there, alone and unafraid, letting the tide take her further and further out to sea, washing her clean of everything she had done, absolving her sins as it washed the dirt from her body. The light faded as the sun dipped further and further beneath the horizon. Darkness spread in from the edges of her vision, and she was asleep without knowing she was asleep.

For the next few hours Violet was lost in a slow kaleido-scope of dreams, sometimes surfacing enough to be aware of where she was, sometimes submerged in the moments and the memories, attempting to make some sense of their fragmentary chaos.

Rising from depths of sleep where she had been lost and stumbling in an art gallery full of portraits of people she did not know, she found herself on a beach of pebbles in various shades of grey and ochre. Somewhere out in the darkness, waves crashed on shingle, rattling as they withdrew and then crashing again, relentlessly, mindlessly, over and over again.

Tock.

Startled, she turned around. Nothing was moving. The pebbles ranged away from her in all directions. Somewhere over to her left there was a sketchy indication of a breakwater, but that was the only thing to stand out in this otherwise featureless place.

Tock.

She turned again, in a full circle. There was nothing to see but pebbles and darkness, nothing to hear now but the waves.

Tock.

That had come from the ground, by her feet. Glancing down, she was shocked to see a pebble move. Rounded by the sea, dark red in colour, it suddenly lurched towards her on tiny feet. Violet backed away rapidly, faster than the pebble could move. It had tiny claws which it waved at her, and she could almost swear that it had a tiny face between the claws, a wizened little face with two eyes buried in puffy, criss-crossed flesh.

Tock. Tock-Tock.

Behind her now. She turned again, heels catching in the shingle. Two more pebbles were scuttling toward her, waving their minuscule claws. One had a little curl of grey hair hanging between its eyes.

Terrified, she edged backwards.

Something moved beneath her heels.

Tock-Tock. Tock.

The shingle heaved beneath her. She felt herself tumbling, screaming as she fell into their claws, into their tiny, tiny claws—

Violet jerked awake, heart racing, breath rasping in her throat. The bedroom was black, washed with amber from the street lamp. *Tock, tock, tock,* went the alarm clock, one *tock* for every two thumps of her heart. She lay there, gradually relaxing back into the bed, until sleep claimed her once again. Deep, dreamless, anonymous sleep.

She woke, as she usually did, at half past seven in the morning. The street outside was as busy as she had ever seen it. Every few minutes a front door closed behind someone in a suit or smart clothes, heading for the bus stop or the station. She stood in the window, one of Daisy's dressing gowns wrapped around her. She loved watching people. Their unconscious grimaces and their little sideways glances when they thought nobody was looking fascinated her. They always had, ever since she was a child.

A man, still half asleep, yawned as he locked his front door behind him, covering his mouth with the back of his left hand while he manipulated his keys with his right. Violet raised her own left hand to her mouth, touching her lips against the skin on the back in the same way he did, counting the seconds silently, feeling her breath tickle the fine hairs on her skin, until he lowered his hand and turned to leave. A woman on one side of the street carrying a thin briefcase on a strap over her shoulder cast sideways glances at the door of a house on the other side, hoping someone was going to come out. Violet practised those same darting looks under half-closed eyelids, knowing and yet not knowing that she was doing it.

Yes, she loved watching people. But even more than that, she loved *being* them.

Breakfast was a slice of toast with butter and a smear of

marmalade along with a cup of tea – made with Daisy's teabags, not the tea leaves she had brought with her the day before. After breakfast she set a match to the items in the metal bin in the back garden and, while they burned, set to work searching the house.

She started at the bottom – literally. The cellar hadn't seen light for many years. The cobwebs hanging from the crude wooden rafters were so burdened with dust they looked like grey chiffon scarves. Apart from a patina of coal dust that glittered in the light from the naked bulb there was nothing for Violet in that dark, dead place. She didn't even go all the way down the stairs. At the back of her mind there was a nagging fear that her feet might sink into the coal dust up to the ankles, and all she would hear would be the dry rustling of thousands of insect carcasses crushed beneath her soles.

The parlour was old, familiar territory, but she searched it anyway, just in case she had missed something along the way. The bureau was stacked with crockery, cutlery, glassware, old music manuscripts and cuttings from newspapers dating back twenty years or more. The newspaper cuttings she threw on the bonfire; the rest of it looked worthless, but might fetch a few pounds somewhere. If not, she could always donate them to charity. One had to do one's part, but charity did begin at home.

The kitchen yielded nothing unexpected. Violet had spent so many hours in there, boiling the kettle for one of Daisy's endless cups of tea, retrieving biscuits from the cupboard ('Arrowroot, m'dear – helps my digestion!') and grilling the occasional fish finger or, if it was a special occasion, piece of cod, that she knew the contents of every cupboard and drawer like she knew the pattern of freckles on her arm. There were a couple of Apostle teaspoons that bore further investigation, to judge by their hallmarks, but nothing else. Nothing that would give her purchase on Daisy's bank accounts or other financial assets.

The dining room was just that: it contained the dining table and a rosewood cabinet in which the best china and silverware were stored. There was nowhere for any paperwork to be kept, but Violet paused in the doorway, wanting to leave but unable. The dining table pulled her back. The black dining table.

Violet shook her head convulsively. No time for dilly-dallying. 'Take time by the forelock', as the old adage went.

She quickly headed up the stairs and gave the bathroom and the front bedroom – her bedroom – a thorough going over. The bathroom didn't take long, but the bedside cabinets contained piles of letters and postcards that Daisy had, presumably, lain in bed reading. These Violet put to one side. She already knew everything that was in them from the endless monologues that she had encouraged with brandy and the occasional weak infusion of flowers from her garden – the names and addresses of old friends, the background details of Daisy's previous life that could be dropped in conversation or used to deflect questions – but it was worth going through them, just in case. One could never be too careful.

Finally, Violet turned her attention to the back room. The storage room. Previously, when Daisy was alive, she had only been able to stand in the doorway and look around, but she was pretty sure that most of Daisy's paperwork was kept there. What little paperwork Daisy had, anyway. That's why she had left it until last.

There was a truckle bed against one wall, and bookcases flanking the door, but Violet's attention was fixed immediately on the desk that sat beneath the window. The chair in front of it was, disconcertingly, a 1970s-vintage secretary's swivel chair with upholstery patterned in a psychedelic swirl of green and blue. Heaven alone knew where Daisy had got it from – or indeed why. With some qualms, Violet sat in the chair and methodically went through the desk drawers.

And it was all there. Building society statements, showing that Daisy was in the black to the tune of several thousand pounds. Mortgage details – and it turned out to be the case, as Violet had strongly suspected but needed to confirm – that the mortgage was freehold and had been paid off many years before. The deeds on the house. An insurance policy on thick parchment that had been taken out in the 1930s and would, presumably, pay out a pretty penny now, if Violet wasn't intending to keep Daisy alive – at least, as far as the rest of the world was concerned. Some premium bonds that might be worth investigating, and perhaps cashing in. Some certificates almost certainly inherited or acquired by Daisy's deceased husband that gave Daisy shares in companies that, to judge by their names (Amalgamated Nickel Engineering, Imperial Celluloid), had probably gone to the wall many years beforehand. Still, she put them to one side. Best to be sure. For all she knew, Amalgamated Engineering might have changed its name to British Steel and the shares could be worth millions now.

She leaned back in her chair and gazed out of the window. From this perspective she could see the entire length of the garden: unkempt, overgrown but potentially quite attractive. She might spend some time out there later on, trimming the bushes with her secateurs. Perhaps plant a few nice flowers in the borders as well. And while she was at it, there were people who would come in and spring-clean the house. The wallpaper and paintwork were old-fashioned, to be sure, and the kitchen could certainly do with bringing into the twenty-first century with a new cooker, new refrigerator and new cupboards and work surfaces, but those were big jobs that would require careful planning. And they might not be necessary.

Once she had finished searching the house – and it suddenly occurred to her that she needed to take a quick look in the attic, just to be absolutely sure she hadn't missed anything – Violet decided that she would take a wander down to the High Street. She could treat herself to a cup of tea and a steak pie and some new potatoes in one of the department stores, and then take a slow walk along the row of estate agents. What she needed was one slightly down at heel, one that specialised in lets and sub-lets rather than actual sales. And – although this might require some careful observation from a seat in a coffee shop – one that dealt more with what Violet thought of as the lower end of the social spectrum. Immigrants. Students, perhaps. If the rent was set low enough – and Violet wasn't greedy, far from it – then she was sure that tenants wouldn't mind an old-fashioned kitchen and some faded wallpaper. It was probably better than they were used to.

The best thing was, the estate agents would make all the arrangements, choose the tenants, collect the rent and just forward it to wherever she wanted, after taking their cut, of course. And Violet didn't begrudge them their cut, considering the load they were taking off her shoulders.

Streamers of smoke drifted up past the window. Somewhere down below, on the concrete patio, Daisy's clothes were burning away to ashes. Violet didn't like using the word 'evidence' – it sounded so harsh – but she was comforted to think that soon the events of the previous day would have vanished into the air.

And soon, after the house had been sorted out and whatever assets were in the house had been converted to cash, so would Violet.

The drifting smoke drew her gaze up into the sky: a deep cloudless azure that seemed to go on for ever and ever. She wished that, when she brought her gaze back down again, instead of overgrown bushes and thin trees she might see a glorious stretch of turquoise water, with the wind blowing spume off the crests of the waves and distant container ships breaking the straight line of the horizon.

And she decided there and then that she'd had enough of the small towns she had been hiding in for so long. She longed for the seaside, and that's where she would go next.

As she was descending the stairs, the telephone rang. Without even thinking, she picked it up off the table in the hall and said, brightly, 'Hello. Daisy Wilson speaking.'

CHAPTER FOUR

The mortuary was located between a park and a fire station on the outskirts of Braintree: a nondescript two-storey building that looked as if it had originally been intended as a temporary measure but now just sat there, set back from the road, fading further and further from people's minds. It was, Detective Chief Inspector Mark Lapslie decided as he pulled off the road and parked in one of the designated spaces, the closest thing to an architectural blind spot it was possible to get.

He wasn't in the best of moods. The morning before, after Emma Bradbury had driven off from the forest where the body had been discovered, Lapslie had hung around, waiting for the forensic pathologist to arrive. The press had turned up in the early afternoon, just before Jane Catherall, tipped off, he suspected, by one of the paramedics. By the time he had dealt with them and spent half an hour on the phone to the Crime Scene Manager she had already departed with the bodies, leaving him furious. Some mix-up in the admin had resulted in most of the uniformed police being pulled away from the crime scene in order to cover a local football match. And Superintendent Rouse had not called back. All in all, it had been a frustrating day.

Emma's Mondeo was two spaces across from his car. This time, it was empty. No strange men in the passenger seat, waiting for her to return and whisk them away.

The front door had a push-button combination lock. He'd known the combination once, but he'd forgotten it several times over the years, so he did what he usually did: buzzed the intercom. It was a good minute before anyone answered.

'Detective Chief Inspector Mark Lapslie,' he said, bending down to the level of the intercom. Why was it they were always installed by dwarves? Or did the installers expect lots of school parties to visit the mortuary unaccompanied?

The door buzzed, and he pushed it open.

Despite the summer sun outside, the building was pleasantly cool. The hallway was carpeted with tiles that had, over the course of the years, picked up so many coffee stains they were piebald. The walls were plastered and painted in a muted shade of blue. A young man wearing a white coat over jeans and a T-shirt was waiting for him.

'DCI Lapslie?'

He handed his warrant card across. The man inspected it carefully, although Lapslie was pretty sure he wouldn't have been able to tell the difference between a proper warrant card and a Scotland Yard gym membership.

'This way, please.'

He led Lapslie down a corridor and gestured for him to go ahead through a set of double doors. The temperature dropped appreciably as Lapslie pushed the doors open, and he became aware of a strong smell, like bleach that had been poured down a blocked drain and allowed to fester. The smell was so strong, so cloying that he could taste it at the back of his throat. His synaesthesia momentarily went into reverse; the taste of the disinfectant, or cleaner, or whatever it was, overlaid on the smell of decay filled his head with deep, sonorous chimes. It didn't happen very often, and he staggered slightly, one hand to his forehead, disoriented.

'Are you all right?' asked an unfamiliar voice.

'Fine. Fine. The smell just got to me for a moment.' He blinked a couple of times, forcing the sound of church bells to the back of his mind.

The room he had entered was large, and tiled in white

from top to bottom. Several large ventilation units had been fixed to the ceiling, positioned above stainless-steel tables that stood in the centre, as organised and as massive as ancient obelisks. Each table had a raised lip around the edge and a tap with an attached hosepipe and shower head, also in stainless steel, at one end. Two of the tables had shrouded bodies on them; one much larger and more irregular than the other.

The woman standing between the tables was smaller than him, with a stomach so pronounced and so rounded that it was almost as if she had thrust a basketball under her white coat, and bulbous blue eyes that gazed at Lapslie with disconcerting mildness. She smiled, and Lapslie thought that he had never seen such a sweet smile on a woman.

'Polio,' she said, her voice tasting of brandy and soda.

'Pardon?'

'I noticed you looking over at me yesterday, when I finally arrived at the scene of the crime. You were probably wondering what caused me to look like this. The answer is polio. I contracted it as a child. I was probably one of the last children in England to catch it.'

'I'm – sorry.' He wasn't sure what she wanted him to say.

'Six months flat out in a hospital bed, and several operations to fuse my spine together. It could have been worse. Of course, if I'd been born a year or two later, it could have been a lot better. Such is the uncertainty of life.' She held out a hand. 'We've not met. Doctor Jane Catherall. Pleased to meet you.'

She walked towards Lapslie with jerky steps and held out her hand. He shook it, noticing as he did so that she had double cuffs on her shirt, pinned together with delicate gold chains. A woman who cared about her appearance. 'DCI Lapslie,' he said.

'I've been expecting you. Your colleague is already here.' She kept hold of his hand, and Lapslie had the absurd impression that she was expecting him to bend down and kiss it. 'I wouldn't want you to think I always greet everyone with the unfortunate story of my health,' she added. 'I wanted to make the point that our bodies are a permanent record of everything that happens to us. Broken bones, illnesses, diseases ... they're all there, preserved in the flesh. And if all we have to work with is the flesh, then we can work backwards and recreate the person from the list of things that happened to them.'

'Thank you for the lecture.' He could feel her charm beguiling him, but he wasn't going to succumb. 'We didn't get a chance to talk yesterday,' he said tersely. 'I was too busy dealing with the press when they turned up to deal with you when *you* finally turned up.'

Dr Catherall looked away. 'I apologise for arriving so late. Alas, one of the physical effects of the polio is a weakness in the intercostal muscles. I have to wear a face mask connected to a respirator when I sleep. It maintains a positive pressure in order to ensure that I keep breathing but it does lead to a very disturbed night's sleep, and I find it difficult to wake up in the mornings. I missed the first four calls on my mobile.'

'Then buy a louder mobile,' Lapslie said unsympathetically.

Dr Catherall gazed up at him with those disquietingly mild eyes. 'The victim had been there for many months,' she said. 'Two more hours was not going to compromise any evidence on the body, and it ensured that when I did arrive I was not making any mistakes through lack of sleep. Let me do my job, Detective Chief Inspector, and I will provide you with everything you need to do yours.'

The long silence that grew between them was broken by the doors to the mortuary opening and Emma Bradbury entering the room. She didn't look like she had taken her suit off since the day before. The mortuary assistant who had let Lapslie in was following her.

'Boss,' Emma acknowledged.

'Sergeant. Been here long?'

'Half an hour or so. Dr Catherall let me use her office to make a few calls.'

Lapslie nodded. 'Well, shall we get on with it?'

Dr Catherall led Lapslie and Emma over to the first table and nodded towards the shrouded body. 'Your crash victim,' she said. 'I took the liberty of conducting the post-mortem this morning, before you arrived.' She glanced sideways at Lapslie. 'As I understand it, he was the victim of a car crash, rather than of a suspected murderer. It occurred to me that you would not want to be stood around waiting while I fiddled about in his innards.'

'Correct. Was there anything unusual about the body?'

'Nothing that caused me concern. Bruises and abrasions caused by the crash, some burning from the airbag, and a massive trauma to his neck, cutting through his carotid artery. All consistent with what was found at the scene. I have, of course, sent blood samples off for testing. We may get traces of alcohol, or drugs. Happy?'

'Ecstatic. What about the other one?'

With a flourish, she pulled the white cloth off the bulky, irregular shape on the second table. '*Et voila!*'

Seeing the corpse in the forest, a natural thing nestled amongst other natural things, had seemed almost normal. Seeing her here, laid out naked on harsh metal, surrounded by the plastic sheets that had been disinterred with her and crusted with dirt, Lapslie was struck by a sense of wrongness. Nobody deserved to be left like this. Death should have some dignity, surely.

What remained of her was mottled grey, and dry. Her hips and shoulders made tent shapes under her skin, and her stomach had decayed away, or perhaps been eaten away, to reveal the lumpy shape of her spine. Her face was dominated by the rictus-like grimace of her mouth, where the skin had pulled back to reveal black gums.

Framed in the plastic sheets, she seemed smaller than she had done in the forest.

'Well,' Dr Catherall said quietly as her assistant wheeled a stand supporting a tray of surgical instruments across to her. 'With no further ado, let us commence.'

For the next hour, Lapslie and DS Bradbury watched from the sidelines as Dr Catherall painstakingly unwrapped the sheets and cut her way through the old woman's cadaver, taking samples as she went and talking quietly into a minidisc recorder while her assistant took occasional photographs. Her work was meticulous and detailed, and her manner was more like a woman doing a difficult crossword puzzle than a medical expert slicing up a body.

Lapslie felt himself falling into an almost hypnotic trance as he watched, lulled by Dr Catherall's effortless technique. He had expected her hands to be clumsy, based on her shape and her medical history, but her movements were precise to the point of minimalism. Every gesture was exactly what was needed, no more and no less.

Emma Bradbury, on the other hand, fidgeted endlessly. After a few minutes she found a laboratory stool and perched on it, but she couldn't seem to get comfortable. Every now and then she would shift position, scratch her head, tug at her ear or search her pockets for something that she never seemed to find. She was plainly bored, and not very good at disguising it.

After twenty minutes or so, as Dr Catherall had penetrated to the last layer of plastic sheet around the body, she suddenly stood back. 'Good Lord,' she murmured. She leaned closer to examine something within the sheets. 'Good Lord,' she said again, and gestured for her assistant to move closer. He started taking photographs as Dr Catherall carefully removed a number of objects from between the plastic sheets and the corpse and transferred them to the third post-mortem table.

'You might want to take a look at this,' she said, turning to

Lapslie. He moved to join her, but before he could get to the table his mobile rang. Dr Catherall cast a dark glance at him.

'DCI Lapslie,' he said.

'Lapslie?' The voice was familiar: dry, like grass cuttings, and slightly tinny, which probably meant that he had Lapslie on speakerphone. 'Alan Rouse. You called yesterday.'

Dr Catherall gestured abruptly towards the door.

'Sorry, sir – could you hang on for a moment. I'm in the middle of a post-mortem.' He strode towards the door and out into the corridor. 'That's better,' he said as the doors swung shut behind him. 'Sir – it's been a long time.'

'Too long.' Lapslie could imagine Rouse leaning back in his chair in his white, glass-walled office. 'How's Sonia?'

A stab of unexpected pain; an icy knife in his heart. Lapslie's breath caught in his throat. 'She's – okay.'

'And the kids?'

'Fine. Thanks for asking.'

'And what about your … ah, medical condition?'

'Unchanged – which is why I was startled when I got a call from a young copper attending a car crash.'

'Ah yes. She called me when your name popped out of the computer.'

'That's one of the things I wanted to ask you about. Why was my name in the computer in the first place?'

There was a pause on the other end of the line: the aural equivalent of a shrug. 'I'm not entirely sure,' Rouse said eventually. Lapslie found that his tongue was tingling, as if he'd dipped it in something mildly spiced, but he wasn't sure what that meant. 'Presumably something about the case resonates with some previous investigation you've been involved with. Some unsolved murder, or suchlike.'

'I can't say I can hear the sound of bells ringing.'

'Perhaps it's a glitch. Computers are the bane of a policeman's life, these days.'

Another momentary silence, but this time Lapslie had the

impression that Superintendent Rouse was waiting for him to make some comment. 'I was under the impression that I was on indefinite sick leave,' he said eventually. 'You know that my synaesthesia makes it difficult for me to work in an office environment.'

'I know that's what we talked about, Mark, but you understand that we can't have you off sick indefinitely. We've been looking for some kind of job you can do without being in the office, but it's not been easy. I know you've written a couple of reports for the Chief Constable, but there's pressure from the Home Secretary to get as many people back in work as we can. So when your name was flagged up as someone who might be able to contribute to this case, well, I took it to be a sign. A sign that it was time you came back to us. I've arranged a desk for you here in Chelmsford, and you'll have access to a Quiet Room if you need it. We'll sort out something for you once this case is over.'

'And until then I'm the investigating officer?'

'Correct.'

'As DCI? Isn't that over-egging the pudding a bit?'

'Look on it as a way of easing yourself back into harness.'

'Nice talking to you, sir.'

'Pop in, when you're in the office. Let's have a chat.'

Lapslie slid the mobile back into his pocket and took a deep breath. It looked like he was back on the job. Not entirely unexpected – he'd been waiting for something like this to happen – but not entirely welcome either.

Sighing, he entered the pathology lab again.

Laid out on the stainless-steel table were the objects that Dr Catherall had removed from the stomach of the dead body: five desiccated corpses of what were either field mice or voles, along with two rats and something larger that Lapslie assumed was a polecat, or a ferret, or something along those lines. The smaller animals looked to Lapslie like no more than matchstick bones in twists of matted fur.

'Apparently we're looking for a serial killer, sir,' said DS Bradbury dryly.

Dr Catherall favoured her with a level glance. 'These animals had managed to worm their way through gaps in the sheeting and get to the old woman's body,' she said. 'I found them clustered around the stomach area, where they had started eating their way through. And they all died before they could do much damage.'

'Died how?' Lapslie asked.

'That,' Dr Catherall said, 'we will determine in due course. For now, I have a post-mortem to complete. It is not the kind of thing that you can come back to later.'

She worked in a logical progression, starting at the crown of the corpse's head and finishing at the soles of its feet. Half way through the process, the cadaver was splayed open, with Dr Catherall wrist-deep in its dry innards examining whatever remained of the organs, but by the time she had finished, the corpse was very nearly back to the condition in which it had started the post-mortem, albeit with a massive Y-shaped incision, stitched up with thick black thread, marring the body from groin to chest, where it split and continued up to either shoulder, passing above the flaps of its breasts.

As Dr Catherall finished with the body, Lapslie thought that she looked smaller: drained by the process. It seemed to him as if she didn't have much in the way of stamina within that diminutive frame of hers.

'What can you tell me about her?' Lapslie asked, as Dr Catherall washed her hands thoroughly and wearily.

'Let us start with the state of decomposition,' she replied. 'The body is in remarkably good condition, considering where it was found. The plastic sheeting in which she was wrapped would have provided something approaching an anaerobic environment, which would have slowed decomposition down and deterred all but the most determined or –' she indicated the small corpses on the next table '– smallest predators. Given the condition of the skin and the flesh, and taking account of the effects of the environment, I would estimate that she has been dead for between seven and ten months.'

'Which is about what we thought,' Emma said.

Dr Catherall sniffed. 'Sometimes pathology is about confirming the obvious, rather than bringing rabbits out of hats. Judging by bone density and porosity I would put her towards the end of her natural life, somewhere between seventy and eighty years of age. The progression of arthritis in her joints confirms this. Her lungs had been damaged by childhood rheumatic fever, and she had suffered from numerous other diseases during the course of her life – rickets, some small skin melanomas and so on – but none of them carried her off. She had also been suffering from low-level malnutrition for some years, I would estimate, but that did not carry her off either.'

'Then what did?' asked Lapslie.

'I'll come to that in a moment.' She leaned forward and indicated a puckered scar on the corpse's neck, sitting in the notch of the breastbone. 'This scar indicates the insertion of a breathing tube at some stage early on in her life. Without seeing her medical records it is difficult to be sure, but I would lay odds that it is the result of childhood diphtheria.' She paused for a moment, considering the body. 'The hips are worn, but they are hers, rather than replacements. Apart from the normal signs of extreme ageing, there are no indications of any age-related issues that might have caused her death – no tumours, no evidence of a stroke. And, as far as I can tell this far after death, she had a heart like a horse. In fact, if I were her doctor, and if she were still alive, I would say she had several years left in her yet. She did not die of the set of symptoms we collect together under the aegis of "old age".'

'Then—'

'I am getting there.' Dr Catherall rubbed a hand across her

chin thoughtfully. 'Exposure cannot be entirely ruled out. The degeneration of tissue means that I cannot definitively test for shock or circulatory collapse, but for reasons I will explain in a moment I do not believe that exposure is probable – at least, as a primary cause of death. It may, of course, have been contributory.'

'Of course,' Lapslie murmured. Dr Catherall gave the impression that she had either been rehearsing her little speech all the way through the post-mortem or that she carefully structured her thoughts down to subordinate clauses and subjunctive moods even as she spoke.

'To cut a long story short,' she said, seeing the look in Lapslie's eyes, 'you probably noticed yourself when you examined the body yesterday that there was some damage to the back of the skull. This was not accidental. I would estimate that she was battered once or twice, shortly before death, with a blunt object.'

'Nothing was found at the scene,' Emma murmured from beside Lapslie.

'Any other damage to the body?' Lapslie asked.

'No stab wounds, no fractures, if that's what you mean.'

Lapslie frowned. 'I was thinking more of the fingers.'

Dr Catherall nodded slowly. 'A strange one, that. The fingers on the right hand appear to have been removed by some sharp object. I'll have to do further tests in order to determine whether they were sawn off, cut off or bitten off, but they're certainly missing and I'm reasonably sure it was done after death. They certainly weren't removed surgically – there was no attempt to close up the wounds.'

'And the left hand?'

'Intact,' Dr Catherall said. 'Which is, of course, a little odd.'

'Does that mean anything to you yet?' DS Bradbury asked.

Lapslie thought for a moment. Apart from that maddening faint taste of lychees, caused more, he suspected, by the memory of a sound than by the sound itself, there was nothing more than a nagging familiarity. He'd talked to someone about missing fingers before, but where? When?

Silence filled the room. Lapslie eventually broke it by tapping the metal lip on the autopsy table with his hand. 'Do you have any idea whether the place where we found her was the actual scene of the crime? Did she die there, or did she die elsewhere and was moved there afterwards?'

'That's more a question for the CSIs to answer,' Catherall said judiciously.

'Doctor Catherall – Jane – I get the feeling that you've never stinted from venturing an opinion, especially when you have evidence backing it up.'

'Ah, how well you know me after such a short acquaintance. There were traces of earth and vegetation beneath the nails of her left hand, which indicates to me that she was alive when she arrived in the forest. More than that, I cannot say.'

'We still need to establish the identity of the victim. Did you find any clues on the body or in the clothing?'

'Her clothes were badly affected by the time she had spent in the forest,' Dr Catherall said. 'I will send them to the forensic team, of course, but I would be surprised if there was any usable evidence on them. The labels indicate that they came from a range of department stores, although the general style and colour, as well as the patterns of wear and the repairs that had been carried out on them, suggest that they had all been worn for a number of years.' She paused for a moment. 'I realise that it is not my area, but I did notice cotton threads hanging from a button here, or a zip there. I suspect you may find that many of the clothes were bought second hand, perhaps from charity shops, and the threads were the remnants of the labels. Just a suspicion of mine: Forensics will have more to say.'

'Doctor Catherall, I can't imagine *anyone* having more to say than you,' Lapslie said, smiling.

'You're too kind,' she murmured.

'So, we're no closer to discovering her identity.'

'That is not entirely the case.' She turned away. 'Dan, could you bring me the evidence box over by the fume cupboard?'

Lapslie looked over his shoulder. The young technician was busy putting the surgical instruments into an autoclave for sterilisation. At Dr Catherall's request he walked across to a large glass-fronted box on one side of the room and retrieved a plastic box with a standard CJA label stuck to the top.

'Take a look at the victim's mouth,' Dr Catherall said to Lapslie. 'What do you see? Or, rather, what do you *not* see?'

Lapslie bent closer to the skull-like head, catching a whiff of something unpleasant as he did so. 'I don't see any teeth,' he said.

'Indeed.' Dr Catherall opened the plastic box with a flourish. 'She had lost all of her teeth somewhere along the way, and replaced them with these!'

In the box Lapslie could see a set of dentures: bright and sparkling. Bizarrely, he wanted to laugh. They looked more like something from a joke-shop than something a person would put in their mouth.

'And these help us how?'

Dr Catherall carefully picked the dentures out of the box and turned them over. 'Because they have a serial number,' she said, indicating what looked to Lapslie more like a set of small scratches than anything meaningful. 'And that special ortho-dontic design serial number, which is unique to these dentures, will allow us to trace them back to the dental technician who made them. And that will allow us to identify the body.' She smiled that sweet smile up at him. 'And when I say "will", what I mean is "already has". Young Dan over there made some phone calls earlier on, and we now know who this lady is.'

'Doctor Catherall, I am amazed. Truly amazed. All you have to do is tell me who killed her and we'll have solved the entire case without leaving the room.'

'In true Nero Wolfe style,' she said, blushing at Lapslie's praise. 'Sadly I cannot help with identifying her murderer, but at least I can provide some of the information you need. Her name was Violet Chambers. She was seventy-nine years old, and she lived in Ipswich. That is all the information I have: I did not want to trespass too much on your undoubted area of expertise.'

'Doctor Catherall, you are truly amazing.'

'Please, call me Jane.'

'Even more amazing is the fact that you knew who she was and what killed her before I even walked into the room, and you still gave me the entire performance.'

She shrugged: a contorted movement of her shoulders. 'It is so rare that I get an appreciative audience. I have to take advantage where I can.'

'Jane, it's been a privilege being taken advantage of by you.'

'Then perhaps I could lure you into my office, where I could offer you a cup of coffee and show you what little information young Dan here has been able to unearth about Violet Chambers.'

'Are you propositioning me, Doctor Catherall?'

'Oh, I was taught never to end a sentence with a proposition,' she said, smiling.

Lapslie turned to where his DS sat. 'Emma, head over to Forensics. Find out whether they discovered any skeletons of animals around the crash site.'

Emma nodded and left, obviously grateful for the chance to actually do something, rather than just sit there watching someone else doing something.

'Dan,' Dr Catherall said to her assistant, 'could you organise two coffees for me? Cream and sugar to the side. We'll be in my office.'

She gestured to Lapslie to precede him. For a moment, Lapslie thought she wanted him to take her arm. He still wasn't sure quite how seriously Dr Catherall took herself, but he suspected he might wound her pride if he laughed.

Pushing the double doors open, he walked out of the post-mortem room and turned instinctively to his right, where a side corridor ran off the main spine of the building. As Dr Catherall let the doors close softly behind her, he moved along the corridor – slowly, so that she could keep up.

The doors he passed were closed, labelled 'Laboratory', 'Stores' and 'Evidence'. At the far end, a fire-door with a push-bar across it gave access to, presumably, the rear of the building. Just before the fire-door, to his left, was a door that had been left a few inches ajar. The sign said, 'Dr J. Catherall, Senior Forensic Pathologist'. He waited for her to join him and, when she gestured for him to enter the office, he pushed the door open and walked inside.

Based on his short experience of Dr Catherall, Lapslie had expected papers and books to be scattered all over the desk, the bookshelves, the filing cabinets and the floor. Instead, he was pleasantly surprised to find it was almost bare. A book-case held copies of medical journals and some reference works, but apart from that there was nothing but plain work surfaces and a Dell computer sitting on the desk, its screen-saver running.

No, that wasn't quite all. On top of the bookcase, next to the computer's printer, was a framed photograph of a young man with black hair. He was smiling at whoever had taken the photograph. Something was written across the bottom, but Lapslie didn't like to look more closely. It would have seemed too intrusive for such a short acquaintance.

Dr Catherall gestured to a chair and said, 'Please, take a seat. I will just be a moment.'

He did so. Dr Catherall pulled open a drawer and rummaged around inside, and Lapslie was irresistibly reminded of how, less than an hour before, she had been doing much the same thing inside a dead human body. Eventually she pulled out a thin folder.

'Here – this is what Dan discovered about her identity, along with a list of the clothes and possessions we found,' she said, handing it over. 'I'll print another copy off for you to take away.'

Lapslie opened the folder and leafed through the pages. Some had obviously been typed up – probably by Dan, the Doctor's assistant – but others were copies of emails. He started to read, then looked up, aware that the atmosphere in the office had changed in some subtle way.

Dr Catherall was staring at the computer.

'Anything wrong?' he asked.

'I have not used the computer this morning,' she said. 'I did not even switch it on when I arrived.' She nudged the mouse, and the screen flickered to life.

There, on the screen, was an open word-processing program, with the file that Lapslie was reading prominently displayed.

'Someone has been playing around with my computer,' Dr Catherall snapped, her mild demeanour changing suddenly to something much darker. 'Dan!'

Footsteps in the corridor, and the Doctor's assistant arrived carrying a tray with two cups and saucers, plus a sugar bowl and a jug of cream. 'Yes, Doctor?'

'Have you turned my computer on today?'

Dan shook his head. 'Definitely not.'

'Do you know who did?'

'There's only been you and me in this morning. And the Detective Sergeant, of course, but she spent most of her time in here reading the paper, as far as I could tell. The computer was off when I last checked.'

'Well it's on now.' She turned her gaze towards the bookshelf. 'And the printer has been turned on as well. Someone has been in here and printed off a copy of the information we discovered about Violet Chambers!'

'That's impossible,' Dan blurted, putting the tray down on the desk. 'What would they want to do that for?'

'And why leave the computer on?' Lapslie asked, frowning. 'Why leave the file up on screen?'

'Perhaps whoever it was got disturbed when Dan brought your DS in here,' Dr Catherall said. 'Perhaps they had to get out in a hurry and did not have time to close the computer down. They could have got away through the fire door outside. If they'd parked their car in the car park they could have been back to it in a handful of seconds.'

Lapslie looked from the computer to the printer and then to the file he held in his hands. It didn't make any sense. An elderly murder victim buried in the woods, *that* he could understand. It was the kind of thing that had happened before. A break-in at a pathology laboratory in order to copy a file, that he could understand as well, albeit at a stretch. There had been cases – usually gang-related murders – where there had been pretty sophisticated attempts to tamper with the evidence, including in one instance, he recalled, someone setting fire to the laboratory where the post-mortem was taking place. No, it was the combination of the two that was throwing him. Why would the murder of an elderly lady be so important that someone would gain access to a pathologist's office to look at her file? It was like a collision between two entirely unrelated cases.

He looked at Dr Catherall, whose face was contorted into a thunderous scowl. 'I'm having a hard time believing this,' he said. 'Are you sure you didn't leave your computer on last night when you left?'

Dr Catherall said something scathing in reply, but Lapslie didn't catch it. Something she had said earlier was biting at the back of his mind. Something about whoever had gained access to the office and turned the computer on – if indeed she hadn't forgotten to turn it off the night before, or Emma Bradbury hadn't turned it on herself for some unknown reason – parking their car in the car park outside.

And then he realised what it was. When he visualised that car, he imagined it as being a black Lexus with a shaded windscreen.

Just like the one that had been parked near the place in the forest where Violet Chambers' body had been discovered. The one that had driven off before he could find out who was inside.

CHAPTER FIVE

Daisy Wilson left her car – or *Violet*'s car, as she was already thinking of it with a mixture of nostalgia and distaste – in a side-street in Colchester. She could have driven it all the way, but something made her stop twenty or so miles short of her eventual destination and complete her journey by train. Partly it was the usual caution that had served her so well for so long. There was something about leaving her car where it might be connected to her that made her feel itchy and vulnerable, despite the anonymity that her new identity afforded her. Mainly, however, it was the fact that driving made her nervous, while trains calmed her down. If she was going to live in this area for a while, she wanted her first impressions to be happy ones.

Leaving the relative anonymity of the A12 dual carriageway she drove cautiously through the outskirts of town, looking for the nearest station. She had a pretty good idea that the trains to Leyston-by-Naze stopped at Colchester on their way, although she wasn't entirely sure how she knew. The problem was, Colchester seemed to have three different stations, and she didn't want to end up too far away from the right one. Eventually, after driving past Colchester Station and North Station, and having detoured around the plain architecture of the Dutch Quarter and the contrasting ornate Gothic monstrosity that was the Abbeygate arch, she ended up at Colchester Town, chosen by the simple expedient that it was the closest station to the road signs that pointed to Leyston-by-Naze.

She left her car parked in a disabled spot outside a quiet row of shops with two storeys of flats above them, taking with her only a small suitcase and her handbag. She had a disabled badge for the car, although she wasn't actually disabled, and she left it on the dashboard before wiping over the places she had touched with a damp cloth soaked in sugar soap and locking the car up. She glanced around, as if looking for a particular shop front: florists, second-hand bookshop, laundrette, bookmakers, small supermarket. Nobody was watching. Nobody would be able to describe her later. Despite its closeness to the station it was a quiet location, out of the main flow of traffic. The car should be safe there for a few days before anyone became suspicious, and she fully intended to be back to collect it before then.

Daisy patted the roof of the car absently with a gloved hand. An F-registration Volvo 740 in a dull shade of bronze – 'Champagne', she believed it was called – she had obtained it at some stage in her travels and kept it because it was so completely undistinguished. Nobody would give it a second glance. And nobody was likely to steal it. For a start, it didn't even have a working radio, let along anything more modern.

Then again, if someone did steal the car it might actually help. Loath as she was to find a new one, Daisy was becoming increasingly aware that the Volvo was a link to Violet Chambers – a link she really should consider breaking. It wasn't as if she was emotionally attached to the car – Daisy knew, without any great upheaval of the heart – that she wasn't emotionally attached to anything in the way that she supposed other people to be. It was more that the car was the perfect blend of blandness and reliability. It was also an automatic, which made her feel a lot more comfortable when she drove.

Locking the car, she walked briskly away towards the station, suitcase swinging from her left hand. Time and tide waited for no woman, and she was impatient to see the sea.

According to the notice boards in an anonymously modern station – all girders and columns and glass – she had a half-hour wait before the next train, so she bought her ticket with cash and had a bland, milky cup of tea in the station café. The place smelled of strong coffee and hot pastry. Nobody gave her a second glance: a small woman in a tweedy jacket and hat sitting by herself, sipping at her cup. She was well aware of the impression she gave – or failed to give. It was something she consciously cultivated.

For some reason Daisy had expected an old 1950s vintage British Rail diesel pulling four dusty blue coaches, but the train she boarded was a bland, white, modern train with electric doors covered in graffiti. Regardless, the sight of the train pulling into the curve of the station filled Daisy with nostalgic longing, although she was disturbed to realise that she wasn't sure exactly what she was being nostalgic about. Perhaps it was just for the past itself.

Daisy settled herself down into an empty second-class compartment. A small mist of dust and stuffing rose from the upholstery as she sat, the strangely familiar smell suddenly provoking a memory of … of what? Her, sitting on a train, looking out at an ocean of red poppies. How old was she? *Where* was she?

She shook her head. No time for memories now.

The train started with a jerk, and Daisy felt her breath quicken with anticipation as her carriage pulled out of the shadow of the station and coasted gently through the outskirts of the town before accelerating into the countryside. For the next half hour or so she gazed raptly out at rolling fields and hills, haystacks and barns, and at small towns with evocative, perfectly British names like Wivenhoe, Alresford, Great Bentley, Weely and Kirby Cross.

She saw her first seagulls just as the line split, the right-hand arc heading off towards Clacton, the left-hand arc towards Frinton-on-Sea, Walton and Leyston-by-Naze. They sat in groups on the roofs of houses and wheeled slowly above the Essex marshes, great grey and white birds with tiny black pearls for eyes, and beaks hooked cruelly, like fish-knives.

By the time the train stopped at Frinton she could smell the sea itself prickling her nostrils, salty and cool, a smell like nothing else on earth. A smell that hadn't changed since a time before houses, farms and people, before cars and tractors and trains. Perhaps the only original smell left on the face of the planet.

The door to the carriage slid open and an elderly woman stepped in. Despite the thinness of her arms her skin sagged beneath the bones, and the veins on the backs of her hands were knotted and twisted like the roots of a storm-weathered tree. Beneath the hand-knitted hat that covered her hair, her eyes and face seemed carved into a perpetual smile.

'Good afternoon,' she said. 'May I join you?'

'Please do,' Daisy said automatically, although she could feel disappointment seeping through her body and souring her mood. 'I was feeling quite lonely, sitting here.'

The woman smiled and sat down opposite Daisy. Without thinking, Daisy arranged her hands in her lap in the same way as her new travelling companion.

A whistle blew somewhere down the platform, and the train began to pull away.

'On holiday?' the woman asked, glancing at Daisy's suitcase.

'My cousin has been taken ill,' Daisy replied. It was her standard cover story. She tapped her chest vaguely. 'It's her ... you know. She's in and out of hospital, and I thought I'd pop down and make sure she was all right.'

The woman nodded. 'Terrible,' she said, nodding. 'Still, it's amazing what the doctors can do these days.' She leaned forward, extending one of her gnarled hands. 'My name is Eve,' she said. 'Eve Baker.'

'Daisy Wilson – pleased to meet you.' Daisy shook the offered hand, feeling the way the papery skin moved against the bones. She could take Eve's wrist in her left hand and push those fingers back until they snapped, one by one, leaving Eve breathless with pain and shock. If she wanted. The feeling excited her.

'And what about you?' she asked instead. 'Are you on holiday as well?'

If she was, Daisy had no use for her. Although she usually

waited until she had got her bearings and somewhere to stay before she started looking around for her next victim, there was no point in passing up a perfectly good opportunity if it presented itself. All is fish that comes to the net, as they said.

'Oh my, no,' Eve laughed. 'I live in Leyston. I've lived there since I was a child.'

'Really?' Daisy allowed her face to adopt an encouraging expression.

'Oh yes.' Eve leant forward confidingly. 'I was evacuated here during the war, you see, and while I was here my home in London was bombed during the blitz. My family was killed, so I stayed with the family I had been placed with.'

'I'm sorry to hear that.'

'Oh, it was all such a long time ago, now. I was educated here, I married here and I brought up three children here.'

The little spark of interest that had begun to flicker in Daisy's breast guttered in a discouraging wind.

'You have three children?'

'Oh yes. They've all moved away, of course, but they still visit every week or so. One of them works in a bank, one works in computers and one is a school secretary. And they've given me so many lovely grandchildren.'

'That's wonderful,' Daisy murmured, letting her gaze slide away from her travelling companion and alight again on the flat, green countryside that was rolling past the window. Children and grandchildren. Family. People who would notice if she vanished. People who would care.

'Where does your cousin live?' Eve asked brightly.

Daisy paused for a moment before replying, just long enough to give the impression that she had thought the conversation was over. 'Near the church,' she replied vaguely. There was bound to be a church in Leyston.

'Which church?'

'The Methodist one, I believe.' That should still be safe. How many Methodist churches were there likely to be?

76

'Ah. I see.' Eve subsided back into her seat, looking disappointed that her new friend didn't want to continue their conversation.

The train began to slow, and Daisy's heart began to beat faster. It was always like this, coming into a new town, a new home, for the first time, but there was something else as well, a feeling that this time she really *was* coming home. It was something to do with the briny smell of the sea, the plaintive cries of the seagulls, the feeling of almost infinite space just beyond the bushes that lined the track. And then they were pulling into the tiny station, just two tracks separated by a platform between them.

The train lurched to a halt, and Daisy was surprised, looking away from the window, to see the little old lady still sitting opposite her. She had almost dismissed her from her mind.

'Nice to meet you,' she said.

'And you. I hope your cousin … you know.'

'Thank you.'

Daisy allowed the old woman to disembark first, then, as the woman scurried towards the metal and glass ticket barrier, so different from the solid red-brick one she had expected, she busied herself for a few moments with her suitcase, allowing some distance to grow between them before she moved off.

Daisy walked out into the sunshine, and stopped to drink in the view. To her left, a row of three-storey houses with tall windows curved leisurely out of sight. To her right, a public house named, of course, The Station Hotel. And ahead of her, across a triangular green fringed with bushes, lay the North Sea, heaving and billowing like a grey-blue sheet that had been fastened between the buildings on either side and allowed to ripple in the wind. She walked toward the seafront, entranced. How long had it been since she had seen the sea? She couldn't even remember. All the places, all the names and the faces were blended together in her mind. She knew she must have been to the seaside at some stage in her life, but she couldn't remember when.

Daisy took a look over her shoulder, a valedictory farewell to the life she was leaving behind, and found her vision filled with a block of flats in Victorian design: red brick, tall windows and a massive front door. She had walked around it to get from the modern glass ticket office to the green, but it looked so much like the older ticket office she had been expecting that she had to blink and look again, just to check she wasn't imagining things. And then, noting the location of the flats in relation to the building, she realised what must have happened. The building had once actually been the ticket office, but it had been closed up and converted into flats. Presumably it was worth more that way. Now the way into the station was through an anonymous building built from a kit, and the people who lived in the old ticket office now had no idea about the history they were walking amongst.

The short walk from the station brought her out on the esplanade. Directly ahead of her was the pier: a long wooden road leading out into the sea, supported on an elaborate truss-work of poles and struts. To her left was a row of hotels and guest houses, receding into the distance. To her right was what looked at first glance like a whole pile of children's building blocks in bright colours, piled higgledy-piggledy, one on top of the other. It took Daisy a few moments before she realised that they were beach huts: simple wooden sheds painted in reds and greens and yellows, set into a sloping hillside and separated from one another by concrete walkways.

But it was the sea that kept pulling at her attention. The restless sea, a thousand shades of blue and grey, all blurring together as the waves crashed onto the sand and ebbed back again, only to gather their strength for another assault. She could feel the sea-spray in the air, pricking at her skin. So chaotic, so relentless and so endlessly fascinating. She could watch it for hours.

But she still had to find somewhere to stay. The drive from the London suburbs to Colchester followed by the train journey had taken it out of her, and she craved nothing more than a long, hot bath and a long, dreamless sleep.

The best thing she could do, she decided, was to find a nice hotel for a few nights. That would allow her to take her time looking for something more permanent – a flat, perhaps, on the ground floor of an old house somewhere within walking distance of the beach. As long as she had a kitchen where she could cook and a bed where she could sleep, she would be happy. A lair, from which she could emerge to hunt. First, as the old proverb had it, catch your hare.

A garden would be nice, but not essential. After all, the trunk of her car, still back in Colchester, was filled with various twigs, leaves, flowers and roots that she had picked from her *real* garden, her *proper* garden. That should be enough to keep her going.

Slowly, and with increasing tiredness, Daisy turned and wandered along the line of hotels and guest houses. The first few looked as if they were designed to catch the first people off the train: bland, plastic affairs with no character and nothing to recommend them apart from their proximity to the station and the beach. The next one was a large public house with rooms above the bar: too noisy, she decided. And then, a little way on, she discovered a small Edwardian frontage, four storeys high, which advertised itself as *The Leyston Arms Hotel*. She stood for a few moments, looking it over. The windows were clean, and the front steps were spotless.

Someone in there knew about soda crystals, she thought.

Decision made, she walked purposefully up the steps and into the foyer. The carpet had been freshly vacuumed, and she could smell furniture polish in the air. These were all good signs. The man behind the front desk was impeccably dressed in dark trousers, white shirt and maroon tie. The twin folds down the front of his shirt indicated that either this was the first time he had worn it or he had his cleaning and ironing done professionally, but she could forgive him that by the way he smiled at her.

'Good afternoon, madam. Can I help you?'

'Do you, by any chance, have a room?' she said, smiling back.

'We do,' he said. 'How many nights will you be staying?'

She thought for a moment. 'It might be up to a week. Would that be all right?'

'Let me check.' He looked down and consulted what Daisy suspected was a computer screen hidden below the level of the desk. Computers were everywhere, these days. How had the world managed to function without them?

'We have a room overlooking the beach, or one at the back of the hotel,' he said eventually. 'They're both the same price.' His eyes flickered to a velvet-covered pegboard, the same colour as his tie, which hung to one side. On it were displayed the prices for single rooms, twin rooms, double rooms, family rooms and for breakfast. Daisy took the information in for a moment, suspecting that the man was already wondering, based on her age and her clothes, whether she had enough money to pay for the room.

'Is there any difference between them?' she asked.

'The one at the back of the hotel gets less traffic noise, especially in the mornings, but it doesn't have quite the same view,' he said, smiling again.

'Then I'll take the room at the front.'

He nodded. 'May I take a credit card?'

'Oh,' she said, 'I don't have a credit card.' Forestalling his surprised reaction, she quickly added, 'I don't like them. I've never needed one, and I don't see why I should start now.'

He was momentarily nonplussed. 'We normally require some form of … surety,' he said eventually.

'Could I pay for two days in advance?'

He thought for a moment. 'That will be fine,' he said. 'If you could fill out this form for us ...' He reached down under the counter and retrieved a clipboard with several pre-printed forms attached to it. Sliding it around so that she could see it properly, he added, 'Just put down your name and address – I'll do the rest.'

A pen was attached to the top of the clipboard by a length of chain. Taking it gingerly, Daisy placed the tip of the pen against the paper and started to write her name.

And realised with horror that she couldn't remember what it was.

Who was this woman, standing in the hotel foyer? Daisy Wilson? Violet Chambers? Jane Winterbottom? Alice Connell? How did she sign her name: simply, ornately or in copperplate handwriting? Her mind whirled with the flotsam and jetsam of too many abandoned lives. She was paralysed with indecision. Her hand trembled, making small patterns on the form.

'Is everything all right, madam?'

She took a deep breath. 'I'm sorry – it's been a long day.'

Work backwards. Where had she driven from? What did the house look like? What did the street look like? *Who was she?*

'Daisy Wilson,' she said firmly, grasping onto the nearest, the most recent memory as it floated past. 'My name is Daisy Wilson.' Quickly she filled out her name and, with some misgivings, Daisy's address. It was a trail, of sorts, but it couldn't be helped. After all, she was going to be playing Daisy for a while yet.

'Thank you,' he said as she slid the form back and delved into her handbag for her purse. 'I've taken the liberty of putting you in room 241. The bar is to your left, the dining room is to your right. Will you be requiring dinner tonight?'

She thought for a moment. It had been a long drive, and she didn't particularly want to wander out looking for a civilised restaurant. 'Yes, that would be lovely. About half an hour?'

'I'll make sure a table is available,' he said. 'I hope you enjoy your stay.'

Daisy took her suitcase up to her room. It contained a bed, a desk and chair and a small armchair, all arranged in the smallest possible space without actually looking cramped.

Another hotel. Another town. Another identity.

A wave of ... something ... rose up unexpectedly and crashed around her. It wasn't quite grief, or sadness, or regret, or anything in particular. It was more as if a low-key version of each of those emotions had been blended together to form something new, something with no name: a general feeling of sad disconnection from the world. For a moment she was lost and drifting. For a moment.

'Focus,' she murmured. 'Focus.'

She washed quickly and, taking a pen, notebook and a pile of plain stationery from her suitcase, she headed down to the dining room.

Dinner was two lamb chops with asparagus spears and potatoes dauphinois, simply prepared but very pleasant. She followed it with a trifle – something she hadn't had for years. It was what she considered to be 'nursery food' – plain but comforting – and none the worse for that. The portions were small, but enough was as good as a feast, as she always said.

While she ate, she started on the next phase of her task. Before leaving the house in London in the tender care of the estate agents, she had carefully combed through Daisy's letters for the names of friends with whom she was in intermittent contact. Some of her correspondents had drifted away or died over the course of the years, but Daisy was still receiving Christmas cards and the occasional round-robin letter from seven people – old friends or work colleagues with whom she had shared some part of her life. Taking several sheets of stationery, Daisy carefully wrote the same message to each person or family in the almost perfect copy of Daisy's scrawled handwriting that she had worked on whilst dancing attendance on the old bitch.

I'm sorry that I haven't been in touch for some time, but life has been rather complicated. I don't know if you remember my cousin Heather, but she has recently been taken ill. She is currently recuperating at home, and she asked me to come down and look after her and her cats. I don't know how long I will be away, but I suspect it might be some time. I have let the house out while I'm gone – I was worried that it would be empty, but at least this way I know it will be looked after, and I'll get some (much needed!) income.

I'll let you know when I have more information – in the mean time, if you get around to writing to me then please use the address above.

On each letter, Daisy added in the names and some personal details and questions she had gleaned from the letters, in an attempt to make them all seem more personal. She left the tops of the letters blank. When she had settled down somewhere local then she could fill the return address in. Or, if she wanted to really play it safe, she could use a PO Box number.

She read through the letters again. She wasn't sure if they were too formal, too carefully worded. Daisy had been quite demotic in her speech, but what little writing of hers that Daisy had seen betrayed a sharper mind and a trained writing style. Having been through the house and seen Daisy's choice in books, Daisy had revised her opinions of the woman. Daisy, she believed, had been putting it on a little.

After dinner she dropped the letters off in her room and walked through into the hall, intending to go for a quiet stroll around the town. The sun had gone down since she had arrived, and the indigo sky of sunset that had acted as backdrop to the drama of the sea was now a black curtain against which the glowing bulbs of the esplanade's lights were displayed. The bar, however, was just to her right, and she decided that she deserved a drink before setting out. The day had gone pretty well, all things considered.

The room itself was furnished with cane chairs and low glass tables. It wasn't quite her 'scene', but she persevered, walking steadily up to the long bar and asking the barman – a lanky youth who was probably a third of her age – for a small dry sherry.

His thick brows contracted into a single line. 'Don't think we do sherry,' he said without even looking at the bottles.

Daisy was not going to be put off. 'Then I will have a Dubonnet with lemonade, please.'

He poured it with bad grace, and she took her drink to a table over in one corner from where she could see the entire bar area. It was pretty empty – most people had probably gone out on the town – but one or two of the tables were occupied. A middle-aged woman in a shawl was sipping on a gin and tonic at one table. Her husband, dressed rather uncomfortably in a suit, was sitting across the other side of the table. Neither of them was talking. The woman was staring at her glass as if it contained the secrets of the universe, and her husband fidgeted as if he was constantly on the verge of saying something just in order to break the silence and then reconsidering at the last moment when he realised how banal it would sound.

Daisy found herself holding her Dubonnet like the woman at the table was holding her gin, and she forced herself to stop. She'd already had one moment of slippage. She had to keep a grip on who she was, lest it all slide away from her, leaving her with no character at all. Or a faceless stranger, perpetually reflecting every character she came across.

At another table a lone man sat, nursing a pint of dark liquid. He was burly, florid, with more hair on his knuckles than on his head. A flat cap sat on the table beside him. There was an air about him that made Daisy think he was drinking something old-fashioned and manly, like mild and bitter, or brown ale. She wondered briefly whether she should engage him in conversation, but she decided against it. She never stalked men: it was almost impossible to strike up a friendship without the sexual element creeping in, and there was always that ever-present worry that they were stronger than her should her little poisons not work quickly enough. And, of course, taking on their identities directly was almost impossible: she would have to find some sideways approach to realising their assets when they were gone, and that itself was adding an extra risk to the proceedings. No, best not.

Delicately she drained the last drops of her rather tart Dubonnet and gathered her handbag and coat together. A little walk around town and then bed, she decided.

The air outside was cold. Across the road she could see the metal railings of the esplanade but behind that, where earlier there had been the beach and the sea and the sky, there was nothing. A black void, immense and empty. It was as if the world ended at those railings, and an unwary pedestrian might stumble and fall, pinwheeling for ever through space until the end of time.

Daisy shook herself. Really, the thoughts that were entering her head. It wouldn't do. It really wouldn't do.

She let her feet guide her, not planning where she was going. A side street led away from the esplanade and deeper into town. She crossed what she assumed was the High Street – occupied mainly by teenagers who appeared to be migrating from pub to club and back again – and found another side street that was lined with antique and curio shops. Something was pulling her on, some deep, primal attraction towards something sensed but as yet unseen. She stumbled on, letting the shop fronts and the lights all blur together.

Until she found herself in front of a gaudily lit frontage, all blue neon and yellow letters. It looked as if it had once been a cinema, but now it was used for another kind of entertainment.

Bingo.

A session had obviously just finished, and a crowd of women was descending the steps. Some were wearing wraps, some coats, some just low-cut silvery tops and skirts. They were laughing coarsely. *Secretaries*, Daisy thought, dismissively. Behind them came a gaggle of older women in long coats and woollen hats, walking in ones and twos, and suddenly Daisy's senses came alert. Her mouth went dry, and every detail stood out as if spotlit. She could *smell* the lavender perfume, lovingly dabbed on from bottles bought twenty years beforehand. She could *feel* their rough, hand-knitted cardigans and scarves. She could *see* the surreptitious gleam of their scalps through their carefully coiffured hair. As they went their separate ways, with goodbyes and waves and little pecks on the cheek, Daisy noted which streets they went down, which directions they left in, who leant on a cane for support and who didn't, who left in company and who left alone.

These were her natural prey.

And tomorrow, the hunt would begin again.

CHAPTER SIX

It was several weeks after the autopsy that Mark Lapslie and Emma Bradbury drove up to Ipswich together in Emma's Mondeo. Technically, Ipswich was outside their manor, falling within the boundaries of Suffolk Constabulary, but Lapslie had made some phone calls before setting out and they'd been given permission to continue with their inquiries. The roads were busy, but Emma managed to weave her way through the mass of other cars, overtaking where necessary and under-taking where she had to, in order to get them there in good time. Lapslie just let himself sink back in the passenger seat, eyes closed, the roar of her engine sending pulses of marmalade through his mouth and provoking his salivary glands into spasm. He was so used to the sound of his own car engine that he couldn't taste it any more, but he hadn't spent long enough in Emma's car to get used to the noise, or to be able to screen it out. He'd wanted to drive up himself, but it made no sense for them to take two cars on the journey, and police etiquette demanded that a DS drove a DCI, not the other way around.

Once she reached out to switch the radio on. Firmly, he switched it off again. She glanced uncertainly across at him, but said nothing.

After a series of turns separated by shorter and shorter distances, Lapslie opened his eyes to find Emma slowing down to look for a parking space. They were in a wide road lined with a mixture of silver birch and lime trees and, behind the trees, semi-detached houses built some time around the 1970s. Most front gardens had bikes, or scooters, or wheeled toys shaped like small tractors or lorries abandoned on them. The area gave off a welcome sense of prosperity and supportiveness. Not like some of the sink-hole estates that Lapslie had visited over the years. That was the trouble with being a policeman. You ended up getting a distorted view of the world.

Emma parked in a space under a lime tree. As she and Lapslie got out, Lapslie glanced behind them. There were no other cars driving along the road. He wondered what exactly he had been looking for. A black Lexus perhaps? He shook his head and turned back to Emma. He was beginning to take this conspiracy thing a bit too seriously.

Emma cast a dark glance at the overhanging branches. 'This tree's going to drip sap all over my car,' she muttered. 'I know it is. Sticky sap. It's a bugger to get off, but it stains the wax if you don't.'

'It's okay,' Lapslie said soothingly. 'We'll stop off at a car wash on the way back.'

She frowned. 'This car's never seen the inside of a car wash, and I'm not about to start now. Do you know what those rotating brushes do to your paintwork? I might as well take a scouring pad to it.'

The nearest house had a plate attached to the gatepost with the number '58' attached. A metal climbing frame sat on the recently cut front lawn: fronds of longer grass and a handful of daisies poking up around the frame where it touched the ground. 'That's Violet Chambers' last known address,' Emma continued. 'Doesn't look abandoned. Also doesn't look as if an old woman lived there.'

'If she lived with her family then someone should have reported her missing some time ago,' Lapslie said.

'Which they didn't, according to the records.'

Lapslie walked up towards the house. A bedroom window was open, and a maroon Toyota Camry estate sat on the drive. The rear section contained two backwards-facing seats just large enough for two six-year-olds.

The warm taste of vanilla flooded his mouth, and for a moment Lapslie wasn't sure why. Then he heard the sounds of children shouting from the back of the house. The sound and the taste and the memories they evoked made him suddenly dizzy: he reached out to hold onto the frame of the swing to steady himself.

'Are you okay, sir?'

'Fine.' He straightened up. 'Let's get on with it.'

Emma rang the bell, and they waited for a few moments. There were sounds of movement inside the house, then the door opened. A woman in her thirties looked at them curiously. Her brown hair was tied back into a pony-tail, and she wore a flowered silk blouse, tied loosely beneath her breasts, and cord culottes. Her feet were bare. 'Hello?' she said cautiously.

'Detective Chief Inspector Lapslie, Essex Constabulary,' he said, holding out his warrant card. She glanced at it blankly. 'And this is Detective Sergeant Bradbury. Sorry to bother you, but we were looking for the house of Violet Chambers.'

The woman shook her head. 'I know most of the families around here,' she said. 'And I've never heard of a Violet Chambers.'

'She was an elderly lady. In her seventies.'

'We've got mostly families around here. There's an elderly couple across the road – number sixty-seven. They might know her.'

Emma stepped forward, tossing her hair back with a flick of her head. 'How long have you been living in the area, Miss—?'

'Wetherall. Mrs Suzy Wetherall.' She smiled at Emma, and Emma smiled back. 'We moved here six months ago. We're renting, but we love it here so much that we're hoping to buy a house in the road if any come up for sale.'

'What made you move here?' Emma asked.

'My partner's job relocated from London. We thought we'd

take the chance to find somewhere nicer to live.' She made a vague gesture towards the garden. 'And we succeeded.'

Lapslie smiled in response. 'Who are you renting the house from?' he asked.

'An estate agents near the station. I can't remember the name.'

'Do you know who was in the house before you?'

She shook her head. 'No, but they left it absolutely spotless.'

'And what about the owners of the house?'

'I assumed the estate agents owned it.' She shrugged. 'I suppose they could be renting it on behalf of someone else, but they never told us who. We just pay them every month.'

'And you've never heard of Violet Chambers?' Lapslie asked again, just in case the conversation had dislodged a random fragment of memory from the woman's mind. He'd known it happen before.

'Never. But ask David and Jean over at number sixty-seven. They might be able to help.'

'Thank you for your help,' he said, smiling.

Emma extended her hand towards Mrs Wetherall. 'Thanks,' she added, squeezing the woman's own hand.

They turned to leave. As the door closed behind them, Lapslie said: 'Instinct?'

'She's telling the truth. We can check it with the estate agents—'

'And we will.'

'—but I don't think she's stringing us along. Looks like the family moved in a couple of months after Violet Chambers died, assuming the post-mortem results are accurate. So – what's the next step, boss?'

'We talk to the neighbours over at number sixty-seven to see whether they remember Violet, and then we drive down to the nearest station and check with the estate agents to find out who is renting the house out.'

Vanilla suddenly exploded across his tongue as if someone

had squashed an ice cream cornet into his mouth. On the back of the explosion came the sound of shouting from the garden: a sudden argument, a fight, or just a moment of triumph in a game. The shock made him stumble: he caught his stride again but his ankle turned slightly and he staggered sideways, into the grass, before he could catch himself.

Emma was at his side in a moment, holding his arm.

'Sir – are you all right?'

He felt his face warm up as he blushed. He hated showing weakness. But he probably owed her an explanation, especially if it stopped rumours spreading that he might be alcoholic, or mentally unstable.

'Let's get to the car.'

Leaning with his back against Emma's Mondeo, the heat of the sun-warmed metal comforting through his suit jacket, he took a deep breath. How best to start?

'Look, sir,' she said, standing with her hands on her hips and staring out along the road, 'if you want to talk about it, that's fine. If you don't, that's fine too. Either way, it goes no further.'

He nodded, and took a deep breath. 'I've had it for as long as I can remember,' he said quietly. 'For a long time I assumed everyone was the same as me, but when the kids at school started teasing me, and saying I was crazy, I stopped talking about it. "Crazy bonkers", they used to say. "Mark's gone crazy bonkers".'

'And the Force know about it? Whatever it is?'

He nodded. 'Don't worry – it's not depression, or psychosis, or anything like that. I'm not going to suddenly sit in a corner and sob for hours on end. My doctor's aware, but there's nothing he can do. Nothing anyone can do. It's not life-threatening, or even life-changing, or anything that would make them do anything about it. It's just … part of me. Part of who I am.'

Emma nodded, but she looked like she wanted to shake her head instead. 'So – what exactly is it then?'

'It's called synaesthesia. Nobody knows quite what causes it, but it's as if the nerves in the brain have got short-circuited somehow. Signals going in on one route get rerouted to somewhere else. The best theory is that it all starts in infancy. Babies perceive the world in a mish-mash of sensory impressions, because their brains are not completely developed and they can't separate out smell, taste, touch and so on – they're all mixed up. As the brain develops, the senses start to separate from one other. For people like me this separation may not take place for reasons we don't understand. Some people see different colours when they listen to music. There was a Russian composer called Alexander Scriabin, for instance – he could tie particular notes and chords to different shades of colour, and composed his music not just to sound good, but to *look* good as well – at least, to him. Others can actually feel tastes. Roast chicken might be sharp spikes on the palms of their hands. Orange juice might cause the feeling of soft balls rolling on their scalp.'

'You mean—' She paused, grasping for the right words. 'You mean like some people say that something's making them feel blue? Like that?'

'Not like that. That's just people using examples. Blue just means depressed. These are real feelings.'

'Hallucinations?' Emma asked, frowning. 'Surely it must just be hallucinations?'

'If so, they're consistent. The same things always provoke the same responses.'

'And what is it with you? Lights or feelings on your hands?'

He laughed, bitterly. 'Those I might be able to ignore. No, with me, certain sounds translate into tastes. If I ever hear "Ticket To Ride" by the Beatles, it's like I've just taken a bite out of a rancid chunk of pork.'

Emma ventured a smile. 'I thought everyone reacted that way to Paul McCartney.'

'Yeah, but when my cell-phone rings it tastes like I'm

drinking a mocha coffee.' He nodded towards the house. 'And the sound of children playing always makes me taste vanilla. Sometimes it just takes me by surprise, that's all. Overwhelms me.'

Emma glanced at him. 'And there's nothing that can be done?'

'Nothing. It's not going to kill me, and it's not stopping me from working. My doctor's suggested acupuncture, which shows how desperate he is, and the neurology department of the local hospital are more interested in studying my brain than they are in finding a treatment. So I just keep on going. Most of the time it doesn't change anything. I can still work. It's just that ... every now and then, it's like I get ambushed.'

'Ambushed by a taste?'

He glanced over at her. 'Ever bitten into an apple and found it had gone rotten inside? Ever taken a bite of a chocolate and found it was coffee flavour rather than strawberry? Sometimes, flavours can surprise you. Sometimes, they can shock. That's why I had to take time off work – go on gardening leave. Things at home weren't going well, and my synaesthesia took a turn for the worse. I couldn't stand to be in an office, *tasting* everyone else's chatter, banter, lies and deceits. I was overwhelmed. The Chief Super signed me off for a few weeks. A few weeks turned into six months. I've been doing little odd-jobs for the Chief Super ever since – writing reports and conducting studies into how we can do policing better – but this is the first time I've been on active duty for a while.'

'And the family, sir? You said things weren't going very well.'

'They got worse,' he said shortly. 'The synaesthesia got to the point where I couldn't even bear to hear my kids playing in the garden any more. I couldn't listen to their voices without wanting to throw up. It was ... difficult.'

An understatement. It had nearly driven him to suicide. And it had driven him and his wife apart.

Emma shrugged. 'Well, thanks for telling me. I won't mention it to anyone.' She ran a finger across the roof of her car, rubbed her fingers together, and grimaced. 'Bloody sap. Careful of your jacket – dry cleaning won't get this stuff out. Shall we get on with talking to the old couple across the road? If you're all right, that is?'

'I'm fine.' He straightened up. 'Thanks.'

'No problem.' She hesitated. 'Do I taste of anything?' She suddenly blushed. 'I mean—'

'I know what you mean. Lemon, most of the time. Lemon and grapefruit if you're in a good mood; lemon and lime if you're not.'

She looked strangely pleased. 'Could be worse,' she said. 'You know what they say: if little girls are made of sugar and spice and all things nice, then why do women taste of—'

'Anchovies. Yes, I know.'

They walked across to number sixty-seven. The lawn was so close-cropped that it might have been cut with nail scissors. There were no toys in the front garden; instead, a cast-iron bird bath took pride of place. The curtains twitched as they approached.

'Detective Chief Inspector Lapslie,' he introduced himself to the tall, white-haired man who opened the door. 'And this is Detective Sergeant Bradbury.'

The man nodded. He was dressed in pressed slacks and a blue shirt. The skin around his neck had sagged into set folds. 'Is this about the Neighbourhood Watch? It's taken you long enough.'

'No sir, it's not about the Neighbourhood Watch. We're making inquiries about Violet Chambers. Did you know her?'

'Violet?' He looked surprised. 'Yes, of course. She lived opposite.' He glanced back over his shoulder. 'Jean, put the kettle on, will you? We've got visitors.' Turning back, he added, 'Would you care for a cup of tea. Or coffee? I know you're on duty, so I won't offer you a sherry. Name's Halloran. David Halloran.'

'A cup of tea would be most welcome.' Lapslie followed Halloran into the hall, wondering if anybody under the age of seventy still drank sherry. Emma followed them both.

Mrs Halloran was standing in the living room, which ran through the house from the bay windows at the front to a conservatory at the back. A backless set of shelves extended half-way across the room, dividing it roughly in two. A sofa and two armchairs covered in flowery material sat in an L-shape facing a rather old television set. The walls were decorated with Regimental badges and pictures of men in uniform. 'Did I hear you say you were with the police?' she asked.

'Asking after Violet,' her husband said. 'Violet Chambers.'

'Poor Violet,' Mrs Halloran said enigmatically, and vanished into the kitchen.

Mr Halloran gestured for them to sit on the sofa. He sank into one of the armchairs. 'Army days,' he said, nodding at the photographs. 'Everything from Korea through to Northern Ireland. Spend my time worrying about the little bastards playing hide-and-seek in my hedge now. Funny old thing, life.'

'About Violet Chambers...?' Lapslie prompted.

'She was here when we moved in, twenty years or so ago. Her and her husband – Jack. He died a few years later. Heart attack, the doctors said. Went quick, whatever it was. One moment he was weeding the garden, next he keeled over like he'd been shot.'

'And Mrs Chambers?'

'She stayed on in the house. Mortgage was paid off. I suppose she could have moved away, but they had no children. She seemed to manage okay. Pottered down to the shops once a week. We offered to help, but she was a bit stand-offish. Didn't like to socialise. I think she thought she'd married beneath her when she married Jack. I don't think we ever saw inside the house. Not once, in twenty years. That's why it seemed so odd.'

Emma leaned forward. 'What seemed odd?'

Mrs Halloran arrived from the kitchen with a tray which she put down on a small table between the armchairs. 'Well, one day she popped a note through our door saying she'd had to go away,' Mrs Halloran said. 'Which was unusual, as she'd never bothered telling us about anything like that before. Apparently her sister had been taken ill. We didn't even know she had a sister. She said she was going to look after her. We never saw her again – not that we ever saw her much when she was there. But the next thing we knew, someone else was moving into the house.' She looked up, eyes meeting Lapslie's as she poured the tea. 'We presumed she died.'

'She did,' Lapslie confirmed.

'And what about the sister?'

'I really don't know.' Lapslie glanced across at Emma, hoping she could pick up the story. Mrs Halloran's face, so close to his, was mildly off-putting.

'There's some question about the estate,' Emma took over smoothly. 'We're just making routine inquiries. You say she kept herself to herself, and you very rarely saw her. Did she have any visitors that you noticed?'

Mrs Halloran handed Lapslie a cup of tea. 'I can't really say.'

'There was someone,' Mr Halloran said suddenly.

His wife eyed him. 'Was there?'

'A woman. Saw her a couple of times leaving the house. Thought she was a home help or something, although come to think of it she was a bit old to be a home help.'

Mrs Halloran frowned as she handed Emma her cup of tea. Emma looked at it as if she had never seen one before. Perhaps it was the bone china that was putting her off. 'Now you come to mention it, I think I might have seen her once. She was carrying something out of the house. I assumed she was from the social services.'

'Did you know her name?' Lapslie asked.

'Oh no. We never got to talk to her.'

Lapslie slurped his tea back quickly. 'Thanks for your help. If you remember anything else ...' He made to get up, but something in Mr Halloran's eyes kept him sitting.

'Didn't we get a Christmas card?' he asked his wife.

'You're right,' she said. 'I think I still have it.' She headed for the back half of the room. 'Give me a moment and I'll find it.'

'She keeps everything,' Mr Halloran confided. 'We've got Christmas and birthday cards dating back to when we were married.'

'And the card – that was sent *this* Christmas?' Emma asked.

'That's right.'

Emma glanced over at Lapslie. He knew what she was thinking. Violet Chambers had died somewhere in the region of nine months before. When people had been cheerily singing Christmas carols and exchanging presents, when they had been watching the Queen's Speech or sleeping off a surfeit of turkey, Violet Chambers' body had been slowly decomposing, returning the stuff of which she had been made to nature. Small animals had been burrowing through her innards.

So who had sent the card?

After a few moments rummaging in a cardboard box, Mrs Halloran returned triumphantly, holding not only a Christmas card but a postcard as well. 'I'd forgotten this,' she said, waving it in her husband's face. 'It arrived a week or so after she left.'

Lapslie looked at the Christmas card first. Mass produced for some charity, the picture on the front was so generically festive as to be laughable. Some people, he reflected, went through years studying graphic arts at college with high hopes of working in advertising or magazine design, only to end up churning out endless paintings of robins and snowmen and snow-laden branches. Probably in July, so the cards could be ready in time. What happened to these people? Did they eventually die of a broken heart, their dreams of a high-profile career dashed, or did they end up committing suicide, depressed by all the production-line festivity they had to create? He'd have to ask Dr Catherall whether she had a glut of dead graphic artists in her mortuary come the autumn.

Thinking of Dr Catherall made him realise that he needed to talk to her about the results of the tests she had ordered on the samples from Violet Chambers' body.

All that was written in the interior of the Christmas card was a signature, appended to the usual meaningless printed message. The writing was cursive, rounded, done with a fountain pen. The postcard had, to all appearances, been written with the same fountain pen. It was a plain, white card with no picture on it. The Hallorans' address was written on one side, and the message on the other simply said: 'Dear David and Jean. I don't know how long I will be away, but I suspect it might be some time. I have let the house out while I'm gone – I was worried that it would be empty, but at least this way I know it will be looked after, and I'll get some (much needed!) income. Take care, Violet.' The stamp on the front was a standard first-class stamp, and the postmark was blurred into incoherence.

'And this is the only communication you've had since she left?'

'That's right,' Mrs Halloran said.

'What about the writing? Is it Violet Chambers'?'

'I really wouldn't know. I don't think she ever wrote to us when she was here.'

Lapslie passed the two items to Emma. As she examined them, Lapslie asked: 'I don't suppose you kept the envelope the Christmas card came in, by any chance?'

'Why would we?' Mr Halloran replied, genuinely surprised.

'No reason,' Lapslie sighed. 'No reason at all.' He made as if to get up. 'Well, we won't take up any more of your time. Thanks for the tea.'

'A couple more questions, if I might,' Emma said, still sitting. Lapslie sank down heavily in his chair again. 'Do you have any photographs of Violet Chambers?'

Mrs Halloran shook her head. 'No, my dear. I can't think of any reason why we might.'

Emma nodded. 'What about her appearance, then? Was there anything out of the ordinary about her? Any distinguishing features?'

As both the Hallorans considered, Lapslie nodded at Emma. Good question.

'There was a scar,' Mrs Halloran said eventually.

'On her neck,' Mr Halloran confirmed. He tapped his own neck, just below the Adam's apple. 'Just here.'

'Thanks,' Lapslie said again. He glanced over at Emma. 'If there's nothing else ...?'

She shook her head, and they left, taking some time to disengage themselves from the Hallorans' hospitality. For one horrible moment Lapslie thought they were going to be invited to stay for lunch, but fortunately it didn't happen.

Walking back to Emma's car, Lapslie said, 'That was good thinking about the distinguishing features. I'd forgotten about the scar on the corpse's neck. Diphtheria, wasn't it?'

'Breathing tube inserted when she was young,' Emma confirmed. 'At least, according to the pathologist. It gives us some additional faith that the body is Violet Chambers.'

'Were we in any doubt?'

'Well, all we had were the dentures.' Stopping to unlock her car, she said: 'Where do we go from here, sir?'

Lapslie looked up and down the road, thinking. 'The estate agents near the station – the ones that have been renting Violet's house to the Wetheralls since she disappeared. At the very least, they can tell us where the rent is being paid to.' He sighed. 'I feel as if we're getting more and more information without making any progress. We know that Violet Chambers died in the middle of a forest. Someone must have left her there, even if they weren't responsible for her death – and we still don't know how she died. We can assume that the same person sent the postcard and the Christmas card to the

Hallorans. There might be more cards floating around as well, if she had other friends. Either way, it looks as if someone is trying to keep Violet Chambers alive, at least in people's minds. Why? What's in it for them? I can't imagine that the rent coming in from the house is enough to justify the risk, no matter how nice this area is.'

'Then how do we proceed, sir?'

'That, Detective Sergeant Bradbury, depends on two things: what we find out from the estate agents, and whether the good Doctor Catherall has managed to establish a cause of death yet.'

They found the nearest station within ten minutes. It was just off a crossroads of shops, wine bars and restaurants. There were three estate agents' premises within a short walk of one another, and Lapslie and Emma had to check all three before they struck lucky. Lucky, Lapslie reflected, was a relative term. According to the girl they talked to, the house had been put up for rent less than a year before. She hadn't been working there when the house had come onto their books, but according to the computer files – which she consulted with rather bad grace after repeated prompting from Lapslie – the owner, a Mrs Violet Chambers – had completed most of the paperwork by post. The rent money – minus the standard cut taken by the estate agents – was paid regularly into a building society account. And that was that.

They drove back in silence from Ipswich, each concerned with their own thoughts. As they hit the motorway, Lapslie's mobile bleeped. The taste of chocolate in his mouth made him realise that they hadn't eaten lunch yet.

The message on the mobile's screen said: *You may wish to revisit the mortuary. I believe I have established the cause of Violet Chambers' death. It is not –*

The message stopped there. Trust Dr Catherall to avoid the contractions and short cuts of texting and over-run the number of characters allowed in a message. A few seconds later, with another beep, a second message – or, rather, the continuation of the first – appeared.

– exactly what I had been expecting. I will be working late. Arrive whenever convenient. Jane Catherall.

'Head back to Braintree,' he said, deleting the messages. 'Doctor Catherall's found something. And if you know of any decent pubs on the way, stop off. I could do with a bite to eat.'

Following a quick cheese and ham baguette at a white-washed pub just off the A12, they made good time. Emma brought the Mondeo to a halt in the mortuary's car park just short of three in the afternoon.

'Do you want me to come in, sir?'

Lapslie considered for a moment. Emma didn't particularly like standing around listening to technical talk: that had become clear last time. 'No,' he said finally. 'Check the building society account the rent is paid into. I want to know who's spending that money. I'll get a car from the station to pick me up.'

Dan, the mortuary attendant, let him in when he buzzed. Lapslie quickly strode ahead and pushed his way through the double doors, eager to discover what Dr Catherall had found out.

The mortuary tables were empty. Dr Catherall was over by a small autoclave, leafing through a sheaf of pink paper, her polio-ravaged body dwarfed by the size of the tables, the cabinets that lined the room, the air-conditioning pipes in the ceiling. The ever-present background smell, cloying and faecal, made his throat tighten. He forced the reaction down. How did she ever get used to it?

'Doctor Catherall?'

She looked up from the papers she was reading. He had forgotten how mild and blue her eyes were. 'Ah, Detective Chief Inspector.'

'Mark.'

'Mark it is, then.'

'You texted me.'

'I did. A hateful thing, texting. It encourages lazy writing and imprecision of thought. It is, however, too useful to lose.'

Impatiently, he cut through her stream of consciousness. 'What else have you found?'

'You will remember,' she started, placing the papers down on top of a cabinet, 'that the body had been subject to slow, anaerobic decomposition and to a certain amount of animal activity. This made the examination problematic, to say the least. There were, however, no immediate signs of heart attack, stroke or exposure as far as I could tell. Given the fact that the body was found in a shallow grave in the middle of a forest, with no obvious means of transport around, wrapped tightly in plastic sheeting and with the fingers on the right hand removed by a pair of sharp, opposed blades, like a pair of chef's shears, I am inclined to rule out natural causes.'

She smiled. Lapslie just sighed quietly to himself. God save him from pathologists who liked to give lectures.

'Now, apart from the damage to the back of the skull, which could have resulted from the car crash that excavated her body, there are no signs of pre-mortem attack – no fractures, no stab wounds, nothing that would account for a sudden collapse.'

'Doctor, you've spent the past few minutes listing every possible thing that *didn't* kill her, with the exception of a freak meteor shower and an attack by crocodiles. If I don't find out soon what actually did the job then I'm going to strap you to one of those spare tables and prod you with your own surgical instruments until you tell me.'

She had the good grace to laugh. 'Very well. You will recall that we found the corpses of several small animals nestled within her chest cavity. This started me thinking. What could have caused them to die, and die so quickly that they could not escape? To cut to the chase, I tested the poor lady's stomach contents – at least, what remained of them – for toxins. And I found some.'

'*Poison!*' That was the last thing Lapslie was expecting.

'Indeed. To be more precise, her stomach lining, liver and kidneys were saturated with colchicine – a drug used in small doses to treat gout.'

Lapslie shook his head slowly. 'So she accidentally overdosed on her own medicine? In the middle of a forest?'

'I have no idea how she got into the middle of a forest,' Dr Catherall replied with asperity, 'but she certainly did not overdose on her medicine. Firstly, she was not suffering from gout, nor was there any evidence she had ever done so. Secondly, her stomach contents indicate that the poison was not administered in the form of tablets, which is how colchicine is most often given, but in what I can only describe as its raw form.'

Lapslie was beginning to feel like the straight man in a double act, feeding Dr Catherall lines so she could get to a punch-line. 'You're going to have to explain that, as well.'

'Colchicine is derived from the seeds of a plant known as the meadow saffron, otherwise known as the autumn crocus, although, strangely enough, it is not actually a crocus. Despite the passage of time, there are still traces of seeds in the stomach. My best guess – and it really is a guess – is that she somehow ingested enough meadow saffron to provide a lethal dose of colchicine.'

'Accidentally?'

She shook her head. 'I really cannot see how. For a start, meadow saffron does not grow anywhere within fifty miles of where she was found. And besides, there were enough traces of other substances in the stomach contents that I can be reasonably certain that the plant was administered in the form of a cake.'

It took a few moments for Lapslie to fully understand what he was being told. He understood the individual words, but putting them all together in the form of a sentence, even one as convoluted as Dr Catherall preferred, took him to a place he really didn't want to go. Despite the coldness of the room he could feel a prickly kind of heat across his neck and upper arms. This was deliberate. Worse than that, this was planned as some kind of domestic *event*.

'Let's be clear, Doctor,' he said finally. 'You know what you're saying?'

'I do,' she said. 'Colchicine overdoses of the size I believe occurred here are particularly painful and protracted. If done deliberately, it verges on torture, I would say.'

Silence filled the room.

'This now becomes a murder investigation,' Lapslie said.

CHAPTER SEVEN

As Daisy Wilson awoke from a deep sleep, troubled by dreams of a long dining table around which faceless figures sat in uneasy silence, she rose through a series of previous identities like a balloon floating up through layers of cloud.

For a while she was Alice Connell, a former librarian in Epping, living alone but for a white cat in a small house near a canal. She liked walking along the canal in the afternoons just to be able to see other people and to smile at them. Sometimes the cat would walk along with her. Then Alice was left behind and she was Jane Winterbottom, an obsessive collector of Victorian hairbrushes who kept her collection in her flat on the bottom floor of a Victorian block in Chelmsford and who had nobody to whom she could show it. Jane, too, receded into the distance, and she was Violet Chambers, a widowed old lady living in a house too big for her, too proud to make friends with her neighbours, sitting at her living room window and watching the world pass her by. And then Violet was falling away, and she was Daisy Wilson, an old woman with ulcerated legs, dreaming of her glory days as a dancer in West End shows.

And as Daisy emerged from sleep, the cocoons of her previous existences sloughing away from her, she dimly remembered that there had been others as well, others before Alice Connell. The names were vague now, but she could just make out the dim outlines of stolen memories: an old, cobbled street somewhere in south London with rusted tram lines running down the centre; a familiar seat in a public house with a half pint of Irish stout set on the table; a grey room with a grey metal bed; a powder-blue eiderdown coat; a tortoiseshell comb; an Aga. No faces, no names, just snatches of things seen and half-remembered. Fragments of too many lives; a pile of different jigsaw puzzles, fallen to the floor and mixed together, never to be undone.

And behind all of those, a long dining table, set with bone china cups, and those silent figures. Those silent, waiting figures.

She lay there for a while, the sunlight playing on the ceiling of her room, letting her mind idly sort through the fragments until she could reassemble herself. Daisy Wilson. She was Daisy Wilson, and she was establishing a new life in a small seaside town named Leyston-by-Naze, on the east coast. She needed a place to live, she needed to make some friends, and she needed some money. Those were the priorities of the day.

Eventually, she got up out of bed and gazed out of the window of her hotel room. It was still early. There was barely any differentiation between the water and the clouds; one blended into the other in a continuous sheet of grey. Only a large container ship, crawling infinitesimally right to left, marked the location of the horizon.

Daisy washed, dressed, left her room and headed down to the restaurant where she had eaten on the previous night. The tables had been stripped and reset for breakfast, with small pots of jam, saucers of butter and steel cutlery stark against white linen. The ghosts of old coffee rings were still visible on the linen. Small signs marked which tables were reserved for which rooms. She located the table for room 241 – set for one – and sat down. Within a few moments, a tired-looking young girl in a black skirt and white blouse came over to her.

'Good morning, ma'am. Would you like tea or coffee?'

Daisy considered for a moment. Was she a tea or a coffee person? 'Tea, please,' she said eventually.

'And would you be wanting a cooked breakfast?'

Less of a hesitation this time. 'No, thank you. Just toast, please.'

'Fruit juice?'

'Yes please – grapefruit, if you have it.'

'If you want cereal, it's on the table over by the window.'

'Thank you, m'dear.'

The waitress left. As Daisy waited for the toast to arrive, she glanced around at the other hotel patrons. The couple from the night before – the man in the suit and the woman in the shawl – were just finishing their breakfasts. They were still failing to find any topics of conversation. The florid man with the flat cap was absent, but a family of four – mother, father and two children, both girls – were making a big production number over swapping knives, buttering toast and cutting up fried breakfasts so that the children could eat them. The girls were dressed in identical outfits: white cloth patterned with green leaves and vines, like something one might use as a curtain. Daisy wondered if their mother had made the clothes herself.

'Your toast, ma'am. Tea's on the way.'

The waitress had reappeared by Daisy's side. She placed the toast on the table, then headed over to help the family sort out the mess they were making.

Daisy felt a prickle on the back of her neck. Turning casually, she saw an elderly woman enter the restaurant. She was elegant, with a long green dress cinched in at the waist and covered with a long cardigan made of wool. The necklace circling the corrugated skin of her neck might have been pearl. Daisy would have to get closer to be able to tell for sure.

Daisy tracked her progress across the room. Knowing in her heart that the woman was probably on holiday, which more or less ruled her out as a prospect, Daisy was nevertheless unable to stop herself. It was like those lions one saw on wildlife documentaries: an antelope walks past and the lions look up, watching the animal move, calculating the line of least effort between them and their prey. It doesn't matter that they aren't hungry, it just matters that they are lions and the thing going past is an antelope. Instinct overrules everything.

Her heart beat a little faster as the woman seemed to be heading for a table with a single setting, but slowed as she bypassed it in favour of a table set for two. The woman sat down, and a few moments later a man in a cream-coloured jacket, walking with a cane, entered the room and followed her.

Probably for the best. One should never foul one's own nest, isn't that what they said?

The tea arrived and she poured herself a cup, breathing in the rich, aromatic steam. It was a blended tea, half Ceylon and half Darjeeling, as far as Daisy could tell. She was good with tea. She had, after all, made enough of it, over the years, including her own special blends.

Daisy spread a thin layer of butter over the toast and took a delicate bite while she considered her options. At some stage she would have to visit an estate agents and arrange to rent a property in the area. After all, she couldn't live at the hotel for ever. A predator needed a trap, and the hotel was too public, too exposed. The problem was that she knew little about the town: where the best areas for retired folk were, which were the noisy public houses and which were the quiet ones, and so on. Her usual tactic was to buy as many local papers as the area could support and read through them a few times, getting a feel for wherever she had ended up. She had found, through long experience, that the classified advertisements and the announcements provided a lot of useful background information, not the least of which was the section devoted to forthcoming funerals or the anniversaries of deaths. After all, one had to start somewhere, and widows were easy prey.

Finishing her toast, Daisy got up to leave. Nobody in the restaurant bothered watching her go, and that was the way she liked it.

Outside the hotel, the weather was warm despite the grey,

cloudy sky. The tide was on its way in, creeping slowly up the sandy shoreline. Off to her right, the pier jutted out into the water; a bridge heading into nowhere. Pulling her cardigan closer about her, she turned left and walked along the sea front. Ahead of her the esplanade curved away to the left, hiding all but the next row of houses, bars and hotels and making it appear as if the sea lapped directly against the buildings. Far away in the distance the shore curved back into sight again, rising into a knob of land that towered above the town – the Naze itself, named, she assumed, from the French *nez*, meaning 'nose', which is what it actually resembled.

As she walked, she realised that she had turned left with deliberate purpose, as if she was heading for somewhere in particular, but when she examined her motives she realised that she didn't really know where she was going. She had approached the hotel from the other direction the day before, and when she had gone for her evening walk she had turned right, back towards the station. Now, heading in an unknown direction, she had the distinct feeling that there was something familiar around the curve of the road: something that she wanted to see, if only she knew what it was.

A few steps, and she could see further around the bend. And there was a public garden: a small walled area on the corner between the esplanade and what she thought might be the High Street. As she approached, she saw that it had benches around the edge, and was planted with rows of brightly coloured flowers. It was a small oasis of calm amid the seaside bustle.

Rather than keep on going around the corner and into the High Street, Daisy cut through the garden. With practised eye, she identified the plants that she passed. Over by the brick wall of the next building, pennyroyal plants were reaching upward, their little bursts of pink and white blossom separated by stretches of stem. Next to them, Daisy spotted the dark red, five-petalled flowers of a row of delphiniums reaching toward her. Both of them were poisonous, although the essential oil would have to be extracted from the pennyroyal first: a fussy process that Daisy would rather not have to do again. There were other plants in the garden as well, but she had less interest in those. They might have looked nice, they might even have smelled nice, but they had no practical purpose. They couldn't be used to kill anyone.

It reminded her of her own garden. She smiled for a moment, recalling the dark scents and the glistening flowers that she had left behind. When she had taken Dais— no, *she* was Daisy – when she had taken the *body* away and left it where nobody would find it, she had taken the opportunity to tend her garden, to remove some of the weeds that were growing up around the mulch and to cut back some of the more extravagant growths. It made her feel calm. It made her feel centred, somehow.

Leaving the garden behind her, she turned into the far end of the High Street.

The road was long, and lined with shops of various kinds. Every second one appeared to be selling something to do with the beach: swimwear, sticks of rock, inflatable rings and mattresses, towels – all the paraphernalia of a day by the sea. In between these holiday-specific shops were the ones she would expect to find in any small town: newsagents and banks, florists and shoe shops, bakeries and butchers: the kinds of shops that, in some bigger towns, had been rendered obsolete by hypermarkets and telephone banking, but managed to survive in places such as this like barnacles clinging to rocks while the tide of progress tried to wash them away.

She popped into the first newsagents she came to and bought one of the three local papers that were sitting on the lowest shelf. A few yards along the High Street she found another newsagents, and she bought the second of the local papers. Buying three local papers in one shop probably didn't count as suspicious behaviour, but she didn't like leaving a trail, even if that trail was only one of memories. Daisy far preferred to slip unnoticed through people's minds; just one more little old lady living her life one day at a time.

A little further along the road, she found a W. H. Smith. There she bought the third local paper, and managed to get a plastic bag to go along with it. Now, with all three in her possession, she needed to find somewhere to sit down and read them. For a moment she hovered on the verge of turning around and heading back to the public garden she had discovered, but she knew the intoxicating smell of the pennyroyal and the delphiniums would just distract her. A café would do just as well.

Walking further along the High Street, Daisy found herself turning left into a shop doorway before she knew what she was doing. It was only when the burnt sugar smell of candy floss hit her that she looked up and realised she was in a gift shop. What had made her think this was a café? Smiling vaguely, she backed out and kept walking, looking around more carefully this time.

She almost missed the place across the road. It was part of a building that extended from one street corner to another, built out of the same red brick and with the same buff adornments on the corners. The building had once been a large post office: it still was, at one end, but the other end had been converted into a genteel coffee shop advertising gateaux and pastries, espresso and cappuccino on a chalk board pinned to the red brick wall.

She entered the coffee shop and looked around. It had the same kind of dated feel as her hotel: backward looking, rather than forward, with lace doilies on the tables and sepia-tinged photographs in frames on the wall. A perfect place to sit and read. She found an empty table and perched herself on a chair. Having established from the plastic-covered menu on the table that she could, in fact, order tea as well as coffee, she asked the waitress for a pot and then spread the first local paper, the *Tendring Gazette*, over the table.

Dismissing the headlines, which involved accusations of fraud in the Council and blocked inquiries into the sale of school fields in the vicinity, she concentrated on the later pages. The local stuff. There were small news paragraphs of course. One of them, headlined 'Milk and Beer Taken', reported on how thieves had broken into a local garage and stolen a bottle of beer and a bottle of milk from a fridge, drunk them both, and then smashed the milk bottle, which Daisy decided summed up perfectly the parochial approach of local newspapers to events. The world might be heading for ecological disaster, nations might be at war, but as long as one local journalist was on the job, no case involving a stolen milk bottle would go unreported. Another paragraph reassured readers that a horse that had been stuck in mud had been freed by fire-fighters. It wasn't until page twenty-two that Daisy found a section headed 'Neighbourhood News', which listed the activities of various local organisations such as the Fuchsia Club, the Bridge Club and, of most interest to her, the Widows' Friendship Club. Anyone who was a member of a club, of course, was, by definition, bound to know people there, but Daisy knew that she could quite easily befriend one of the widows, separate her from the flock and gradually take over her life. The other widows might wonder from time to time what had become of their friend, but they would probably only make cursory attempts to check she was all right. Once a couple of telephone calls had been missed, once a few knocks on the door had gone unanswered, they would give up. It was human nature.

The next page listed local churches and services, and Daisy made a mental note of their locations and the types of activity they undertook. She didn't want to stumble into anything evangelical, after all. Still, she was pleased to see that there were plenty of Methodist churches. Her spur-of-the-moment story on the train the day before was safe.

Three pages of death notices followed, and Daisy read through them all in detail. The words were much the same, as if they all followed a small number of templates, and she sneered to herself at all the various euphemisms employed. 'Died peacefully.' 'Passed away unexpectedly.' 'Taken from us in the prime of life.' All ridiculous. How many of the notices covered up days of messy, agonised and undignified writhing on the part of the dear departed? How many of the fond remembrances covered up neglect, abuse, even murder?

Her tea arrived, late, and Daisy poured a cup, added milk and took a sip. It was stewed. The girl had obviously left it somewhere and forgotten about it. What was the world coming to? If she was that careless, perhaps Daisy should come back one day and slip something into one or two sugar bowls whilst nobody was watching: a fine sprinkling of white powder that would be undetectable when it dissolved in tea or coffee, but which would cause agonising convulsions hours later.

She wouldn't, of course. That would draw too much attention. But it was nice to dream.

Towards the back of the paper, the *Gazette* had ten pages of property adverts. The first eight pages were houses and flats for sale, but the last two covered rental properties. She scanned them with as much care, and as much emotion, as she had read the death notices. The going rate seemed to be between five hundred and seven hundred pounds per month: not a rate she wished to sustain, but something she could manage while looking for a proper house that she could slide into. An occupied house. A house that would soon be hers.

Finally, Daisy came to the classified ads. She loved looking through these sections. It was like getting a small glimpse through the curtains and into somebody's life. Just a small glimpse, open to all sorts of interpretation, as you were walking past. What to make of: 'Family-tree historian seeks f, to form a new branch and dig up some roots together'? Would he ever get his wish? Was the 'Tall, medium-built postman, cat owner, seeks compatible female' giving away too much information?

And then there was 'Happy, lively lady, 50s, seeks male companion and escort for boot fairs, garden centres, etc.' That one looked promising. If she was advertising in the newspaper then it implied she had given up on clubs, or church, or any of the other ways mature women made friends. And that meant she was likely to be isolated. Daisy made a careful mental note of the response number at the bottom of the ad. She was familiar with the process: it varied little from town to town. The number would be a message line run by a company on behalf of the newspaper. Verbal messages could be left, or text messages could be sent. The text messages were preferable as far as Daisy was concerned: if she wanted to lure this woman out into the open and befriend her, she would have to identify her. And that meant she would have to arrange a date at some convenient location, and observe from afar when the woman turned up and waited in vain for her erstwhile paramour to arrive.

Erstwhile paramour. The words made her smile. She'd never had a paramour, erstwhile or otherwise, and had no intention of ever acquiring one, but she knew enough about the relationship between men and women to send a convincing text message.

The remaining two papers – the *Leyston Recorder* and the *Walton and Leyston Post* – were much of a muchness with the *Tendring Gazette*. The story of the horse stuck in mud appeared in both of them, while the one about the stolen bottles of milk and beer was in the *Recorder* but not the *Post*. Of the three, Daisy decided that the *Tendring Gazette* probably had the most to offer. Already it had yielded several leads.

She left enough money on the table to cover the cost of the tea, but without leaving more than a few pence as a tip. Waitressing of that low quality did not deserve a reward.

Leaving the coffee shop, Daisy continued right along the High Street, as much to reconnoitre the area as for any other reason. Across the other side she could see, in the distance, the

Bingo Hall where, the night before, she had caught her first scent of prey. The type of shop between her and the Bingo Hall was shifted slightly away from the holidaymakers and towards the more utilitarian: a hairdressers, an ironmongers, and so on. Coming up to a corner with a florists on one side and a Visitor Information kiosk on the other, she paused. The road off to the right led away from the High Street, away from the sea front and from Daisy's hotel, but she decided on a whim to take a wander and see what was down there.

The road curved away to the right, and all Daisy could see for the first few minutes as she walked along were detached and weatherworn houses on either side. The gaps between the paving stones were caked with sand, brought in from the beach by wind and by storm, she presumed.

After a few hundred yards, the houses on the right-hand side gave way to an earth bank, taller than she was and covered with grass and more sand. Every so often, concrete steps led up the side of the bank, vanishing into mystery at the top.

Ahead, the road came to an abrupt stop at a wire-mesh gate. A sign hanging from it read, 'Leyston Yacht Club' in large letters, and then in smaller letters underneath, 'Members Only'.

Daisy took a few more steps towards the gate. A yacht club might be a useful thing to know about. At the very least, it would give her an immediate social veneer. She knew little about boats, but she was sure she could learn. A few hours in the company of a yachtswoman, or even a few hours spent in the same room, and she would be moving and talking as if she had been on boats all her life.

Daisy turned away from the Yacht Club, and gazed absorbedly at the grass bank to her right. It lay there, the faint wind-stirred movements of grass on its flanks like the slow, deep breaths of some recumbent beast. From somewhere beyond the bank she could hear the screeching of gulls, like screaming children. The sound made her unaccountably nervous: she had never had children, never even felt the touch of a man's hand, but something about that sound made her want to scream.

The nearest set of steps was only a few yards away, and with mounting nervousness she walked up them, taking small bird-steps.

As her head rose above the top of the bank, the first thing she saw was a line of houses, far in the distance, and then, as she reached the top, her breath suddenly fluttered within her chest as she saw the stretch of calm water that lay between her and them. The bank dropped down on the other side to a concrete dock, and the water stretched from the dock all the way across to the far side, a misty grey-blue surface, a wash of colour.

It was a marina, a place for boats to tie up, and there were hundreds of them there, hulls painted white and bows sharp and somehow cruel to Daisy's eyes. Somewhere nearby there must have been a channel or a river that led to the North Sea, allowing the boats access. Now they sat still, watchful, waiting for their owners to come and untie them and take them out into the rough ocean.

Daisy walked down the steps on the other side and up to the edge of the dock: slow, unwilling steps, as if something were pulling her forward against her will, or something were pushing her back from a long-sought goal.

Bending down, she could see her reflection in the water: a figure, outlined by blue sky, one hand resting on the dock, the other reaching out to touch the water.

But it wasn't her.

The figure looking up at her from the water of the marina was a young girl with red hair, tied back in a pony tail. She was wearing a checked dress. There was something covering the front of the dress: a stain, like jam, or fruit juice.

Or blood.

Daisy staggered to her feet, backing away from the edge of the concrete. Whatever she had seen in the water was wrong. So very wrong. And it had perverted everything around her as well. She hadn't noticed before, but it was obvious to Daisy now that the concrete had crumbled in places and cracked in others, and the various chains and rings that had been set into the concrete were leaking orange rust. The boats looked sorry for themselves; behind the cruelly curved bows their hulls were dirty and their ropes hung limp.

Above the boats, and between them, seagulls either hung precariously upon the breeze or bobbed on the water, hoping for a morsel of food to float past. Their cries were making Daisy panicky, and she turned away and ran up the concrete stairs of the bank as fast as she could.

Catching her breath at the bottom of the bank, she composed herself and walked back the few hundred yards to the High Street. Somehow, it felt as if she had crossed between two worlds.

Daisy was keeping her eye out for a library, and found one a little further down the High Street. It was a single-storey building, built out of a sandy stone. Once her breathing had returned to normal, she went inside.

The library was bright and airy, built on two levels with a ramp in between. Daisy spent ten minutes or so wandering around, familiarising herself with the layout. Fiction at one end, non-fiction at the other, with a space in the middle for the sadly omnipresent internet terminals and DVDs. Books seemed almost to be a secondary concern for libraries, these days.

A door leading out of the library led not, as she might have expected, back to the street but to a courtyard nestled between the library and the building behind it. Roses had been planted in pots, and benches artfully positioned around. A few people were sitting out there, reading books they had brought out of the building.

Within moments, Daisy had identified three women over sixty sitting alone, reading.

With studied indifference, she went back into the library and wandered along the shelves until she found a book entitled

Leyston-by-Naze: A Personal History. Always good to know something about the place you were going to be living in. Daisy had lived in some anonymous towns in her time, and she was quite looking forward to somewhere that actually did have a history. She took the book outside, found a bench with nobody sitting on it and started to read, making sure that she was scrunched up enough at one end that someone could sit comfortably at the other. If she was lucky, they could strike up a conversation. If she was really lucky, the other person would be an elderly widow with no friends and no social life.

For the first ten minutes or so, Daisy paid little attention to the book. She was more concerned with the comings and goings within the courtyard; the little courtesies, the way small customs appeared to have sprung up amongst the regulars. But after a while, as nobody came to sit with her, she began to get absorbed into the book.

It had been written by a local historian, and privately printed as far as she could tell. There was certainly something less than professional about the typeface and the way the pages were cut. The author knew his subject, however, and he could turn a good phrase. Daisy actually found herself becoming interested in the details of how the beaches of Leyston had become a key source of hardcore aggregate for the building industry, and how the local station had been a marshalling yard for transporting the broken rocks into London. Who would have guessed?

Other chapters dealt with Leyston during the war, and then the expansion of Leyston as part of the Tendring Hundreds area. History seemed to have pretty much bypassed the town for a long time; small events took on a greater significance, just because there was so little else that happened. Daisy already knew that, of course – any town where the theft of a milk bottle and a beer bottle made headlines in the local paper was not making its mark on history – but the book's author had to scrape the bottom of the barrel in order to come up with inter-esting stories.

At least, that was what Daisy thought until she turned a page to find a chapter about sensational crimes in the Tendring Hundreds area. To illustrate it, there was a photographic reprint of the front page of a newspaper dating from the 1940s. The headline said, simply, 'Local Woman in Murder Tragedy'.

And beneath the headline was a black and white photograph of the girl whose reflection she had seen in the water of the marina.

CHAPTER 8

Once upon a time, before he had made Detective Chief Inspector, Mark Lapslie's office had been a small, rectangular room in a monolithic 1950s building on the outskirts of Chelmsford, with a grim view across the police station car park and plasterboard walls that showed signs of continual over-painting in a variety of colours. Triangular pieces of sticky tape, yellowing with age, had adorned the walls, though the posters and photographs they had secured had long since been removed. Angular metal conduits, studded with rivets, had been fixed along the skirting board at some stage in the past to take electrical cables and sockets; more conduits had been added at waist height at a later date to take computer network cables. The building had no air conditioning, but the policemen and women who had worked there had quickly learned which windows to open and which to leave shut in order to create a continual cool flow of air through the corridors. In winter, Lapslie had kept cartons of milk out on the window ledge. A lady with a trolley used to come through, once at eleven o'clock and once again at three, selling sticky buns and stewed tea. Another lady with a trolley would come through half an hour later to empty the out-trays on the desks and deliver any new post.

Now, Lapslie had a desk on the eleventh floor of an open-plan office in an architecturally award-winning office block built only a few years before in the redeveloped town centre. Incoming post was scanned in and delivered electronically to the computers on every desk. Outgoing mail had been replaced with outgoing email. The windows were coated with metallic film, for security and energy efficiency, and they couldn't be opened. Nobody was allowed to stick anything to the walls, and the notice boards were pruned once a month for offensive or out-of-date items. All of the electrical and ethernet cabling ran under the raised floor. So did the ventilation: small, circular vents every few yards provided an almost unnoticeable flow of fresh air. The chairs were state-of-the-art, like black sculptures: plastic mesh on a metal frame, promoting comfort and coolness. A cafeteria in the basement sold *venti lattes* and almond croissants at grossly inflated prices. A chalkboard sign on one wall compared their grossly inflated prices with those of other coffee bars in the locality and came to the conclusion that the coffee there was just cheap enough that it made no sense to go out for one, unless you just wanted a walk. They had a gymnasium, a dry-cleaners and a hairdressers actually on the premises.

And Lapslie hated it. He hated it with a passion beyond telling. The noise of thirty or so officers and civilians of various ranks, all talking to one another, talking to themselves or talking on the telephone was distracting beyond measure. To Lapslie it had been like having the taste of blood in his mouth for the entire working day. Following a letter from his doctor to the Assistant Chief Constable, Lapslie had been allowed to use one of the Quiet Rooms – usually set aside for confidential discussions – as a surrogate office if he needed a break. The rest of the time, he wore earplugs.

Still, there were some consolations. Shortly after the force had moved in, some of the lower-ranking officers had discovered that if they covered the floor-based ventilation grilles in a line at the same time, leaving the last one uncovered, then the resulting air pressure out of that vent could quite easily lift a skirt high above the waist on any passing woman. That had kept them amused for a while, until a circular came round forbidding the practice.

Now he sat in the Quiet Room, reading through Dr Catherall's final autopsy report. He'd spent several weeks chasing her to get it finished, and eventually, and with bad grace, she had complied.

There was no doubt – Violet Chambers had been murdered. The cause of death was uncertain – she had certainly been poisoned, but she also appeared to have been struck on the back of the head. Either could have been the fatal occurrence, although the dirt under her fingernails matched the ground in the vicinity, meaning that she had still been alive when she had been dumped in the forest. The fingers on the right hand had been removed by a sharp, bladed object like a pair of scissors, but that had been done at some stage after Violet Chambers had died, and so blood loss could be ruled out.

Lapslie put down the autopsy report and picked up the report on the area where the body had been found. Tests on the plastic in which she had been wrapped were inconclusive: it was a standard make, available from any large DIY store, and both time and weather had erased any fingerprints that might have been there. And, based on some complicated calculations involving insect pupae and moss, it had been definitively established that her body had lain there for more than eight but fewer than ten months before having been so rudely excavated by a crashing car.

Which still left the two big questions: who had killed her, and why?

Something moved in his peripheral vision, and he twisted around. Emma Bradbury was standing just outside the glass door to the Quiet Room, waving at him. She was wearing a pinstripe trouser-suit offset by an orange sash tied around her waist. He gestured her to enter. She pushed the door open, and Lapslie could immediately taste blood as the susurration of the open-plan office washed over him, as if he'd suddenly bitten his tongue.

'What's up, Emma?'

'Message from the Super, sir. Could you give him an update on the case? Apparently his PA has been trying to get hold of you, but you haven't been at your desk.' The saltiness of the blood receded, replaced by lemon and grapefruit. For a moment the two tastes combined in his mouth: something exotic, like lemongrass, only deeper and more intense. Emma closed the door behind her.

'An update on this case? The Violet Chambers one?'

'Yes, sir.'

'Bit beneath his level of interest, surely?'

Emma shrugged. 'Not for me to judge. Oh, you asked me to trace where the rent from Violet's house was going, sir. Turns out it's going into an account opened some years ago in the name of J. Chambers.'

'Jack Chambers?' He remembered the name from the interview with the elderly couple living opposite what had been Violet's house. 'Violet Chambers' husband?'

'That's right. According to the bank, when he died, back in 1984, she had the account transferred across into her name. And she used it intermittently right up until we know she died, ten months ago. And, bizarrely, she's been using it since as well.'

'Someone's been taking money out of the account? That would certainly track with theft being a motive, but I can't imagine it's a whole load of money. What is it – a few hundred pounds a week?'

Emma nodded. 'Something like that, sir. I've known murders happen for less.'

'In the heat of the moment, yes, but this has the hallmarks of something longer term. Something premeditated. I can't see anyone taking a risk like that for a few hundred pounds a week. How has the money been taken out? Cashpoint, debit card or cheque?'

Emma consulted a sheet of paper in her hand. 'All of the amounts taken out have been cashpoint withdrawals from a variety of banks scattered around London, Essex, Norfolk and Hertfordshire. No cashpoint machine was ever used more than once, as far as I can tell.'

Lapslie leaned back in his chair and ran a hand through his hair. 'All right, let's summarise where we've got to. The crime scene where we discovered the body is a bust – the evidence has just been washed, carried or blown away over the past ten months. The body is a bust – we can't say for sure how she died, and there's no trace evidence. The victim's background is a bust – there's nothing there that could give any cause for murder, apart from this trickle of rent. The only thing we've got is this woman who may have been seen going in and out of Violet Chambers' house before she died, and that may be completely innocent. We could spend the next few months tracking down a chiropodist, if we're not careful. So what's left? Where do we go from here?'

'The nature of the crime itself. Poison is generally a woman's weapon, and the fact that it may have been administered in the form of food indicates a domestic setting – something casual. The murderer was known to the victim, and trusted enough for her to take a slice of cake or whatever it was that the murderer had baked.'

'Okay – it's something to be going on with. Set up a house-to-house in the neighbourhood around Violet Chambers' place. Ask anyone if they remember Violet having any regular visitors in the month or so before she disappeared. Check local shops to see if they recall any women who appeared around that time and then vanished again. Pharmacies and off-licences might be a good place to start. Check with the local surgery as well – whoever this woman was, if there was a woman, she might have taken Violet to an appointment at some stage. Or made one herself.'

'Will do. Anything else?'

Lapslie thought for a moment. 'Yes – run a check into unsolved poisonings. See if this ... colchicine ... has been used before. It's a long shot, but we might strike lucky. I can't imagine it's a common poison, all things considered.'

Emma nodded, and headed off. The door swung shut behind her, and Lapslie was cut off from the noise of the office. Cut off from all noise apart from the sound of his own breathing and the rustle of his clothes as he moved. And if he kept very still, then even that was hushed to the point of silence.

Silence. The blessed state that he craved above all else, and so very rarely achieved.

When Lapslie explained his synaesthesia to most people, they either didn't believe it or they were fascinated. They asked him questions about how it felt, and they sympathised – as much as they could – but they never really understood. Not even the doctors and the psychiatrists, who spent their time reading textbooks and devising experiments to help them understand what synaesthesia implied about the way the brain worked. They never appreciated how it felt to be constantly battered by sensations you weren't expecting. Constantly ambushed by unplanned floods of flavour – some pleasant, some sickening, but all of them unwelcome.

How could you explain that you could never listen to the radio? Never watch the television? Never attend a sporting event or a concert, for fear that a stray taste provoked by an unexpected sound could make you throw up? How could you tell them that you couldn't spend your evenings in the pub with the lads because the raucous atmosphere was like a stream of rancid fat in your mouth, masking the taste of the beer, the whisky or whatever else you tried to use to cover it up with? He'd got a reputation in the force for stand-offishness, for being remote and aloof. The truth was, he just couldn't do it. He couldn't join in. He felt as if he was slowly going mad.

Even eating out was difficult. When they first started seeing each other, he and Sonia had tried to go out for the occasional meal, but they'd had to look for restaurants with no back-ground music. Even then the murmur of other people's conversations underpinned the whole meal, from starter to coffee, with the flatness of blood. No matter what main course he ordered, the meat always tasted raw. After a while, they stopped going out entirely, apart from on Sonia's birthday, when Lapslie steeled himself for an unpleasant evening. And, frankly, that just wasn't fair on her.

It wasn't only one way, either. Over the years, Lapslie had found himself eating blander and blander food, if only because his working life was a morass of clashing flavours. Sitting in a silent house, eating rice or pasta, was the ultimate in luxury for him.

A quiet house. A house without a wife, without children.

Sonia had tried to understand. Not one for going out much herself – her job as a nurse took up most of her time, and resting took much of the remainder – she valued the peace they had together. They went for long walks in the woods. He read, sitting quietly in an armchair, while she did needlepoint and crosswords.

A little island of peace and contentment, which had lasted until precisely the moment when Sonia unexpectedly fell pregnant. With twins.

Lapslie loved his children desperately. He also hated them; or, rather, he hated the constant noise, the squalling when they were young and the shouting and arguing when they were older. Earplugs helped; working late in the office and going out for long walks alone helped even more, but that just put more strain on Sonia, who had to look after the children and the house by herself. And slowly he found himself losing touch with them. Watching from a distance as they got on with life without him.

He couldn't now remember whether it was he or Sonia who had suggested splitting up. They had obviously both been thinking about it for some time, and when one of them broached the subject, almost in passing, the other leaped on it. 'A trial separation', they had called it. And, as with many of the trials that Lapslie had been involved with over the years, it was getting increasingly rancorous and there seemed to be no sign of it ever ending. They were still in contact, but they were drifting apart. Through no fault of his, and no fault of hers, they were just drifting apart.

He sighed. Better go and see what the Superintendent wanted.

He chose a route to his office – one of the few actual offices in the entire building – that minimised the number of people he had to pass on the way. 'Office' was a bit of a misnomer – in fact, it was just a section of the office 'floorplate' , as they called it, separated off by frosted glass panels – but at least it was something. When he arrived outside, the Super's personal assistant glanced up at him from her desk. She was frowning. 'I've been trying to get hold of you,' she said.

'Sorry,' he murmured. 'I was caught up.'

'He's got someone with him, but he'll be free in a moment.'

Lapslie stepped away from the desk and over to a nearby notice board. While he waited, he let his gaze flicker across union notices, fire alarm reminders and cards offering rooms to rent and laundry services. So much information, these days, he thought. So many signs everywhere to read. How could any ordinary person keep all that information in their head without going mad?

A sudden increase in noise made him turn his head. Superintendent Rouse stood in the doorway of his office, saying goodbye to two men. They were both in their late thirties, short-haired, and wearing black suits with a subtle pinstripe. The Superintendent was, as usual, in full uniform.

The two men moved away, and the Superintendent bent to have a quick word with his PA. As the men passed Lapslie one of them turned his head slightly. Lapslie glanced sideways, and the two gazes met with a noticeable jolt. The man raised his eyebrows slightly, involuntarily, as if he recognised Lapslie. Then he was gone, and Lapslie was left with his interest heading one way and his body heading another.

When he turned his attention back towards the way his body

was moving, the Superintendent had re-entered his office. His PA gestured Lapslie in. 'Ten minutes, then he has to leave for another meeting.'

He knocked and entered. The Superintendent had sat behind his desk and was rearranging a sheaf of paper. The desk was placed so that the office's window was to his right, and the light cast one side of his face into a flattering glow and the other into sharp and craggy relief. His face had once been memorably, if uncharitably, described by a young DS as looking like a bag full of spanners. He was older than Lapslie by a few years, a battle-scarred veteran of police politics and in-fighting who had worked his way up the ranks, regardless of prejudice and the old-boy system, to a position of relative authority. Despite the fact that he was Lapslie's boss, and obviously had one eye on the next job in line, Lapslie liked him.

'Mark, thanks for popping along.'

'I understand you wanted an update on the Violet Chambers case, sir?'

Rouse's gaze flickered down to the sheaf of notes in front of him. They were hand-written. Lapslie had often seen Rouse make similar notes in meetings, a contemporaneous record of what was being said to remind him later, something between a set of personal minutes and a stream of consciousness. Had he made the notes during the meeting that had just finished? And, if so, why was he consulting them now?

'That's the woman whose body was found in the woods? Quite decayed?'

'That's the one.'

'Has the coroner been able to establish a cause of death?'

'It's a toss-up,' Lapslie replied, moving across to the window and gazing out at the surrounding landscape of office blocks and, off to one side, an elevated slice of road visible between two buildings. 'She was poisoned, but she was also bludgeoned on the back of the head. It's going to be impossible to determine which one caused her death.'

'But it's murder?'

'Either that or the most elaborate suicide I've ever seen.'

His gaze dropped to the car park below. He could see his own car, parked off to one side. There were too many Mondeos for him to be able to tell where Emma had parked. He could hear the Superintendent making notes as they talked.

'Any suspects?'

'Not as yet. We've finished processing the crime scene – or at least, the location where the body was found. We have yet to establish whether she was killed there. We're currently checking into Violet Chambers' background, in case there's something in her past that would explain her murder.'

Two figures had just left the building, far below. They were heading for the spaces reserved for visitors.

'Do you think there's a realistic chance that you can catch whoever is responsible?'

He shrugged. 'Too early to tell, sir. We've not run out of leads yet, if that's what you mean. Not quite.'

The two figures down in the car park had separated now, and were moving either side of a black car. It was difficult to tell from where Lapslie was standing, but it might have been a Lexus.

The scratching of the pen stopped for a moment. 'I was wondering whether the relatively low chances of success in this particular case mean that you should scale down the investigation. Concentrate on something else, where you're more likely to make an arrest.'

As the car below them started off and drove out of the car park, Lapslie turned to meet Superintendent Rouse's gaze. 'Are you suggesting that I should let the case drop, sir?'

'I would never suggest we let a case drop, Mark. I'm merely asking whether our priorities are arranged correctly.'

'I think it's too early to tell,' he said, knowing he was prevaricating. There was a strange flavour in his mouth: something like nutmeg, although he couldn't quite place it. He'd tasted that flavour before. Usually it was during an interrogation, when some toerag was lying to him about their whereabouts, or trying to convince him that the top-of-the-range BMW they'd been trying to get into at three in the morning had been loaned to them by a friend whose name they had temporarily forgotten. It was the taste of lies; or, at the very least, it was the flavour of evasion. Of someone saying one thing to avoid saying another. But why would Superintendent Rouse be evading his question?

'I can let you know in a few days whether I think there's any realistic prospect of a conviction,' he said.

Rouse nodded. 'I think we may be devoting too many resources to this problem,' he said, pursing his lips. 'It's an old case, and there's precious little evidence. Perhaps we should scale down the team.'

'The *team*,' Lapslie said levelly, 'is one Detective Chief Inspector who's been pulled back from sick leave and one Detective Sergeant who has an attitude problem. Unless you want to swap Emma Bradbury for Mary from the canteen, it's hard to see how much less effective the team could be.'

'Very well,' Rouse said, avoiding Lapslie's gaze. 'We'll keep things the way they are. For the moment.' Putting his pen down, he leaned back in his state-of-the-art chair and gazed at Lapslie, smiling slightly. 'We've both come a long way, haven't we, Mark?'

'Since Kilburn CID, back in the eighties? Since those nights we spent arresting crack dealers and Yardies and breaking up three-day-long raves? It's like another world now.'

'I'm surprised you keep going – especially with your problems. Have you thought about taking early retirement?'

He shrugged. 'Who hasn't at our age? Watching the sun rise from your desk for the tenth time in a month? Finding out that an overtime ban means that all the hours you've been putting in are for free? And knowing that my particular ... problems ... aren't enough to get me pensioned off, but they are enough to stop me getting promoted again? The thought has crossed my mind more than once.'

'Then why stay around?'

Sighing, Lapslie turned to gaze out of the window again, not at the car park this time but out past the elevated section of road, towards the nearest thing to a horizon one could see from this office. 'Where would I go?' he asked, more to himself than to Rouse. 'What exactly would I do? I'd be yet another retired cop in a land full of them. I just haven't got the energy to set myself up in business as a security consultant, or head up the investigation branch at one of the big banks. I'm a cop, sir. That's what I do. That's all I can do.'

'What about—'

'Sonia? She's not coming back. Neither are the kids.' And this time it wasn't a sound, but the memory of a sound, that filled his mouth with the taste of vanilla. The memory of his children playing in the back garden, calling each other silly names, screaming as they chased each other around the car. The memory of them calling to him as they ran through the woods, their voices hanging directionless on the wind. The memory of them crying as they fell over and grazed a knee, and laughing as they tried to catch birds on the lawn. Odd how time could freeze around a few moments, projecting them backwards and forwards through his memories. For Lapslie, his children were always the age they were when they left. He couldn't really remember how they had looked when they were born, or when they were crawling around the house. And, despite the occasional visits and the photographs that Sonia sent through, he found it hard to keep a grip of what they looked like now. It was their faces on those last few days, playing in the garden, running through the woods, that he would always remember.

'It's a shame.'

'That it is,' he said heavily. 'That it is.'

'If there's anything I can do to help …'

He nodded. 'Thanks for the offer,' he said. 'But what about

you? Is your star still in the ascendant? Are you still managing to keep your grip on the greasy pole?'

Rouse smiled, and for a moment the years dropped away and he looked much like he had back in Kilburn, all those years ago. 'I'm considering my options,' he said judiciously. 'There's an offer on the table from the Serious Organised Crime Agency for me to take over their counter-terrorist section. And I've heard that there's a team being put together to look at the security implications of the London Olympics. Either of those would suit me.'

'On promotion, of course.'

'Of course. There's only two directions to go on the greasy pole – up or down. Staying still isn't an option.' Rouse gazed up at him, and his eyes crinkled in what might have been the beginnings of a smile, or the beginnings of a worried frown. 'Let's do lunch soon. We should talk about the future. *Your* future. I'll get my PA to arrange it.'

He turned his eyes back to the notes in front of him and started writing. It was a dismissal. Lapslie glanced once more out of the window and then left the office, closing the door behind him. He felt slightly floaty, slightly disconnected from the world.

Outside, he paused by the PA's desk.

'Those two men who left just before I went in,' he said. 'I could have sworn I recognised one of them. I think we were on a course together at Sandridge. Who were they?'

The PA consulted her computer. 'They were visitors from the Department of Justice,' she said. 'Mr Geherty and Mr Wilmington. Which one was your friend?'

'Oh, I didn't say he was my friend,' Lapslie said quietly. 'Thanks for your help.'

Geherty. There couldn't be too many people with a name like that working for the Department of Justice – assuming that's where they actually came from.

Returning to his desk, grimacing at the salty wash of blood in his mouth from the general hubbub of conversation, he looked up the switchboard number for the Department of Justice's new offices in London on his own computer, then dialled it.

'Good morning,' he said, when the call was answered, 'Could you put me through to Mr Geherty, please?'

There was silence for a few moments as the receptionist presumably checked her screen for details. Lapslie wondered idly whether she was actually in the Department of Justice building, or whether she was based in a call centre in Mumbai, perhaps, or New Delhi, and spent her lunch hours laughing about the strange names of people in England.

'I'm afraid I'm getting no answer,' the receptionist's voice said. 'Shall I put you through to Mr Geherty's voicemail, or would you like to speak to someone else?'

'Actually,' Lapslie said, 'I need to put something in the post to him. Can you confirm his title and department for me?'

'Yes, of course. It's Martin Geherty, Assistant Director, PRU. Do you need the full address?'

'That's okay,' Lapslie said, 'I know where he is.'

PRU? What did that mean? Assuming that the black Lexus in the car park and the black Lexus that he had seen back at the place Violet Chambers' body had been discovered were the same – an assumption that would need to be proven – and assuming that the two men coming out of Superintendent Rouse's office were the ones who had got into the Lexus in the car park – again, something he could work with but which would require evidence backing it up – then it looked as if there was some kind of parallel investigation going on. But what interest could the Department of Justice – and in particular the PRU, whatever that was – have in the murder of an old lady? And why had Superintendent Rouse been trying to subtly manoeuvre him off the case, first by asking whether he had too much work on to undertake the investigation properly, and then by suggesting early retirement to him and trying to get Emma

Bradbury reassigned? If Rouse wanted things dropped, why not just order him off?

Presumably, because he would have to give reasons.

And he couldn't.

The noise was getting too much for him, and Lapslie headed back to the Quiet Room, hoping that nobody had nipped in for a quick snooze whilst he'd been gone. Friday afternoons were particularly bad: once he'd found three officers sleeping off a lunchtime drinking session: one in the chair, one flat on his back on the desk and one curled up underneath it.

Fortunately, he was in luck. The room was still empty.

He shut the door and leaned back in the chair, letting the silence slide over him. Slowly his breath, which he hadn't even realised was tight, relaxed.

He found his thoughts turning back to the mortuary, and the question of whether there had been an intruder going through Dr Catherall's files. He hadn't mentioned it to Emma Bradbury. Although she had been alone in Catherall's office for a while and, by any theoretical analysis of the situation, was a potential suspect, Lapslie had discounted her immediately because she was a police officer, because he knew her and because she had no apparent motive. Now, suspecting that his own immediate superior knew more about the case than he should and could therefore have asked his Detective Sergeant to do some undercover work for him, Lapslie paradoxically trusted Emma even more. If Superintendent Rouse was involved then so were the two strangers from the Department of Justice, and it made more sense that they had been going through the files than that she had. After all, it looked as if they had been present at the scene where the body had been discovered.

A disquieting thought occurred to him. Had they been there *when* the body had been discovered? But that was impossible, surely. It was more likely that they had somehow picked up the news from the local police or the journalists at the scene. But in that case, what exactly was it that had triggered their arrival? Did they turn up to every car crash that occurred in the area?

Or did they just turn up every time the body of an elderly woman was discovered?

He thought about letting Emma in on what had been happening, on the basis that she could turn up something about these mysterious strangers, but something stopped him. He needed information, but he had a strong feeling that it needed to be outside normal channels. Retrieving his mobile from his pocket, he scrolled through the list of contacts until he found a name and a number that he thought he'd never have to use again, but had avoided deleting just in case.

'Dom McGinley,' said a voice that triggered an inappropriate but familiar taste across his tongue, like salmon-flavoured bubblegum.

'McGinley? Mark Lapslie.'

'Mr Lapslie. It's been a long time.'

'It's been fifteen years. I probably look now the way you did back then.'

McGinley laughed; a noise that at one time could have cleared a bar. 'I usually only accept calls from coppers when I have something on them,' he said. 'I seem to recall that you and I parted on even terms.'

'Then this is your lucky day,' Lapslie said. 'I need a favour. Can we meet up?'

'Ah, I thought this day would never come. Wednesday – the usual boozer on the Thames. You remember.'

'I try to forget, but I can't. All right – Wednesday it is.'

The phone went dead, and Lapslie stared at it for a moment. A voice from the past, indeed. Dominic McGinley had been a legend in North London, back in the 1970s. He ran most of the drugs, most of the protection rackets and all of the prostitution between the North Circular and the City of Westminster, bounded on the left by the A5 and on the right by the A10. Lapslie had been only one of many policemen to try and get something on him, but McGinley was always several steps removed from the crimes. Tracing anything back to him was impossible.

And now Lapslie needed his help. Funny, the way things turned out.

CHAPTER NINE

Something Daisy Wilson had missed, reading through the local papers covering the Tendring Hundreds area, was the arts pages. It was only later that afternoon, sitting on the esplanade and gazing out across the grey waves, trying to recall where she had seen the face of that girl in the library book before, that she remembered. Delving into her bag, she recovered the *Gazette* and flicked through the pages until she found what she was looking for. Yes! Apart from the usual end-of-pier shows – faded TV entertainers who would attract the wrong type of target entirely – there was a theatre in nearby Clacton which appeared to show real plays. Cultured entertainment. If her previous experience, several victims ago, admittedly, was anything to go by then the pickings at a theatre should be pretty good. Even if she avoided the couples and the coach parties then she should be left with a fair selection of women who had enough money to afford a theatre ticket but nobody to share their evenings with. Perfect!

According to the timetable she had picked up from the Visitor Information kiosk, there was a bus leaving Leyston at six o'clock in the evening that would get her to Clacton in good time for the performance. And fortunately she had packed some clothes that were formal enough to go to the theatre in but casual enough that she wouldn't have any problems catching a bus in a seaside town late at night.

Returning to her hotel, she showered and put on some make-up: not enough to be obtrusive, but just enough to help support the story she would be selling: that she was refined without being posh, that she had money but no friends. The mirror image of the person she would be looking for. People were often, she had noticed, attracted to their own reflections.

The dress she pulled out of her suitcase was black, but not funereal. With a belt, a pair of tights and an overcoat, it would be perfectly acceptable. She cast her mind back, trying to remember where she had obtained it. She certainly hadn't bought it – Daisy tried not to buy anything, if she could possibly help it. Had it belonged to Alice Connell? Jane Winterbottom? Daisy tried to remember their faces, but all she could recall was their clothes with her own features on top, looking back at her. No, Alice had been taller than her, and Jane a lot wider. Was it someone earlier than Alice? She had a vague memory of a woman in Leeds who had died slowly after Daisy had grated yew tree bark into her food over the course of several weeks. She had seemed absolutely fine, to the point where Daisy was about to switch to a different plant, and then she had suddenly dropped dead, apparently of a heart attack. Daisy hoped her heart had been weakened by the yew bark. It would have been a waste of time and effort if she had died of natural causes.

Now what had that woman's name been? Was it another Jane? She really couldn't remember.

No matter. To go with the dress, Daisy chose a rather nice necklace that she remembered had belonged to Violet Chambers, once upon a time. It set the dress off nicely. By the time she had finished dressing, it was almost time to go.

It was nearly night by the time she left the hotel. The pier was coming to life: what had been tawdry paint and worn woodwork in daylight was now hidden by the glare of the light bulbs which surrounded the entrance and were strung along the dark bulk of the pier like sparkling drops of water on cobweb threads. Daisy could hear music too: a regular, hypnotic pounding that echoed back in strange counterpoint from the houses. How could people live here, night after night, with that racket going on?

The bus was on time, and the journey along winding country lanes and through nameless villages was long enough for Violet to fall into a daze. The bus was half full, and the passengers were evenly divided between teenagers and older people, some of whom were probably on their way to Clacton for the play. Daisy deliberately didn't take note of any of them. There would be time enough for that later.

Every so often Daisy would glance out of the window, but the encroaching darkness meant that more often than not she just saw her own reflection. And, as she slipped deeper and deeper into a reverie, her reflection sometimes became that of one of the women she had supplanted in life. Once, when she looked over, the woman looking back was thinner than her, and wore glasses. Deirdre – Deirdre something? Another time, it was the former Daisy Wilson who turned to meet her gaze, her eyes deeply sunk in puffy flesh, her white hair piled high on her head in a sad remnant of the beehive hairdo she had once sported so proudly.

And once, when Daisy opened her eyes and looked into the dark mirror of the window, a young girl was staring back at her. A red-haired girl in a flowery dress, stained down the front with something dark and wet and terrible.

With a jerk, Daisy woke up. Her heart was pounding fit to break. She took a deep breath, having to fight to get it past the lump in her throat. Gradually, her heart eased itself back into its normal rhythm.

Daisy knew that girl. She knew that face, she even knew that dress, but there was something about the girl that she didn't want to think about. When she saw the girl's photograph at the library she had slammed the book shut and left. Now she deliberately focused on the lights outside the window, trying to wipe all trace of the girl from her mind.

The bus was pulling into Clacton now. The lights were brighter than Leyston, the music was louder and everything was more intense. If Leyston was the shy, retiring brother then Clacton was the older, outgoing and rather blowsy sister.

Taking her cue from some of the other older passengers, Daisy left the bus and found herself just a short walk from the theatre. Looking up at the frontage, she realised that she hadn't even checked what play was being performed that night. Now, gazing up at the title, a giggle escaped her lips.

Arsenic and Old Lace.

How apt. How perfectly apt.

The audience heading into the theatre seemed to be mainly people around her own age, and her dress and overcoat did not mark her out from the rest of the crowd. She headed towards the box office and managed to secure a ticket in the balcony. A better class of person went in the balcony, she had found.

Sitting in her seat, with just a few minutes to go before the curtain rose, she gazed around. The theatre was about half full, and she could already see a few good prospects in her vicinity. Best to wait until the interval and see what transpired.

The play was well performed and the set was a convincing reproduction of a down-at-heel boarding house in the 1950s, but Daisy felt her attention wander after a while. She didn't recognise any of the actors – no doubt they were well known from television soap operas or something of the sort, but she rarely watched television. They rushed around the stage, keeping the audience laughing with the story of two old ladies who were killing off the single male guests in their house and burying them in the cellar, but Daisy found it all too frantic and too unbelievable.

There was a woman sitting two rows ahead of her, and just to the left. She was white-haired, and quite stocky. The seat to her left was empty; the one to her right was occupied by a man, but he was younger than her and his head was turned towards the person on his other side. She wore a silk scarf tied around her neck. She was absorbed in the play, and Daisy became more and more absorbed with her as the play went on. She kept glancing at her, taking in the curve of her neck, the shape of her ear, the way the earring she wore sparkled in the light. Daisy felt her pulse quicken: this was the kind of drama she liked.

Come the interval, Daisy quickly manoeuvred out of her aisle and made sure she was slightly ahead of the other woman in the queue for the bar. She wanted to make sure that she had been seen. It was always best if the first move came from the prey, rather than the predator.

Daisy bought herself a small gin and tonic at an extortionate price, then went to sit by the nearest window, making sure there was a second chair at her table. The bar was too warm for comfort, but a cooling breeze came in from outside, flavoured slightly with candy floss and hot oil from the nearby sea front. She composed her expression into one of quiet resignation, and gazed blankly out of the window.

'Excuse me, is this seat taken?'

She turned her head. The woman she had targeted was standing beside the empty chair.

'No, I'm – no. Please, feel free.'

The woman sat down. She was holding a glass of white wine. Daisy could just make out her perfume above the smell from outside. 'My name is Sylvia – Sylvia McDonald. Are you enjoying the play?'

'It's very good. Yes, *very* good,' Daisy replied. 'I don't get to go out much, and I do so enjoy the theatre.'

'So do I. I thought the actors were terribly good.'

'It's such a lovely theatre, too.'

'It is. And so convenient.'

'Do you live nearby?' Daisy asked.

'I live in Leyston,' the woman said. 'I drove in this evening. I'm parked just down the road.'

'Daisy. Daisy Wilson.'

They raised their glasses at each other, and smiled.

'My husband used to love the theatre,' Sylvia said after a few moments.

Daisy looked around. 'Is he—'

'I lost him, nine years ago last month.'

'I'm terribly sorry.'

'And you?'

'Oh,' Daisy said, 'I never married. There was a man, once, but ...' She trailed off, leaving Sylvia to fill in the rest of the story. 'I've just moved into Leyston myself,' she added. 'It's such a quiet place.'

'And it can be quite beautiful,' Sylvia added.

The bell rang for the second act. Daisy realised she only had a few seconds to make her move. 'It can also be so lonely,' she said. 'If you don't know anyone in the area ...' She gazed out of the window, leaving the thought hanging.

'Perhaps you'd like to meet for a cup of tea,' Sylvia offered. 'Let's organise something after the play finishes. Perhaps I could offer you a lift back?'

Daisy finished her drink, aware that the glass was trembling slightly in her hand. And so it began: the long dance of friendship, dependence and ultimately death. She felt as if she was poised on the brink of a long slope. One step, one small step, and she would be committed.

'That would be lovely,' she said.

Daisy hardly noticed the rest of the play. She was too busy rehearsing her own production in her head: practising her lines until the words and the mood were perfect; choosing various locations for the scenes until she found the ones that best conjured up the mood she wanted to create. Following the final curtain, the two of them nattered while walking to Sylvia's car, and nattered more as they drove. And by the time they arrived outside the station, where Daisy had asked to be dropped off, they had arranged to meet the next day at the coffee shop by the post office – the only one that Daisy knew, although she wasn't going to admit that. She went to sleep that night exultant, and she slept the sleep of the dead.

The next morning, Daisy awoke early. She had a lot to do. After a quick breakfast, she made her way through the town until she found an estate agents that met her criteria: not the flashiest, but not the most down at heel either. One tucked away in a side street that catered to local people, not holiday-makers wishing to rent a flat for the summer.

Daisy knew her requirements, and politely rejected every-thing she was shown until the young man helping her showed her a photograph of a house a little way out of town, close to the cliff. Old in style, with a small garden at the back and a passion-fruit climber wrapped around the porch and trailing up to the first-floor window, it was just what she was looking for. The first floor was already let to a foreign girl studying at the local college. The ground floor was available for imme-diate letting. It was, Daisy decided as she looked at the photograph, the perfect web in which to trap the fly she sought. Using bills addressed to Daisy Wilson's old address as proof of identity, she obtained a set of keys and went to view the flat by herself, although the young man offered to drive her. It hardly mattered.

The flat was a little small for her purposes, with a living room at the front, a bedroom at the rear and a combined kitchen and dining room off to one side. At least it had a small conservatory, which made it slightly less pokey. Knowing she wouldn't be living there for long, assuming everything went to plan, Daisy went straight back to the estate agents and put down a deposit. She still had a week or more left at the hotel, which gave her time to obtain some furniture and make the place look as if she had been there for a while. Until then, she would have to make sure that she was invited to Sylvia's place, not the other way around.

Walking away from the estate agents, Daisy identified three shops in the back streets that sold second-hand furniture, and would deliver. She needed things that looked used. Things that she might well have brought with her from somewhere else.

Daisy and Sylvia met for coffee that afternoon. They talked for an hour and a half about inconsequential things: the play the night before, the weather, how lovely the town was. Towards the end, Sylvia told Daisy about her husband, and how he had been a part of the volunteer lifeboat crew for fifteen years until cancer took him away. Her eyes were bright with unshed tears. Daisy risked patting her hand gently and offering her a tissue. Daisy, in turn, explained how she had been a nurse for almost three decades, and how the demands of duty meant that she had never managed to find anyone to settle down with. Using elements of the story that had brought her to Leyston in the first place, she told Sylvia that her sister had been taken ill and that she had moved in with her to nurse her through her final days. It was a calculated risk, and Sylvia did ask what Daisy's sister's name was, but Daisy explained that her sister had been disabled for many years and rarely left the house. Sylvia seemed satisfied with the explanation.

Sylvia insisted on paying for the coffee and the cakes. She used a debit card, which pleased Daisy no end. It meant she was solvent. It meant that she was even more of an attractive prospect than Daisy had originally thought. They parted on friendly terms, having exchanged addresses, and after Sylvia had invited Daisy round for tea the afternoon after next.

Back at the hotel, she sat at the writing table over by the window. From her pocket, she produced the copy of the debit card slip that she had so carefully taken from Sylvia's handbag when Sylvia had visited the ladies' room, just before they left. Using a plain sheet of paper, she copied Sylvia's signature again and again, first slowly and then getting faster and faster, until she could reproduce it perfectly.

Daisy felt like celebrating, that night. Instead of eating in the hotel, she wandered out into the town and found a small restaurant that advertised locally caught seafood. Daisy had scampi and chips, and thoroughly enjoyed it. Even more, she enjoyed the fact that she wasn't watching the people around her, just in case a likely prospect came in. She had found her prospect. Now she just had to follow through.

The next morning, she told the desk clerk at the hotel that she would be leaving at the end of the week. For the rest of that day she visited various second-hand shops along the High Street, ordering furniture to be delivered and buying bits of bric-a-brac, old books, cutlery, plates, dishes and cups, which she ferried back to her new flat on the bus in a wheeled shopping bag that she picked up for five pounds in a charity shop.

Come the evening, Daisy was hungry, but instead of looking for somewhere to eat she found her footsteps turning towards the marina again. Something about the stillness of the water had soothed her, the day before, and she wanted to recapture that feeling. It only took her a few minutes to find the road again, and to walk along it until she found the bank of earth and the gate to the Yacht Club. Slowly she climbed up the shallow concrete steps, feeling the effort more then than she had the day before. At the top, she raised her eyes to take in the expanse of water.

It wasn't there. Instead, Daisy was confronted with a corrugated expanse of greenish-grey mud. She descended the steps on the other side of the bank, trying to work out what had happened. Had the tide gone out? It seemed too dramatic a change to have occurred in so short a time, but she supposed it was the only explanation.

The boats that had sat so calmly in the water the day before were now canted drunkenly on the mud, their masts pointed at crazy angles. Seagulls stalked amid them, pecking at the oozing surface. Daisy could suddenly smell a rank, fish odour that made her nose wrinkle involuntarily.

She walked to the edge of the concrete jetty and looked over into the mud. The sun had baked parts of it to a hard crust, riven by cracks through which glinted an unpleasant wetness. Rusty cans, bottles, pipes and unidentifiable but sharp-edged objects emerged from the mud as if they were part of something larger, buried underneath, that was attempting to pull itself back to land. Small insects skittered across the wet surface, searching for somewhere to lay their eggs. It was hard to believe that something so unpleasant could have been concealed by something so beautiful; that something looking and smelling so disgusting could lurk beneath the pure and glittering surface of the water.

Daisy turned to go. She felt soiled. She would make sure that she never came back to the marina unless it was high tide.

That night, Daisy dreamed of the red-haired girl again. She had been sleeping uneasily since she had gone to bed, repeatedly jerked to the edge of wakefulness by the distant electrical clash of bumper cars on the pier and the sounds of teenagers singing and shouting as they made their way along the esplanade. As time went on, as the pubs and clubs shut their doors and the pier emptied of people, her room grew quieter and she slipped deeper into unconsciousness like a rusty tin can sinking into mud. By midnight, she was oblivious to everything.

In her dream, Daisy was in a dining room dominated by a large mahogany table. Place mats had been set out in front of each of the chairs: cork-backed, with laminated pictures of plants on the front. The room itself was dark, apart from candelabra on the table itself, but Daisy got the impression of curtains in the darkness; soft, velvety curtains, dropping in swoops and furls to the floor, muffling all noise.

Daisy was sitting at one end of the table. The picture on her place mat was of a rhododendron bush. Looking to her left, with the slow, underwater motions of a dream, she could see that the place mat there had a picture of an azalea bush. The one on her right was a mountain laurel.

'Did you know,' said a girlish voice from the other end of the table, 'that honey made by bees who have collected pollen from rhododendron bushes is actually poisonous? I read that in a book, I think.'

Daisy looked up. A girl was sitting opposite her. She was about eight years old, and she had red hair and wore a flowery dress. She seemed dwarfed by the heavy mahogany chair she was perched on.

'What's your name?' said Daisy.

'I don't remember,' the girl replied. 'What's yours?'

Daisy shook her head. 'I don't remember either. Where are we?'

'In my secret place. Do you like it?'

'I don't know, m'dear. I can't really see it that well. What are we doing here?'

'We're having a tea party. We always have tea parties here.'

With no particular surprise, Daisy saw that the place mat in front of the little girl now held a tea pot and two cups on saucers: small cups, small saucers, more fit for dolls' houses than for people. With exaggerated care, the girl filled the two cups with steaming brown liquid, then slipped from her chair, picked one cup up by the saucer and carried it around the table to where Daisy was sitting.

'It's lovely,' she said as she placed the cup down. 'I made it myself.'

'And what did you make it out of, m'dear?' Daisy asked as the girl returned to her chair.

'Sugar and spice and all things nice,' the girl said. 'Like I always do. You have to drink it.'

'I'm not really thirsty.'

'But you have to.' It was less of a command; more a statement of fact.

Daisy found her hand reaching out for the cup. She tried to pull it back, but her fingers closed around the warm china and she lifted it up towards her mouth. 'I really don't think—'

'But you *have* to. It's the game.'

Daisy felt the steam from the tea turn into moisture on her upper lip. She could smell something bitter and unpleasant. 'What *is* this?'

'Don't you know?' The girl smirked.

She could feel the cup in her fingers, feel the increasing heat transferring through to her skin. 'It smells … familiar.'

'It used to grow in your garden. It used to grow all over your garden. You made a drink from the berries. Don't you remember? The gardener called it "belladonna".'

The cup tipped back, and the liquid trickled into Daisy's mouth. She tried to spit it out, but whatever was controlling her hand made her swallow, and swallow again.

'Rabbits can eat it,' the girl said primly, 'and it doesn't affect them. But if you eat the rabbits, you can be poisoned.'

Daisy could feel a burning in her mouth, although the tea wasn't that hot. Blisters were coming up on her tongue and lips, and her forehead was suddenly damp with sweat.

'Apparently, witches used to use belladonna when they were dancing together at night. It made them think they were flying. My mummy says that witches aren't real, but I know they are.'

Daisy's hands put the cup down on the table and folded themselves neatly in her lap, but the fingers were tingling and the palms were wet.

'Roman ladies used belladonna in make-up, to make their skin look really white.' The girl was leaning forward in her chair, her hands clenched on the arms, watching Daisy intently. '*Your* skin looks really white now, but I don't think that's make-up. I think that's the belladonna working.'

Her hands were completely numb, and the room was getting blurry and white. She could just see the girl's outline, but the blurriness turned her fine features into a skull, a red-haired skull, grinning insanely at Daisy.

'How does it feel?' the girl screamed. 'How does it *feel*?'

Daisy shot upright in bed. For a moment she could still feel the blisters in her mouth and the growing burning in her throat, but the sheets were cool beneath her clutching hands and somewhere outside the window she could hear waves on sand. It had been a dream. It had only been a dream.

The next morning, Daisy took longer than usual to get ready.

She was feeling old and tired. Something about this town was sapping her strength; it was as if arriving there had awakened old ghosts and she had to try and lay them to rest if she was going to make any progress with Sylvia.

She spent the morning pottering around the hotel and the town, and after lunch she took a taxi to Sylvia's house. She had already checked where it was on a map of the town she had obtained from the Visitor Information kiosk, which was proving increasingly useful to her, and she knew that she could get a bus that would drop her off ten minutes' walk away, but she wanted to arrive fresh. And besides, it gave the impression that she was used to travelling in some comfort, which would probably go down well with Sylvia.

The house was high up, near the top of the knob of land that pushed out into the sea, north of the town, part of an estate that Daisy estimated had been built in the 1930s. It was well-proportioned and wide, built of red brick, with a garage and a small round window over the front door. It was detached from its neighbours, and set back from the road. As Daisy got out of the taxi and paid the driver, she could hardly take her eyes off it. Of all the houses she had ever lived in, or ever intended to, this was the best. She would enjoy living there, once she had got Sylvia out of the way.

Sylvia was waiting by the front door. 'A taxi,' she said. 'How extravagant.'

'I couldn't face the bus,' Daisy replied, following Sylvia into the house. 'What a lovely place you have here.'

'Would you like a tour?'

Sylvia showed Daisy around with pride. The house was immaculately kept, and there were obviously rooms that Sylvia just didn't go into any more. The kitchen was huge, with wood-panelled cupboards, and the master bedroom had a view between the houses opposite to the sea. It was perfect.

Well, not quite perfect. None of the fixtures or fittings would fetch more than a few thousand pounds, at best. Still, the house itself would be worth quite a bundle when Daisy finally got tired of it.

The weather was warm enough that they took tea in the back garden. Sylvia kept it beautifully tidy, and they spent some time talking about the various flowers. Daisy commented particularly on the well-kept privet hedges, and the morning-glory vine that trailed up the rear of the house.

Sitting in chairs out in the back garden, Daisy said, apropos of nothing: 'It seems awfully quiet here. You must have good neighbours.'

'I don't really see that much of them,' Sylvia admitted. 'There's a family on one side: they go out a lot, and we rarely talk. The man on the other side is a bus driver. He's very quiet.'

'What about the others? The other side of the road?'

'Quite a few of them are new, over the past few years. It's happening everywhere nowadays. It used to be that people would be in and out of each other's houses, offering a hand, having cups of tea, borrowing sugar or milk. Now, people keep themselves to themselves. It's a shame.'

'It is,' said Daisy. 'Everyone needs friends. Life can be so terribly lonely otherwise.'

They talked for a while about the changes they had seen during their lives, and how people today seemed less caring than they had twenty or thirty years ago. The nature of society had shifted, and they felt left behind. Part of the past.

The talk turned to other things. Daisy ventured a comment about her own varicose veins, and how they made walking difficult sometimes.

'I know,' Sylvia said. 'I had one hip replaced, ten years ago, and the other hip done a year after that. I swear that the surgeons put one in shorter than the other, but they won't listen to me. "I'm the one who has to walk on it," I told them, "and some days I feel like I'm walking in circles", but they didn't want to know. Told me it was impossible.' Her face fell. 'Sometimes I just can't get comfortable at night, with these hips. I don't think I've had a good night's sleep since they put them in.'

'You should take something for it,' Daisy said, sensing an opening the way a cat can sometimes sense a mouse without even seeing it.

'Oh,' Sylvia said, 'I don't like the thought of sedatives.'

'I was thinking more of something herbal,' Daisy said casually. 'A herbal tea, perhaps. I could make you some up. If you would like.'

'Oh Daisy,' Sylvia said gratefully, 'you're just killing me with kindness.'

CHAPTER TEN

There was a poem that Mark Lapslie had read once, while searching online for other people's experiences of synaesthesia. It was on a website that noted, with some pride, that there were many artists, poets and musicians who were synaesthetic, although it then went on to admit that this might be because they were more likely to notice and even take advantage of their symptoms. The poem was by a nineteenth-century French writer named Baudelaire, and it stuck in Lapslie's memory. It captured in a handful of words something that he wished he could achieve in his own life – a sense of the beauty and the majesty that synaesthesia could apparently provide.

> *There are perfumes fresh like the skin of infants*
> *Sweet like oboes, green like prairies,*
> *—And others corrupted, rich and triumphant*
> *That have the expanse of infinite things,*
> *Like ambergris, musk, balsam and incense,*
> *Which sing the ecstasies of the mind and senses.*

He remembered the poem again as he made the long drive, under a grey early-morning sky, from his cottage in Saffron Walden to the hospital outside Braintree where he was under the occasional care of the consultant neurologist. *The ecstasies of the mind and senses.* If only that were as true for him as it apparently was for Baudelaire.

Still, Baudelaire had been a syphilitic opium addict with a

drink problem, so Lapslie felt justified in not taking his pronouncements too seriously.

He parked his car near the hospital and walked through the main entrance. Rather than wear a suit, he had chosen chinos, a plain shirt and a moleskin jacket. He'd booked a day's leave for the appointment, and to meet an old friend later on.

The central atrium was tall and airy, surrounded by planters of ferns, with fountains plashing gently in the centre and stone benches all around. Walking through a set of double doors to one side of the atrium, he quickly found himself in the hospital proper: a maze of square corridors that smelled of disinfectant, their walls and linoleum scuffed and scarred by decades of hospital trolleys. The original, 1950s vintage, hospital was hidden behind the impressive new façade in the same way that the ladies of Baudelaire's time used to hide their pox-ridden faces behind caked layers of make-up.

A handful of people were sat around a waiting area, waiting for the neurology outpatients clinic. Lapslie sat and waited with them for his appointment, trying not to make judgements about them. After all, he was on leave, not on duty.

He had timed his arrival perfectly, and within five minutes his name was being called. The consulting room was small, anonymous, with white walls, a hospital trolley, a desk with a computer on it and a couple of chairs. It could have been any consulting room in any hospital or clinic, anywhere in the country.

The young man sitting at the desk was new to Lapslie. He was reading information off the computer screen as Lapslie entered, and he stuck out his hand without taking his eyes off the screen. 'Hello. I'm Doctor Considine. I don't think I've seen you before, have I?'

'Mark Lapslie.' He shook the doctor's hand and sat down. 'I've been seeing Doctor Lombardy for the past ten years or so.'

'Doctor Lombardy retired about six months ago. A very

clever man. Great loss to the hospital.' He consulted the computer again. 'I see you're a synaesthete. We don't get to see many synaesthetes here – estimates of its occurrence vary between six people in a million and three in a hundred, depending on how wide you want to draw the boundaries, but most of them either don't know they have it or assume that everyone does. You, it appears, are in that small subsection for whom the effect of synaesthesia is strong enough to cause problems in your day-to-day life. When was the last time you were seen here?'

'A year ago.'

'And has your condition changed in that time – got worse or got better?'

'It's stayed at the same level.'

'Hmm.' He tapped his fingers on the desk. 'I presume that Doctor Lombardy told you there is no treatment and no cure for synaesthesia? It's something you just have to live with.'

Lapslie nodded. 'He did tell me that. We decided that it was worth me coming back once a year or so to check whether there had been any major advances in the research.'

Dr Considine shook his head. 'Not to my knowledge. It's still pretty much a puzzle. We know from magnetic resonance imaging of the brain, for instance, that synaesthetes such as yourself show patterns of activity that are different from people who are normal – for want of a better word – but we are still trying to work out what that difference means. It's still a puzzle.'

'One that's affecting my career and my personal life,' Lapslie said bitterly. 'It's easy to say there's no treatment, but you don't have to live with it. My career has stalled because I can't socialise the way the others do. I've separated from my family because I can't bear the continual taste in my mouth when they're around. And I can't watch television, or go to see a film or a concert, for fear of suddenly throwing up. Runny egg yolks and chalky antacid tablets are bad enough, but a sudden rush of raw sewage or vomit down your throat can spoil your entire evening.'

'I see.' The doctor wrote a few notes on a pad in front of him. 'And forgive me for asking this, but is there an up-side? Does the synaesthesia bring any benefits with it?'

'I have a very good memory for people – I suspect that's because I can associate their voices with particular flavours.'

'Which makes me wonder – does my voice have a flavour to it?'

Lapslie laughed. 'You'd be surprised how many people ask me that question, when they hear about my problem. No – not all sounds trigger flavours. I don't know if it's to do with pitch, or timbre, or what. Some voices do, but yours doesn't. Sorry.'

'Anything else? Any more benefits?'

Lapslie considered for a few seconds. 'Strangely,' he said, 'I can usually tell when people are lying to me. It's an unusual taste. Dry and spicy, but not in a curry way. More like nutmeg. It's helped me investigating crimes before.' To Considine's raised eyebrow, he added: 'I'm in the police.'

Considine frowned. 'I can just about understand how sounds can be mistranslated into flavours somewhere in the brain,' he said, 'but lying isn't a *sound*, it's got to do with the content, the meaning of what's being said. That's a bit of a stretch.'

'The way I rationalise it,' Lapslie said, 'when people lie, there's a certain amount of stress in their voice, changing the way it sounds in subtle ways. Somehow, I'm picking up on that stress and tasting it.'

'I presume you've been asked to take part in research projects? There are labs all over the country becoming interested in synaesthesia.'

'I've been asked, and I've occasionally taken part in experiments, but it usually turns out that I'm just some glorified lab rat. I want to understand and control my problem, but the trouble is that most researchers want something else. They want to use the synaesthesia as a window into the way the brain operates.'

Considine nodded. 'I can sympathise. There are psychiatric techniques you could use to try and help control the flood of sensations you are getting. Cognitive behaviour therapy, for instance, could help you weaken the connections between stimuli such as particular sounds and your habitual reactions to them. The tastes might stay, but your reactions could be modified. If you want, I can recommend you to a therapist.'

Therapy. Lapslie shook his head. It wasn't for him.

'Thanks,' he said, 'but I think the problem is more deeply rooted than that. Changing the way I think won't affect it.'

'Then you're just going to have to live with it.'

'Thanks for your time.'

'Come back in another year,' Dr Considine said as Lapslie stood up to leave. 'Who knows? By then we might actually know what synaesthesia is and how to suppress it.'

'Who knows?' Lapslie said as he left.

It had rained whilst he was in the hospital. Pools of water congregated along kerbs and in dips in the road. Driving out of the hospital grounds, he headed for the A120, but a small voice in the back of his mind told him that he wasn't too far away from where Violet Chambers' body had been discovered in the forest outside Faulkbourne. Abruptly he turned right instead of left at a roundabout and quickly typed a new destination into his satnav system. He wasn't sure why, but he wanted to take another look at the area. Get a feel for it during the daytime, rather than the early morning. See it when nobody else was there, rather than having it filled with policemen and Crime Scene Investigators.

Accelerating along the road, he let his mind drift, trying to analyse why he wanted to spend what remained of his day off investigating a murder. There was something unsatisfying about the crime. Something slightly out of the ordinary. He had investigated so many murders over the years that he was inured to them, to the sights and the smells, the reasons and the rationales, but this one didn't seem to fit into the usual channels. Partly it was too mannered, too organised. Poisoning was not a crime of passion, but one of meticulous planning. But then there was the blow to the back of the head and the dumping of the body, apparently still alive, in the forest. That spoke of haste, of the murderer panicking and leaving the body behind. The two just didn't go together.

Unless ...

Unless the murderer had been interrupted on their way to dump the body. Perhaps they had chosen a site where they could abandon it with no fear of detection, but something had happened on the way. The poison hadn't worked properly: the supposed body had come back to life again. Lapslie felt his pulse pumping as the thoughts all tumbled together in his mind. The murderer – or, rather, the attacker at this point – pulls over on a deserted road to finish the job with a quick blow to the back of the skull with a handy tool – a spanner, or a wrench, or something – but why not keep on going once the victim was dead? Why dump the body there?

Was there an interruption? Did someone see the car, parked by the side of the road, and pull over to see whether the murderer needed any help? Did the murderer have to leave the body where it was in order to deal with this interruption?

The rain-laden clouds were dark overhead but there was blue sky off to one side. The sun shone diagonally across the landscape, lighting it with a strange golden glow against the dark backdrop. It looked more like a stage set than a real place. Lapslie pushed the problem back in his mind, where his subconscious could chew on it, and set about enjoying the quietness of the drive.

Within half an hour he was heading along the same tree-lined road that he'd been on just a few weeks before. The rain had sluiced the air of dust, and the leaves seemed to glow with a preternatural light as the sun caught them. Shafts of brightness

157

lanced through gaps in the trees, picked out by the moisture in the air. He slowed as he approached the bend in the road where the crash had occurred, pulled over and parked under the trees, his tyres biting deep into the loam.

Lapslie got out of the car and stood for a moment, breathing in the earthy dampness of the air. The CSI team had cleared up and left. Nothing remained of their presence apart from a churned-up area of ground where their tent had been, and some small scraps of yellow tape.

Turning, Lapslie gazed back along the length of the road he had just driven along. If he was right – and it was less of a theory, more of a hypothesis at the moment – the murderer had been driving along that road on their way to dump the body of their victim somewhere. For some reason they had stopped and their victim – who was not quite dead – had taken the opportunity to attempt an escape. A quick tap to the back of the head, and the victim really was dead. The murderer wrapped her in plastic and left her there, rather than drive on to the spot where they actually wanted to leave the body.

First question – why did the murderer stop the car? Three immediate possibilities occurred to him – either the victim had shown signs of life and had to be dealt with immediately, or there had been something at the scene already that had forced the murderer to stop, or the car had developed a fault. Now, which of those possibilities was the most likely? If the victim had shown signs of life while the murderer was driving the car then they might have stopped and hit them hard enough to finish the job, but why dump the body there? Why not keep on driving to the place they had originally intended to dump it? Scratch that idea. If there had been something on the road – a car in trouble perhaps, then why stop? Or, if the murderer had been forced to stop – by a police presence clearing the scene, perhaps – then why dump the body in a place where there were people around? Again, why not just keep going? No, the more Lapslie thought about it, the more he believed that the murderer's car had developed a fault.

In his mind's eye, he could see it happening, playing out against the picturesque setting of the misty road. A lone car, driving carefully, trying not to attract attention. A puncture, perhaps, or steam coming out of the radiator. The car draws quickly to a halt. The driver – a shadowy figure – gets out and checks the tyre, the bonnet, wherever the problem is. Unseen, the back door opens and a form crawls out, heading into the safety of the trees. The driver sees it, follows it across the bracken. A branch is picked up and descends abruptly: once, twice. The driver returns to the car and reluctantly makes a call to the emergency services. Before they can arrive, the driver takes a roll of plastic out of the back of the car and wraps the body up, piling bracken and earth on top to the best of their ability in order to keep it from being discovered. And then they wait for the AA, or the RAC, or whoever to arrive.

It made sense. It was only a possibility, of course, but it made sense. Which meant that the question was: what evidence might there be confirming or denying it?

Lapslie took his mobile from his jacket and held down the button that allowed him to voice-dial. 'Emma Bradbury,' he said, and the phone ransacked its memory for her number. Within a few moments, she answered.

'Sir? I thought it was your day off?'

'It is. I got bored. Emma, I need you to do something for me. I'm at the site where the body was found. I want you to check whether any recovery services or mechanics were called out to a broken-down car on this spot between, say, nine and eleven months ago. Check the police as well: they may have a record of something having happened. Give me a ring back when you have it.'

'Will do. What's this all—'

He cut her off abruptly, not wanting to talk, concerned somehow that if he was to explain his theory – his *hypothesis*

– then it would all crumble to dust and Emma would laugh at him. He would wait until she called back with actual evidence – one way or the other – before he told her what he thought. And while he waited, he decided to take a walk in the woods.

The leaf mulch gave spongily beneath his feet as he walked. All around there was a slight crackle of vegetation drying out after the rain, and the occasional flurry of activity as a bird or a fox moved in the underbrush, but the smell of damp leaves rising from the ground covered any other taste that might have been triggered in Lapslie's mouth. There were no trails, no paths through the bushes to follow. He found himself having to step carefully over fallen trees and skirt around hawthorn bushes in order to make any progress.

Within a few moments he couldn't see the road, or his car. He might just as well have been in the middle of the forest as at its edge, and if he wasn't careful he might just keep walking until he *was* in the middle. There was no way to check direction, and although he tried to catalogue the shapes of trees that he passed, he found they all ended up looking the same.

People talked about cities having personalities, and in his time stationed in London as a Detective Sergeant he had come to know the comfortable excesses of the capital – a raddled old whore who still managed to attract clients – but there was a different kind of personality here in the woods. Something timeless and dark. Whatever it was, it had seen the murder of Violet Chambers and it didn't care, just as it hadn't cared about any of the hundreds, thousands, millions of deaths it had witnessed over the millennia.

Turning back, with some effort, Lapslie retraced his steps as best he could. That tree on the edge of a dip, its roots exposed by storms and animals – he was sure he had seen it before on his way in. That parasitic gall, curled about the trunk of an oak – he surely recognised that. And within ten minutes, he was back at his car again, and it was as if the forest had been a dream.

His mobile rang as he returned to his car: Bruch's 1st violin concerto, and a burst of chocolate.

'Sir? Emma. I've phoned all the recovery and car mechanics firms covering the area. It's something of a blackspot, that curve. Quite a few cars end up coming off it in the wet or if it's icy.'

'How many?'

'In the timeframe in question, there were ...' She paused, consulting whatever notes she had made. '... five incidents where someone was called out to repair or recover a car. Three of them involved families, so I think we can rule them out. One was breathalysed at the scene by police and taken into custody. His car was impounded. I guess we can forget that one as well.' There was something creeping into Emma's voice that made Lapslie pay attention. It wasn't quite nutmeg, but there was something definitely odd about it. She was holding something back. 'The last one was a lady. No age given. Volvo 740, bronze, it says here. Car was repaired, and she went on her way.'

Lapslie thought for a moment. More poisoners turned out to be women than men, and the people living opposite Violet Chambers' house had mentioned seeing a woman going in and out shortly before she left – or disappeared. It was worth following up. 'Did they get a name?' he asked.

'You're going to like this, sir. The woman gave her name as Violet Chambers.'

And that was it. His hunch had paid off. 'Right. It's too much of a coincidence that the real Violet Chambers broke down here shortly before her body was discovered. It's much more likely that whoever dumped her body used her name as well. Get copies of their report form, check the registration number of the car and trace the owner. And, just in case, check whether the real Violet Chambers owned a car.'

'Will do. Anything else?'

'Yes. Put out a general request for assistance. I want to know where that car is now. I'll ring you later.'

He rang off, then pressed the redial button as something else occurred to him. Emma answered, sounding surprised. 'Boss? Something else?'

'Yes. Phone around as many garages and mechanics as you can find within a fifty-mile radius of this forest. I want to know if anyone else has ever been called out to that car, and where it was at the time. If we get lucky, we might be able to tie it down to wherever our murderer lives. Or lived.'

'But there must be hundreds of car mechanics in the area, if not thousands. That's going to take—'

'A significant slice of your time, I know. Just think of the overtime.'

'Any chance you can get a constable assigned to this case, sir?' she said sourly. 'I could use the help.'

'I'll see what I can do,' Lapslie said, ringing off.

The sky was getting darker again, and there was a chill in the air that suggested more rain was on its way. He needed to get away: he had an appointment in London to go to. But for the moment, he found he could not leave. There was something about the spot where he was standing. A person had died there, and yet there was no acknowledgement. No sign. Nothing to mark the passing.

Perhaps that was the state of the world, and the human need to place crosses and markers was just a futile attempt to battle against the tide. The woodlands he was standing in had been there for hundreds, perhaps thousands of years. Possibly they had been there before human beings had moved into the area. If every person's death that had occurred in those woods over the past two thousand years or more was marked by a red spot, would there be any greenery left?

Morbid thoughts. He climbed into his car and drove away, leaving the woodlands and their ghosts behind him.

He left his car at Audley End station, then caught a train to London, grabbing a quick sandwich on the way. The journey took less than an hour, and during the time he looked out of the window at the passing fields and factories and let his thoughts drift. Earplugs cut out the noise of the people talking around him, replacing them with blessed silence. Every time he found his thoughts turning toward Sonia and his children, he stopped and deliberately thought about something else. The pain of that scar throbbed enough; there was no point picking at it any more.

He called DCS Rouse's office from the train. The DCS wasn't available, so he left a message with his PA asking for some extra resources to help Emma Bradbury with her inquiries. He didn't hold out much hope – the top brass didn't seem to want to provide any more resources, despite the interest that DCS Rouse was showing in it – but he had to try.

The train left him at Liverpool Street, and he used the Underground to get across the river to Rotherhide. The earplugs were less effective at blocking out the constant rattling and roaring of the train through the tunnels, and he had to keep swallowing to wash the taste of gorgonzola away. Eventually he slipped a mint into his mouth, just to cover it up with something else.

At Rotherhide he left the station and made his way through cobbled back streets to an old, familiar public house perched on the edge of the Thames. The Golden Hind was tall and thin, slightly lopsided, constructed from blackened timbers and white-plastered brickwork. It looked at first glance like any one of a thousand faux-Tudor inns scattered about England, until you realised that it really did date from Tudor days. Things had been added and subtracted since that time, but it gave off an air of permanence at odds with the buildings around it.

He entered through a narrow doorway and looked around. The interior resembled a collision between three or four rooms of different sizes on different levels. Dom McGinley was sitting in a corner, a half-finished pint of Guinness in front of him. He raised his glass to Lapslie and took a swig.

'A pint of Guinness and a pint of lager,' Lapslie said to the barman. When he turned back with the drinks, McGinley was heading away from the door, towards a small exit at the back of the pub. Lapslie followed on, and found himself on a short pier extending out twenty feet or so into the Thames. Wooden benches were scattered around. There was nobody else out there.

McGinley slumped heavily into a seat. Lapslie put the pints down on the table in front of him, sat on the hard wooden bench and took a sip of his lager. It was largely tasteless, which was why he liked it.

'They found Dave Finnistaire tied to the piles beneath here,' McGinley said eventually. Lapslie felt his mouth prickle with gherkins, pickled onions and piccalilli, and quickly took another sip of his lager to cover the taste. 'Fifteen years back. After your time. The tide doesn't come in too high on a normal day. They reckon he was tied there as a warning. Problem was, there was a surge tide and he drowned. They reckon he might have been hanging there a week before it happened.'

'Didn't he call out?'

McGinley shook his head. 'He probably tried, but after what they did to his tongue he wasn't going to have much luck. Happy days.' He took a swig of his Guinness.

'Happy days.'

Lapslie glanced out into the gathering darkness. The sun was going down, somewhere over the centre of London, and the sky was a glorious set of terraces laid out in scarlet, orange and maroon. The light reflected off the small gold stud that McGinley had in his left ear lobe. For a moment, Lapslie wondered about other synaesthetes, the ones whose senses were cross-connected in a different way from his and who saw colours instead of tasting flavours. Was this the kind of thing they experienced? Was this what *the ecstasies of the mind and senses* meant?

'I was surprised when you called,' McGinley said. 'After all, it's been a good few years since you left Kilburn, and we were never really what you'd call mates then.'

'Strangely, you were the closest thing I had,' Lapslie murmured.

'That's right – you didn't get on with the blokes in the nick, did you? Never went out drinking with them.'

'Not like you did. You were always buying drinks for the coppers. And the occasional car. Favours received, I guess.'

To either side of the pier, old warehouses and new apartment blocks jostled uneasily together, silhouetted against the pastel sky. A tug ploughed gracelessly down river, hooting mournfully. Seagulls rode the waves, their beaks hooked and cruel, their eyes glinting.

'Harsh, Mr Lapslie. Harsh. I've still got a reputation up Kilburn way.'

'But I understand that, what with the Yardies, then the Turks, then the Albanians moving in, then the Turks and the Yardies working together, then the Albanians getting together with the old Maltese gangs in Soho, things have got a little confused since I left. You might have a bit of a reputation, but you haven't got much of a manor any more. What is it down to now – two streets and a stretch of waste ground?'

'Albanians? You're a little behind the times. There's over four hundred different gangs in London and the South East now, all fighting for a little bit of turf and a little bit of respect. In the old days there was maybe four or five main groups. Now you need a computer just to keep up.'

'Makes you nostalgic for the Krays, doesn't it?'

'You can laugh. Latest ones are the Muslim Boys – they claim they're part of Al-Qaeda, but they're just trading on fear. And they're dangerous. Time was when you had to work to get some respect. Now all you need is a knife or a gun, and the willingness to kill someone you've never met and know nothing about.'

'I feel for you, McGinley. I really do.'

'You said you needed a favour. What can I do?'

'What do I have to do in return?'

McGinley gazed at Lapslie over the top of his glass. 'I might need a favour back, some day.'

Lapslie nodded. 'Okay – the PRU. It's a department in the Department of Justice. Know of it?'

'Can't say I do.'

'There's a man works there named Geherty. He's turned up on my patch, and it looks like he might be interfering with a murder case I've got on. I want to know more about him.'

McGinley took another long drink from his pint glass. 'I'll ask around. Give me a day or two.'

Lapslie sank his pint and stood up. 'Phone me from a payphone,' he said. 'There's a rumour around that you're acting as a mediator between some of the main gangs in the capital. Branching out into criminal diplomacy. I wouldn't be surprised if your mobile is being listened to.'

McGinley nodded. 'Why are you telling me that now?'

'Because that,' Lapslie said, 'is the favour returned. I don't like the thought of you holding something over me.' He walked over to the entrance back into the bar, then turned and gazed out over the Thames. It rolled past like a ribbon of tar in the encroaching darkness. 'I heard that it was you that tied Dave Finnistaire to the piles beneath this pier,' he said. 'Any truth in that?'

'No, Mr Lapslie,' said McGinley. 'But I did carve his tongue into strips beforehand. Safe journey now.'

CHAPTER ELEVEN

Over the course of the next week, Daisy and Sylvia met up twice for lunch, and once for a drive out to a garden centre near Frinton so that Sylvia could pick up some plants for her borders. The sun shone down out of a cloudless blue sky as Sylvia drove carefully through the back lanes in her small, but well serviced, Fiat. Daisy gazed out at the fields as they passed. The tall yellow flowers that seemed to be all that was cultivated around here swayed under the breeze. An over-poweringly floral scent seeping in through the windows made Daisy feel dizzy.

Being in the car reminded Daisy of her own Volvo, sitting quietly in a back street in Colchester. She had been neglecting it, and by now it may already have attracted parking tickets, perhaps even been clamped. Retrieving it would be risky, and given that Sylvia had her own car, pointless. Soon this car would be hers, and she could leave the Volvo to rust in peace. It was, after all, a link to a past that she was trying to get away from. Best to let it lie.

Sylvia parked carefully beneath the shade of a large tree outside the garden centre. They went in together, and while Sylvia pottered around looking for something suitable for a herbaceous border, Daisy wandered over to the area set aside for small trees. An entire row was dedicated to yew trees, and Daisy spent an enjoyable half hour wandering along it, noting the differences between the English, Canadian and Japanese varieties, running her hands through the needle-like leaves and across the reddish-brown, scaly bark. Such a versatile tree. So sturdy, so appealing, so deadly if used in the right ways thanks to the high dose of taxine in the bark, leaves and seeds.

Turning her head, she could see Sylvia pushing a trolley along, stacked up with small pots of various types. She let herself daydream for a moment, imagining how she could feed the yew to Sylvia in a variety of ways. The needles alone could cause what she believed was termed anaphylactic shock, if chewed as part of a strongly flavoured dinner. On the other hand, a gradual introduction of powdered bark into Sylvia's food could weaken the heart to the point where it would stop. How delicious.

Growing tired of the yew trees after a while, Daisy went looking for Sylvia. She found her bending over a display of chamomile, trying to select the healthiest specimens.

'Don't they smell gorgeous?' she asked. 'I do so love the idea of a chamomile lawn. They thrive by being trodden on, you know.'

And some people are the same, Daisy thought to herself, anticipating the day when she would be in charge in the house and Sylvia would dance to her tune. A month? Three at the outside, if she didn't rush things. 'Don't you find the smell a little sickening?' she asked. 'I don't think it's quite the right thing for your garden. Let's look for something else.'

'If you really think so ...' Sylvia looked slightly hurt by Daisy's reaction.

'I do. You'll thank me for it.' Turning to the trolley, she noticed the large number of plants that Sylvia had collected. 'Are you sure you can afford all this?' she asked.

'Oh yes,' Sylvia smiled, her momentary hurt forgotten. 'My husband left me very well provided for. The widow's pension I get every month is more than I used to earn when I was working. I don't know what to do with all that money.'

And that, Daisy reflected, was the best news she'd had all week.

While Sylvia pottered about looking at more herbaceous plants, Daisy wandered across to where a fine display of rhubarb was spreading its leaves and nodding gently in the sun. Such a neglected plant. Who, these days, ever cooked rhubarb pie or stewed rhubarb? And did anyone still remember that while the stalks were delicious, the leaves were highly poisonous, if cooked along with them? Oxalic acid, she believed.

Turning away from the rhubarb, Daisy found Sylvia talking to a gentleman in a blazer and sharply creased trousers. They were debating the various merits of bugle and cranesbill as a ground cover plant, and there was an expression on Sylvia's face that Daisy didn't like at all. She was smiling. More than that, she was *radiant*.

'Oh, Daisy,' she said, flustered, as Daisy approached, 'this is Kenneth. He used to work with my husband, years ago. We just bumped into one another, would you believe it?'

'What a lovely coincidence,' Daisy said brightly as Kenneth took her hand. She couldn't help noticing that his gaze only strayed briefly from Sylvia's face. 'My dear, we should really be going if we want to make it back in good time.'

'I thought we might have a cup of tea first.' Sylvia's hand reached out to touch Kenneth's sleeve briefly. 'Kenneth and I have such a lot to catch up on. We haven't seen each other for *years*.'

Reluctantly, Daisy found herself pulled along to the garden centre's café, where she had to endure what at times seemed to her like a long-delayed and very polite courtship. Kenneth was charming, there was no doubt of that, and Sylvia was suitably charmed. Over tea and scones, which Kenneth paid for, Daisy saw her plans begin to erode. By the time the last cup of tea had been poured and the last spoonful of cream had been applied to the last crumbs of scone, Kenneth and Sylvia had arranged to go to the theatre together the following week. Daisy was invited as well, of course, and she accepted in order not to look petty – something might still be retrieved from the situation – but she knew in her heart of hearts that Sylvia was now lost to her. She had another friend now, and that would make isolating her from the flow of the world and making her dependent on Daisy all the more difficult. Perhaps even impossible.

A part of her wanted to cook Sylvia and Kenneth a wonderful rhubarb pie, just to show there were no hard feelings, but there was no point in letting her frustration get in the way of her long-term plans. She would just have to start again.

After they had finished their tea and scones, the three of them parted: Kenneth to hunt down some slug repellent and Sylvia and Daisy to the Fiat, and then back to Leyston-by-Naze. The journey back was rather more strained than the journey there. At one point, Sylvia turned to Daisy and said, 'Are you feeling all right? You're very quiet.'

'I'm just tired,' Daisy said, and she wasn't sure whether she was talking about the day or her life in total.

Sylvia dropped Daisy off just down from the station, after Daisy broke another long silence by saying that she wanted to do some shopping in the High Street. For reasons she couldn't quite explain, Daisy had been reluctant to let Sylvia see where she lived. Now she was grateful for her caution. If she was going to have to break things off and start again, it was best there was no connection between one potential victim and the next – even if that connection was Daisy's rented accommodation. As the small Fiat drove slowly away, Daisy watched it go with mixed feelings. On the one hand, there was the aching loss of the house, the car and the wonderful pension. On the other hand, Sylvia had been quite strong willed. Dominating her would have taken time and energy, and Daisy had the feeling that both of those were in increasingly short supply. Something was pressing her on, forcing her to leave shorter and shorter periods between her murders. Sylvia would no doubt wonder where her new friend had gone, but she would recover – with Kenneth's help. And she would never know what a lucky reprieve she had been given.

Instead of heading down towards the High Street, Daisy found her footsteps leading in a different direction – towards the other side of the pier, where row upon row of beach huts sat in regimented order, looking down onto the beach, waiting until the holiday season when they would open up like flowers, shutters and doors flung wide to catch the warmth of the sun.

From the road above the beach huts, Daisy stared down at the brightly painted roofs – red, blue, green and yellow in chaotic array. Concrete paths wound between the rows, while concrete steps with steel pipe handrails connected them to the beach below. It all looked rather drab and sad now, but in the height of the summer the whole place would be heaving with children and parents, and smelling to high heaven of sun tan lotion.

Carefully, Daisy walked down the nearest stairway towards the beach. Sea grasses were growing up along the edges of the stairs and in between the treads: hardy survivors that would flourish even in the harshest of conditions. Sand had drifted into every crack and every crevice. The doors of one or two of the beach huts had been smashed in by teenagers looking for somewhere to shelter, to smoke their cigarettes and paw their unwilling girlfriends. As she reached the last set of steps, and carefully climbed down to the damp sand below, she could feel the weight of the beach huts at her back, like a hundred staring eyes.

The tide was in the process of going out, and her footsteps squeezed water from the beach as she walked. The receding water had carved the sand into tiny ripples. Small tubes of sand lay curled up every few yards: casts left behind by lugworms searching for scraps of food. Somewhere below the sandcastles and tide pools of the beach there was an entire world of blind, thoughtless life, writhing and squirming away, and yet nobody ever thought about it when they were lying in the sun trying to get a tan, or running around playing volleyball, or throwing themselves into the waves. They weren't aware of the horrors that lay just beneath the surface.

To her right, the dark bulk of the pier dominated the sky: blocking her view of the side of Leyston that she had come to know so well over the past weeks. On a whim, Daisy began to walk across to the massive wooden supports that held the pier up. She could walk beneath it, then find a way up to the esplanade on the other side. From there she could catch a bus back to her flat.

The wooden pilings were each set in a water-filled depression, carved out by the retreating waves as they swirled around the posts. The wood itself was covered, to a height of six feet or so, by seaweed: bladderwrack and various other kinds. Moss-covered rocks littered the waterlogged sand, and Daisy's nose was assaulted by the overpowering aroma of decaying vegetation. She kept walking, avoiding the pools of still water and the stumps of rotted wood that poked out of the muddy sand, holding her breath until she reached the other side.

There, the panorama of the sky and of the esplanade calmed her down somewhat, and she even ventured to walk out towards the retreating tide. A small, still voice in her head suggested that she take off her shoes and paddle in the water for a while, but she knew that she would have looked ridiculous. She kept walking along the beach, the massive promontory of the Naze up ahead of her. Other people were also on the beach, alone or in pairs, walking dogs or just wandering along by themselves. She felt isolated, vulnerable, and yet also somehow anonymous. To anyone on the esplanade she was just another figure walking along the sand.

Daisy reviewed her options. The theatre, she reluctantly decided, was not on the cards, if only for the fact that Sylvia and Kenneth looked like they might be confirmed theatregoers, and Daisy didn't want any well-meaning interference in her stalking. Perhaps the Widows' Friendship Club might be worth investigating. Alternatively, she could always try popping along to one of the local churches on a Sunday evening. Morning services, she found, attracted too big a crowd. Worse, they all tended to know one another and socialise together. Sunday evening services tended to be more for the loners, the people who wanted to worship by themselves, rather than in company. She should be able to find a decent victim there. The problem was that the kind of women who tended to go to worship on a Sunday night were as poor as church mice, pardon the pun. Worse, she would almost certainly be noticed and approached by the vicar, and the last thing she wanted was a well-meaning cleric on her doorstep.

There ought to be a bowls club in the vicinity, Daisy decided. She was pretty sure she'd seen a bowling green from the bus on the way to her flat. Perhaps she should join.

The afternoon sun behind her cast her shadow out across the sand, and suddenly it was joined by another one. She turned her head warily. A small bundle of hair and teeth rushed past her feet and up to the water, backing up suddenly and then rushing toward the waves again, barking.

'Terribly sorry,' said a voice behind her. 'He's always like that. Always racing off, chasing his own shadow. I hope he didn't frighten you.'

Daisy turned. The woman behind her was wearing the oddest assortment of clothes: legwarmers, a billowing skirt, a velvet waistcoat over a denim shirt, and a voluminous coat over the entire ensemble. Her hair, or what could be seen poking out from beneath a shapeless hat, was quite wild, turned gold by the rays of sunshine that spread low across the skyline. Her face, shadowed as it was by the sun behind her, was creased, rather than lined, and her eyes were a faded blue. She might have been ten years younger than Daisy, or ten years older: she had one of those faces that was difficult to put an age on. In one hand she clutched a plastic bag, and in the other a dog lead.

'I said, I hope he didn't frighten you.'

'I'm quite unfrightenable,' Daisy said, staring at this

apparition as if it had arisen from the sand in answer to her unspoken prayers.

'Good for you,' the woman said. 'I'm Eunice. Eunice Coleman.'

'Daisy Wilson.'

'And are you a visitor to this benighted town, or do you have the misfortune to live here?'

Daisy couldn't help smiling at the woman's forthright manner. 'I moved here recently.'

'Then you have my condolences.'

The small bundle of fur and teeth that had rushed past earlier suddenly rushed past again, heading across the sand at breakneck speed in pursuit of the shadow of one of the gulls that hung in the air above them.

'That's Jasper,' said Eunice. 'Named for Jasper Johns, the artist.'

'Is he famous?' Daisy asked. 'I've never heard of him.'

The woman looked at her strangely. 'You've never heard of Jasper Johns?'

'No.'

'You'll be telling me you've never heard of Jackson Pollock.'

'I never have.'

'Joan Miró?'

'Her neither.'

'Joan Miró was a him, not a her.' Eunice shook her head grimly. 'What is the world coming to?'

'Are you an artist?' Daisy asked, feeling as if she'd been drawn into a conversation that was spiralling out of her control.

'I run an art gallery and craft centre,' Eunice said, as if that were the same thing. 'Not that people around here are that interested in arts. Keeps me occupied. Stops me from going doolally.'

'What kind of arts and crafts do you have?'

Eunice shrugged. 'Paintings I've picked up along the way.

Some pottery. A couple of wall hangings. Nothing as tedious as embroidery. That's not art, that's just fiddling about. I do classes as well, or I would if anyone cared enough to come along. Coffee and cakes. All sorts. I've got a converted barn just out of town, next to the house. Off the beaten track, though. Not on the main tourist routes.'

'It sounds rather fun,' Daisy said with as much conviction as she could pull together. 'You must tell me where it is.'

'I've got a map. Somewhere.' Eunice rummaged around in her bag and pulled out a handful of leaflets. 'Printed them myself.'

And Daisy could tell. They had been put together on a computer of some kind, but there were too many different fonts crammed too close together. 'It's ... very impressive,' she said finally.

'No it's not. That's the problem. I can do art, I can do craft, but I can't do advertising. I don't know how people think. No head for business. Accounts just leave me cold. Don't understand cashflow; don't understand the lingo.'

'You need someone to help you out.'

Eunice shrugged. 'I used to have someone to do that, but they left. I have a tendency to speak my mind, you know. Some people respond badly to that. Good riddance to them, I say. Problem is, I seem to have burned my bridges. Nobody here wants to help out any more.'

If Daisy had believed in God, she would have put this meeting down to divine providence. As it was, she could only think that when one door closed, another door opened. 'I was looking for something to do in my spare time,' she said without even thinking. 'Perhaps I could help you out. Design some proper leaflets, get some advertising put up around town, that sort of thing.'

'Are you sure?' Eunice looked doubtful. 'Why on earth would you want to?'

'It'll stop me getting bored.' She looked at the leaflet. 'Should I pop in tomorrow? We could talk it over.'

A smile broke out on Eunice's face. Suddenly she looked ten years younger. 'That would be wonderful. There'll be coffee and cake waiting. There's always coffee and cake, just in case. Mostly it just goes to the birds. The cake, that is. Not the coffee. Ta-ta.' She stomped off, her dog following on behind. Beneath the fringed hem of her skirt and the legwarmers it looked as if she were wearing what Daisy could only describe as 'pixie boots'.

What a strange woman. And yet, what an interesting prospect. Her stream-of-consciousness way of talking would probably drive Daisy to distraction after a short time, but perhaps a short time was all she needed. If she didn't have much of a grasp of business then she would probably welcome Daisy taking control of that side of things, and if she didn't have any friends in the town then she wouldn't be missed if she disappeared. And a barn! Daisy didn't want to get her hopes up – it was probably rat-infested and falling down – but that kind of property was always in demand for conversion into luxury apartments. If nothing else, there was the land.

Feeling a lot happier than she had when she first set foot on the beach, Daisy set off for a celebratory cup of coffee. Not at the post office café, however. Too much chance of seeing Sylvia there now. No, she would have to find somewhere else.

The next day, after a dreamless night, Daisy checked the location of Eunice's arts and crafts barn on her local map. The bus to Clacton went close by, and Daisy set off. It would have been more convenient with a car, of course. Having more or less consigned her Volvo to the past, and having now lost the chance of Sylvia's Fiat, Daisy decided as a matter of some priority to find a car she could use – one with no history that could tie it back to her in the event that anything went wrong. Perhaps Eunice had a car.

The bus journey took half an hour or so, and left Daisy with a ten-minute walk along a rutted country lane. A hand-lettered sign advertising, rather grandly, *Arts and Crafts Centre* had come loose from its fixings, and now pointed vaguely up to the clouds. But it was a glorious day, and Daisy could still smell the sea. She had a good feeling about this.

At the end of the track was a rather grand house, probably dating from the last century: five bedrooms at least, possibly more. Daisy gazed up at it, enraptured. What a prospect for developing into a bed and breakfast establishment. Not hers, of course. That would mean settling down and putting her name on paper in too many places. But someone with vision would pay a lot of money for that house.

Beside the house was a barn: large, long, with a slate roof. The entrance had been closed off with a new addition: a glass and wood double door, open now to provide ventilation to the inside. Daisy approached gingerly and put her head around the jamb. 'Hello?'

'Hello? Who's that?'

Daisy entered the barn. Inside it was surprisingly light and airy. Some considerable effort had been put into painting it and separating areas with partitions on which were hung paintings in various styles. Pots and sculptures sat on pedestals around the space. The floor was covered in cork tiles. Eunice Coleman was sitting behind an L-shaped bench by the door. To her right was a till. In front of her was an open book of black and white photographs which she had been leafing through.

'It's Daisy. Daisy Wilson.'

Eunice's face lit up with recognition. Whatever happened, Daisy reflected as she entered, she would never have any problem in telling what Eunice felt. Every emotion seemed to hit her face and her voice before it actually crossed her mind.

'The woman from the beach! I was worried you might have been being polite, and you weren't going to come.'

'I would never do that,' Daisy said virtuously. 'If I say I will do something then I will do it, come hell or high water.'

'Would you like a coffee?'

Eunice busied herself at a small area at the back of the barn, where four round tables and a handful of chairs were clustered near a serving hatch, behind which Daisy could just make out an urn of hot water and some cakes under transparent perspex domes. Daisy looked around while Eunice prepared the coffee. Appearances had been deceiving: the paintings were badly hung, and the sculptures were covered in dust. There were also piles of newspaper and boxes of odds and ends stacked up in the corners. Eunice was apparently one of those people who considered clearing up to be not only hard work but also difficult as well, in the same way that a crossword puzzle is difficult.

The two of them sat down at one of the tables and talked. Or, rather, Eunice talked and Daisy alternately listened and let her mind drift.

It seemed that Eunice had led quite a free and easy life. The daughter of a well-off family in the Home Counties, she had studied at St Martin's College of Art in London when she was younger, and had lived in various communes and communities for the following twenty years or so, drifting into and out of relationships with both men and women, acting as muse for some artists and model for others, taking soft drugs and generally living the kind of vacuous and unproductive life that Daisy thoroughly disapproved of, although she didn't tell Eunice this. On the death of her father, Eunice had inherited quite a lot of money, and rather than move back to the family home (or 'mansion' as she inadvertently referred to it at one stage) she had arranged for it to be sold, then bought a house close to the sea in the Tendring area with one of her many lovers, with a view to settling into a bucolic farming lifestyle. Farming turned out to be hard work, however; her lover left and she had stayed. Men had come and gone over the intervening time, and those of a practical bent had helped her get the house and barn into some kind of order, turning it into an arts and crafts centre that she was certain would attract patrons and become, in the fullness of time, a mirror image of the artistic communities she had been a part of when she was much younger and much more beautiful. And now she was alone, apart from the occasional passing tourist.

By the time Daisy left she had offered to help Eunice turn the Arts and Crafts Centre into a going concern. She had also developed a venomous hatred for Jasper the dog, who seemed to have as little brain as his mistress without her appealing flashes of sentiment.

Daisy returned the next day and started on clearing the rubbish out of the barn. Most of the boxes were filled with packing material or odd things that Eunice had picked up over the years. These she threw straight out. The newspapers were also old: both local and national papers dating back several months or, in the case of one pile hidden at the back, several years. Daisy could tell how old they were just by the colour and the texture of the paper: in the conditions of the barn, anything dating back more than a few weeks was yellow and stiff.

It was while she was clearing a pile of newspapers near the till that Daisy caught sight of a headline that almost made her heart stop.

Body of Pensioner Found in Forest

Glancing over to where Eunice was oblivious to the world, looking through yet another book of black and white photographs, Daisy bent closer to the newspaper and read quickly through the article.

The body of a 68-year-old woman was discovered yesterday in a forest near Ipswich. The corpse had been wrapped in plastic sheets and buried in a shallow grave.

According to police, pensioner Violet Chambers was discovered by accident when a car came off the road near where she had been buried. The driver was pronounced dead at the scene of the crash.

Violet Chambers had not been reported missing, and police

*are still investigating why her disappearance had not been
noticed before. Sources in the forensic team have said that the
body looked as if it had been in the forest for many months.*

The words on the newspaper seemed to dance in front of
Daisy's eyes.

Violet Chambers. They had found Violet Chambers.

It was the first of her victims to be found. The first link in a
long chain of evidence.

One mistake. Just one mistake, and it could ruin everything.

She glanced up at Eunice. She would have to move quickly.
She needed to get herself established, burrow in and disappear.
She needed to take on a cloak of respectability.

'Is everything all right?' Eunice asked, looking over at Daisy.
'You look as if you've swallowed something nasty.'

'Not me,' Daisy said. 'Not yet.'

CHAPTER TWELVE

The trouble with maps, Mark Lapslie decided, was that they demystified everything.

He was sitting in the Quiet Room, back in the police HQ in Chelmsford. He had an Ordnance Survey map of the forest where Violet Chambers' body had been found spread over the desk, and he was attempting to trace where the car that dumped her body might have been heading.

The forest had seemed so daunting when he was walking through it, waiting for Emma Bradbury to phone back. He'd had the impression that it might have gone on for miles, rolling across the English countryside like a dark stain, ancient and unyielding. There might have been patches of ground in there upon which man had never trod. There might have been monsters. Now, looking at it on the map, he could see that it only covered a few square miles and was bounded on each side by roads, caged in by progress. Somehow, splayed out on paper for all to see, it had lost its enchantment. 'Here there be dragons', the old maps used to say, but the whole point of maps was that they removed all the places the dragons were hiding, making them accessible to any fool with a car and a pair of walking boots.

Jesus, he was feeling cynical. Perhaps it was the effects of meeting up with Dom McGinley. The man hadn't phoned back yet, and Lapslie wasn't even sure he would. The two of them had a certain amount of respect for one another, the same kind of respect that the last two dinosaurs to die probably had, but that didn't mean McGinley would actually do him any favours. It was a long shot, but long shots sometimes worked.

Which was why Lapslie was bent over the Ordnance Survey map, tracing his finger along the road where Violet Chambers' body had been found. The interesting thing was that the road cut through the centre of the forest. Anyone going to any of the big towns in the vicinity would almost certainly have taken the major roads on either side. They were better lit and they were faster. The road through the forest didn't really go anywhere apart from a small set of villages.

A knock on the door of the Quiet Room sent the taste of bacon trickling through his mouth. He looked up. Emma Bradbury was standing outside, holding a piece of paper. He gestured to her to enter.

'Boss, we've got a break,' she said as the door swung open, her words undercut by the sound of chattering from the open-plan office outside. The smoky taste of the bacon hadn't quite faded from Lapslie's mouth before it was joined by lemon from Bradbury's voice and dried blood from the raised level of conversation. And there was strawberry mixed in there as well: a bizarre melange of flavours that could only have been matched in real life by a child mixing their dinner and dessert up on the same plate.

'Great,' he said, wincing and swallowing to try and get rid of the incompatible tastes. 'What's happened? And close the door for God's sake – I'm virtually having a four-course meal in here.'

'Sorry.' She entered the room and shut the door behind her. 'The car that had a flat tyre – the one we thought might have been carrying the body of Violet Chambers ...'

'What about it?'

'We've found it.'

'We?'

She shrugged. 'Well, a copper in Colchester. It had been parked up near the station for quite a while – legally, but nobody had moved it, and it was looking like it had been abandoned. The council were about to tow it away, but this copper who was passing checked it against that call you put out. When he realised that we were looking for the car, he called it in.'

'Good man.' Lapslie leaned back in his chair. 'Colchester's, what, twenty miles away? Okay – I want a full CSI team down there. I want every inch of that car examined *in situ*.'

Bradbury looked sceptical. 'I know you've been out of the loop for a while, boss, but it's more usual to move suspect vehicles to a CSI garage so they can be taken apart under controlled conditions.'

'Thanks for reminding me of standard procedure, but the evidence might be more to do with the place it's parked than the car itself. I know it's been there a while, but there could be a footprint in dried mud, or something fallen out of the car when the driver got out. We can get it to a garage later, but for now I want the whole place treated as a crime scene – car and parking space and all.'

'Okay.' She nodded. 'You want to head out there and see it?'

'Yes.'

Bradbury looked at her watch. 'Almost lunchtime. We could stop for something on the way.'

The abstract mix of flavours was still lingering in Lapslie's mouth, dominated by the taste of Bradbury's voice. 'Thanks,' he said sourly, 'but I've already eaten.'

Lapslie insisted that they took his car rather than Bradbury's. It went against police protocol for a superior to drive around someone further down the food chain than them, but the last thing he wanted at that time was marmalade from her Mondeo's engine purr added to the stuff already in his mouth. Surprised, she agreed.

While they were driving, Bradbury was on her mobile getting the CSI team arranged. It took her five separate calls, plus the possibly empty threat of Lapslie phoning the Detective Chief Superintendent's office and getting him to reprioritise their work, to move his case up their list. At one point Lapslie could taste blackberry wine, very faintly, across the back of his tongue, and he guessed that Bradbury was talking to Sean Burrows, the Crime Scene Manager who had previously been called out to the forest where Violet Chambers' body had been found. He was concentrating on driving, so he didn't catch everything that Bradbury said, but judging by the harsh tone of voice she used she was pressing the point home quite heavily that this was an important case.

Eventually she put the mobile back in her pocket. 'I've been asked to tell you,' she said, 'that by prioritising this case above the rest of CSI's workload you've potentially threatened the investigation into two other suspicious deaths, and you can expect calls from the DCS within the next hour.'

'Life's like that,' Lapslie said. 'A series of choices, each of which has unfortunate consequences. You just have to do what seems best at the time. When will CSI get to the car?'

'They were already on the road to another crime scene. They're turning round and heading for Colchester now. That little Irish git says they'll be there within the hour, which is probably about as long as it'll take for us to get there.'

The roads were relatively clear, Emma Bradbury didn't seem inclined to talk, and Lapslie found his thoughts wandering as he drove. He was working on the assumption that someone – yet to be identified – had killed Violet Chambers and taken on her identity, writing postcards and Christmas cards to make people think that Violet was still alive while he, or she, presumably, plundered whatever money Violet had and rented her house out via an estate agent. According to Bradbury's investigations, the money collected by the estate agents was paid into a separate account in Violet's name from which occasional withdrawals were made in different locations. But as far as Lapslie could see, the money wasn't enough to make it worthwhile killing Violet Chambers for. Perhaps as a crime of passion, a killing on the spur of the moment, but this had all the hallmarks of careful planning and execution. So why go to all that trouble just for a trickle of money?

Lapslie shivered. Somehow, there was more to this crime than they had yet uncovered. He had the distinct impression that the body in the forest, the house that had been rented out and the abandoned car were just the tip of the iceberg. There was a lot more of this case hidden below the surface. And, like an iceberg, it was going to be cold and hard and very unpleasant.

They arrived in Colchester less than an hour after they had set out. Bradbury guided Lapslie in through narrow streets with high stone walls alternating with wider, more modern roads flanked with warehouse-style superstores until they came to the street where the car had been abandoned.

The CSI team had got there before them. Their van was parked near the Volvo and they were already deploying the yellow plastic tent that would keep their work isolated, although Lapslie was aware that the amount of time that had passed since the car had been abandoned meant that most of the evidence would have been blown away by the wind or washed away by rain.

He glanced around, trying to get a sense of the place. They were in a wide street which curved away in either direction. On one side was a row of shops: a florists, a laundrette, a bookies and a couple of unidentifiable frontages that were closed or boarded up. A couple of the shops were selling things that were completely at variance with the signs above them. It was obviously the kind of place where property changed hands faster than the signs could keep up, if anyone bothered changing the signs in the first place. Above the shops were two storeys of flats: windows curtained even in the middle of the morning and grimy with dust and pollution. Overflow pipes projected from the flats like regularly spaced industrial gargoyles. The bricks beneath most of the pipes were green with moss in a sharp triangle, showing where water had dripped or poured on a regular basis over the years. Sheets of newspaper, yellow and crinkled, blew along the pavement and collected in corners. There was nobody about, and a deadness to the air, as if any sound was instantly swallowed up before it could go too far from its source. Even the light seemed grey and tired. The place felt like the end of the world had come early, and it had ended not with a bang but with a whimper.

' "And what rough beast, its hour come round at last, slouches towards Bethlehem to be born?" ' Lapslie murmured as he got out of the car.

'Sorry, boss?' Bradbury said, getting out of the passenger side.

'W. B. Yeats. It seemed apt. I was just wondering what kind of person we're going to find at the end of all this.'

Bradbury gave him a strange look, but said nothing. Together they walked across to where the tent was being erected around the boxy shape of a car.

Sean Burrows was waiting for them. He was dressed in ordinary clothes, but he was holding the papery overalls that all the CSIs wore when they were carrying out their investigations. 'You are aware,' he said with painful sarcasm, 'that we prioritise our work strictly on the basis of importance. An abandoned car that may or may not be connected to a nine-month-old death does not come high up that list.'

'Not your call to make,' Lapslie said. 'Let me give you a couple of reasons why you should do this job as top priority. First: I outrank the investigating officers of all the other cases you have on your list. Second: I can get Chief Superintendent Rouse to give you a call and reprioritise your workload until your ears bleed. And third: I'm the only investigating officer who provides you with bacon rolls while you're working.'

Burrows stared at him for a few moments. 'Sold to the man with the attitude,' he said finally. 'And can we have some sausage rolls mixed in this time? One of the guys is Jewish. Had to eat the roll and leave the bacon last time.'

'Doesn't he know what's in the sausages?' Bradbury asked.

'He won't ask and we won't say,' Burrows answered. 'Trouble is that he can't turn a blind eye to bacon.'

'Can you find a local café and arrange for a regular delivery of rolls and tea?' Lapslie asked Bradbury. She nodded, and walked away.

The tent was up by this time, and Lapslie entered. The dull light from outside was enlivened by its translucent yellow walls, casting a macabre light over the dusty bronze car that sat in the centre. Three of Burrows' people were starting work on the car: one taking photographs and measurements on the inside, one opening the boot while the third opened the bonnet and checked for the serial number inscribed on the engine.

'Any clues as to what we're looking for?' Burrows asked.

'Whatever we can find that will lead us to the driver,' Lapslie answered.

'You think this is the car that old lady's body was dumped from?'

'It's the only candidate so far. And I have a suspicion that the old lady that was found in the forest isn't the only body this car has seen.'

Burrows nodded. 'Volvos, you see. Lots of boot space, nobody ever pays attention to them and they're very reliable. If you're carting dead bodies around, a Volvo's what you want.'

'I sometimes worry,' Lapslie said, 'about what might happen if you guys ever decided to go freelance.'

'We do talk about setting up a murder consultancy,' Burrows admitted. 'But we'd have to register for VAT and everything, and it's just too much trouble.'

The person who had opened the boot was gesturing to her colleague with the camera. He joined her and took photographs of whatever they had found, flooding the tent with the light from the flashgun. Burrows frowned, and walked across to join them. He glanced into the boot, then gestured Lapslie to join him.

'What do you think – a body?' Burrows asked.

'That's all I need right now,' Lapslie said as he walked over towards the car: 'one more body and no more murderers.'

As he got closer to the car he could make out a faint smell of flowers and earth. For a moment he thought it was his synaesthesia reaction to a low-level sound somewhere outside, but when he reached Burrows' side he realised that the smell was a real smell, and it was coming from the boot of the Volvo. The large space was filled with twigs, leaves and colourful petals, all carefully held together with twists of gardening wire.

'Not exactly what I was expecting,' Burrows said. 'I'll have them bagged up and identified.'

Lapslie watched for a while as Burrows' team painstakingly examined the Volvo. They fingerprinted the inside, and picked up samples of hair and lint from the seats. They were, Lapslie thought, like beetles crawling over the carcass of a dead animal, stripping it of whatever flesh it had left. It must have been his imagination, but the car seemed to shrink as they worked, as if the mystery it contained had bulked it out. It occurred to him that Violet Chambers' body must have gone through a process very much like that: plump and fleshy when she was first dumped in the forest beneath a few inches of earth, then progressively stripped of everything that made her human until she was just a collection of bones, tendons and mummified skin, at which time the various scavengers moved on to the next thing on their priority list.

'Apart from the boot, which is covered with a layer of dirt, the car's surprisingly clean,' Burrows said. 'It looks like it's been vacuumed on a regular basis: possibly put through a valet service as well. There's no fingerprints on the steering wheel: my guess is that whoever left it gave it a quick once-over with a J-cloth before they walked away. The outside's been scoured by the elements as well. No chance of getting anything off the door handles.'

'Good work,' Lapslie said. 'Keep going, and if you find anything, give me a ring.'

'Sure,' the CSM said. 'It's not as if I had anything else to do with my day.'

Emma Bradbury was talking on her mobile when Lapslie walked out of the tent. She waved him over, flipping the phone shut as he arrived.

'What's up?' he asked.

'I managed to get a Special Constable to do some legwork on the question you asked me,' she said. 'The one about whether any car mechanic or garage within fifty miles of the forest where Violet Chambers' body was discovered had been called out to look at a Volvo with this licence plate.'

'How did you manage that? I thought there was some unspoken moratorium on getting any help on this investigation.'

'I just didn't tell anyone,' she said. 'Anyway, it turns out that a garage in Malden was called out three years ago to an isolated house in the countryside. This car was there, and it wouldn't start. Turned out that the owner had left the interior lights on by mistake and the battery had run flat. All the mechanic had to do was jump-start it and it was okay.'

'Who was the driver?'

The name on the form is smudged. He can't make it out. He remembers that she was a woman in her sixties, though.'

Lapslie thought for a moment. 'That address might well be where whoever murdered Violet Chambers is living. We need to proceed carefully. Notify Control that we're on our way.' He paused for a moment. 'We're potentially dealing with a murderer here. I think we might need an Armed Response Team.'

Outside, the local police had cordoned off the tent with incident tape, looped around trees and lamp posts and attached to drainpipes. A small collection of people who lived, worked or shopped in the area had gathered, pressing themselves against the tape so they could get a better look at whatever was going on, which was presumably more interesting than anything else they had to do that day.

Lapslie took a deep breath. The air itself seemed listless and insipid. Small flurries of wind, caught in shop doorways, drew up the dust into spirals that looked like invisible animals fighting. They were the most animated things about the scene.

Emma was arguing into her mobile as they walked. Lapslie caught the occasional terse word and suppressed curse. Eventually she flipped it shut and turned to him. 'It's no-go on the firearms team,' she said, face thunderous. 'Apparently they're unavailable. Some kind of counter-terrorism thing in Dagenham. Control reckons that it'll be a day or so before they're free, and even then there's no guarantee that we can have them. Do you want to wait?'

Lapslie shook his head. 'Has it occurred to you,' he asked, 'that we've had to fight for resources at every step of the way in this case? DCS Rouse tried to take you off the case, the uniforms at the crime scene were pulled away to cover a football match, of all things, the autopsy records were interfered with, and any request I make for additional manpower is turned down flat. Something's going on in the background that I'm not privy to, and I don't like it.' He scowled. 'No, I'm going to head over to that address, and I'm going to do it without armed backup. I won't order you to come along, but I could do with the company.'

She nodded. 'Count me in,' she said.

Bradbury was about to say something else when her mobile rang. She turned away to talk, and Lapslie took the opportunity to phone DCS Rouse on his own mobile. Rouse's PA answered, and Lapslie said: 'This is DCI Lapslie. I need to talk to the boss.'

'He's ... out at a meeting,' the PA said, with only a momentary hesitation, but her voice was shaded with dry spice. She was lying. Lapslie had a sudden intuition that Mr Geherty from the Department of Justice was standing over her, listening in. He rang off without saying goodbye.

'I've had Control check the address out,' Bradbury said, flipping her own phone closed. 'It's listed as belonging to a Rhona McIntyre. No records of any incidents related to the address, and she's clear as far as the system can tell. Council Tax is paid off every year, no outstanding mortgage. I've got someone back in the office trying to get a search warrant arranged, but –' she shrugged '– I can't help feeling there'll be an unexpected delay.'

'Just long enough for someone else to get there first,' Lapslie said. 'Okay – let's go. We're half way there already. And if we think there's a crime about to be committed, we can go in without a warrant and explain ourselves afterwards.'

They drove off in silence. Lapslie was glad to put Colchester behind him. He was sure there were some wonderfully historic and picturesque parts of the town to be seen, but there was something about that street that made him think of a whipped dog, too tired to fight, just clinging to existence.

They took a different route out of town, past a series of roundabouts and a modernistic glass and metal station. That was the problem with architecture these days, Lapslie thought as he drove: it was all designed in sections that could be bolted together in a series of shapes. There was no overall coherence, no shape, no structure. Just a set of similar panels, abutting one another, all looking the same.

The drive to the farmhouse took just over an hour, and Lapslie noticed as he drove that a number of road signs were pointing back towards the forest where Violet Chambers' body had been discovered. Depending on where one was coming from, the road through the forest would be an obvious route to take if you were heading for the house. As, he suspected, the murderer was.

There were two possibilities, as far as Lapslie could see. The first was that the murderer lived in the house and was returning there with the body for some reason. The other was that the murderer didn't live there, but wanted to leave the body there anyway. The third possibility was that the house had nothing to do with the murder of Violet Chambers, but Lapslie didn't want to think about that, partly because he desperately wanted there to be a break in the case but mostly because he could taste strawberries, even though the radio was off and Emma Bradbury wasn't saying anything. He was in for a surprise, but whether it was going to be pleasant or unpleasant was still uncertain.

Emma's phone rang. After a few seconds of 'Yes,' and 'Uh-huh,' she disconnected the call and turned to Lapslie. 'Surprise,' she said. 'The search warrant's been turned down.'

'Someone's got it in for us,' Lapslie said bitterly.

The last few hundred yards were along a dirt track that showed little sign of ever having been maintained. Hawthorn hedges flashed past on either side. Through gaps in the hawthorn, Lapslie could see fields that had returned to nature: weeds and grasses predominating over whatever had once been planted there. If there was anyone still at the house, they weren't farming any more. If they ever had.

They found the house around a turn in the track. It was set in the middle of an overgrown grass lawn and was built of red brick, two storeys high, with tall windows and a large portico topped with a pointed wooden roof. The windows were all curtained.

The car stopped in front of the house, on a mossy stone drive through which hardy weeds sprouted. Lapslie approached the portico. Two steps led up to the front door, vertical cracks running through the stone like frozen trickles of black water. Emma Bradbury was just behind him, and she touched his shoulder before he could lift the doorknocker.

'Boss,' she said, 'look over there.'

He followed the direction she was pointing. Off to one side of the house, shielded by a low fence, was a garden. Unlike the drive and the surrounding fields, it appeared to be beautifully kept. Scarlet and mauve flowers burst open against a background of vivid green leaves. Lapslie could see berries of various kinds – red, blue, purple, black – hanging heavily from nodding stems.

'Someone's been here,' Emma warned. 'That garden has been maintained, and recently.'

'It's as if whoever lives here doesn't care about the drive or the fields, but the garden is their pride and joy,' Lapslie said. 'Okay, let's get on with it.'

The door had been painted green at some time in the past, but sunlight and rain had faded it to the point where it was difficult to make out what shade it might originally have been. The wood of the door frame was crumbling along its sharp edges. A window, a few feet to the right of the door, was white with cobwebs, both inside and out. One of the panes of glass was cracked.

He knocked once, twice; the echoes rolling thunderously through the house in search of anyone who might answer. There was no movement, no sound, nothing. Lapslie knocked again. The sounds joined the previous set of echoes, bouncing back and forth, rolling from room to room and from down-stairs to upstairs and back. Still nothing.

Stepping back, Lapslie twisted his body and swung a foot up at the door, his heel hitting it a foot or so below the lock. The wooden door frame splintered. He kicked again, and the door flew open, knocking a pile of letters against the wall. They scattered like snow.

'Police!' he called. 'Come out where we can see you!'

No movement, and no sound. Together, Lapslie and Bradbury entered the house.

An old, unpleasant smell hung in the air, and Lapslie had to fight the urge to brush it aside as he moved. The hall was dark; a faded carpet running its length. Various doors led off the hall. They were all shut.

He approached the closest room – the one whose window he had noticed to the right of the front door – and pushed it open. It whispered against carpet as it swung back. The smell of something deeply unpleasant suddenly intensified.

Light from the cobwebbed window filtered into the room,

illuminating a long dining table set for dinner. Fine porcelain tea cups were placed at every setting. A matching tea pot sat in the centre.

Twelve people sat quietly at the table. They didn't react to Lapslie's entrance: no turning heads, no expressions of surprise, nothing.

'Police,' Lapslie repeated. 'DCI Lapslie. Who owns this house?'

Nobody moved.

Emma Bradbury strode across to the window and brought her hand down, brushing the cobwebs away. Light flooded in.

Lapslie took a step back. Emma gasped. 'Oh good Christ,' she said flatly.

The twelve people sat around the table were all women, and they were all dead. They had been placed in order of death. The body closest to Emma was the freshest, but even so, its raddled flesh had sagged away from the bones, bloated and fly-blown, green and purple and grey. Her eyelids had shrivelled back against empty sockets. The body closest to Lapslie was the oldest: no more than a skeleton whose flesh had been gradually replaced with cobwebs. All of them were ruined things that once may have been beautiful.

'What the hell are we dealing with?' Emma whispered.

' "Why this *is* Hell," ' Lapslie murmured softly, ' "nor are we out of it." '

CHAPTER THIRTEEN

That night, her ceiling dappled with moonlight reflected off the sea, Daisy lay awake. Her sheets were clammy beneath her, and she could feel every fold in the cotton against her old, wrinkled skin. No matter what position she curled into, she could not find that elusive door to sleep.

It was the newspaper report that was bothering her. The report of the discovery of Violet Chambers' body. The first mistake she had ever made, and it was going to come back to haunt her. She knew it would.

The shock of seeing that newspaper headline had sent her into a panic. Eunice had made her a cup of tea and sat with her, not really understanding what had driven Daisy into such a state, but Daisy was frozen, her mind circling around and around like a fly orbiting a light bulb.

And in her mind, the wet *smack* of the branch as it hit Violet's head, caving the bone in. The blood, matting the grey hair. The long gasp as she exhaled her last breath.

And as she relived the memories, as she went back to the time before the branch hit Violet's skull, when she was driving along that country road with Violet Chambers slumped in the passenger seat, she slipped slowly and inadvertently into the long dark tunnel of sleep and the memories turned surreptitiously into dreams.

The sun shining through the leaves made patterns like black lace on the road. She maintained a steady forty-five miles an hour in her Volvo – not fast enough to attract anyone's attention; not slow enough to annoy people sufficiently that they would remember her, and the car, for more than the few moments that it took for them to overtake her.

She had carefully manoeuvred Violet's dead body into the car before dawn that morning, using the wheelchair she had brought in specifically for that purpose. Fortunately the driveway led all the way up to the front door, so she didn't have to wheel the body down to the road, as she occasionally had before. The tricky bit, as always, had been the moment when she had to slide the body from the wheelchair into the passenger seat, but the arm on the wheelchair folded down and the application of a little strength, and the passing of a noisy refuse lorry, had made the job easier.

A tartan blanket over Violet's lap completed the illusion that she was merely asleep. Her eyes were closed, and a little tape laid sticky side out across her gums ensured that her mouth wouldn't gape open at an inopportune moment, such as when they were parked at traffic lights. A thin length of white cotton hidden in the folds of her neck and knotted behind the head rest stopped her head from lolling in an ungainly fashion onto her chest. All in all, Daisy thought as she gazed sideways at Violet from the driver's seat, she looked better now than she had in real life. She certainly didn't look like someone who had ingested a fatal dose of meadow saffron only twelve hours before.

Half an hour after eating the cake into which Daisy had carefully grated several meadow saffron roots, Violet had suffered a series of convulsions while she was sitting in the back garden. Daisy had watched with pleasure as white foam had trickled from Violet's mouth and her lips and skin turned blue. Sweat trickled along the prominent folds in her skin that gave her such a disapproving look all the time. Her hands clutched at the arms of her deck chair, locking on with such force that Daisy had to later use a kitchen knife to prise them off. And then, after a sudden and violent arching of the back, she had subsided, head slumped forward and eyes hooded, breathing her last, few, shallow breaths.

'Of all the women I have ever poisoned,' Daisy had said to her, 'you have been the most arrogant, the most insensitive and the most stand-offish. You seem to believe that you can look down at everyone else because your father had a big house and didn't have to work for a living. In fact, you are a sad, deluded old woman who is dying alone and unmourned. Nobody will know, or care, that you have gone.'

Perhaps her eyelids flickered. Daisy would never know for sure, but she liked to believe that Violet had heard that last valediction, and seen the essential truth in it, before she died. Befriending Violet had been one of the most difficult jobs Daisy had ever done – although she was calling herself Annie then. Annie Moberley. Violet had been stand-offish, suspicious and snobbish, and it was only because Daisy – Annie – hated to break off half way through that she had persevered. She had first met Violet in the local supermarket, where it was obvious that Violet was shopping for one, and wasn't buying the cheapest cuts of meat and the 'reduced items' that pensioners, in Annie's experience, usually selected. They got chatting on the third or fourth occasion that they bumped into each other, and soon she was popping around for coffee. Soon after that, she was collecting Violet's prescriptions for anti-inflammatories from the local surgery.

Violet had been an odd mix. She desperately wanted some human contact, but at the same time she wanted to be able to look down on whoever she was with. For Annie, who automatically looked down on all her victims, the next few months had been amongst the most tiring she could recall, as the two of them vied for dominance without Violet ever consciously realising that a battle was going on.

In the hours that Annie spent driving Violet's body through the early morning she daydreamed about the next few months; of how she was going to progressively strip the house of any expensive items it contained, and raid Violet's building society account of whatever money it contained. And, from small clues that Violet had let slip, she suspected it contained rather a lot. She would take on Violet's identity, like slipping on an old overcoat, letting her current one fall away, and become lost in the past. And then, when she grew tired, she would move on, looking for another victim. Although perhaps one less supercilious this time. Annie had felt for a while that Violet was treating her more as an unpaid companion than a friend, and towards the end more as an unpaid servant than a companion.

The car slipped through forests and past industrial estates as the darkness gave way to daylight. After some unquantifiable time, Annie knew that she was nearing her destination: the place where all of her friends eventually came to visit, and did not leave.

A sudden *bang* from beneath the car startled Annie from her dreams. The steering wheel jerked in her hands, and the car began to drag itself towards the trees just as they were coming up to a bend. Panicking, she slammed her foot on the brakes, and the Volvo slewed violently to a halt, half on the road and half on the grassy verge.

Annie turned the ignition key with a shaking hand. The engine died away. Silence filled the forest.

Eventually, when she could breathe again, when the fluttering of the blood in her neck and her temples had faded, she got out of the car. The front tyre on the side where Violet was sitting was deflated and forlorn, appearing half-melted on the road. She felt panic wash through her. What did one do with a flat tyre? She supposed one had to change it, but how was she supposed to get it off? And where was the spare tyre kept? Was there even a spare tyre in the car? Any tools?

She looked along the road ahead of the car, as it bent to the right, and then back along the direction she had come. There was nobody in sight. No other cars; no other people. She was alone.

What to do? Annie slumped against the side of the car, hearing the clicking and ticking of the engine as the hot metal cooled. Nothing like this had ever happened to her before. So near to her goal, the safe refuge where all her friends ended up, and yet so far. So very far.

In part of her mind Annie knew that she could walk for help, but she couldn't remember seeing any houses for the last few miles she had driven, and she had no idea how far ahead the next set of houses might be. She was old and tired: she could hardly make more than few hundred yards before she would have to take a rest. The next best thing would be to flag someone down, but that could take all morning. And whether she went for help or waited there for it to arrive, the people who helped her would see Violet sitting in the passenger seat. They would ask if she was all right. They might offer her a drink of water. And they would realise, sooner rather than later, that she was dead.

And then it would all start to unravel. Every carefully woven thread of Annie's life.

Whatever she did, she would have to get rid of Violet's body first. For a moment she wondered whether she could manhandle the body into the boot of the car, but she rejected that thought. The spare tyre was probably somewhere in there, and if not the spare tyre then probably some tools or something else that would be needed. No, the boot was too much of a risk. She would have to get the body into the woods somehow, perhaps bury it beneath some bracken, and then come back later to collect it. And all that without making herself look as if she had been dragged through a hedge backwards.

Annie nodded to herself. Hide the body, flag someone down, get them to change the tyre for her, then, when they had gone, retrieve the body and continue on her way. It was a plan.

She pushed herself away from the car and walked around the bonnet. The open passenger door registered in her mind for a good few seconds before she realised the significance of what it meant. Then she noticed the empty passenger seat.

Violet's body had gone. *Violet* had gone.

Annie looked wildly around. She was still alone. For a long moment she was convinced that she had left Violet's body back at the house and somehow imagined that it had been sitting beside her for the past few hours; then she was sure that someone had come and taken the body from the car while she was distracted. It took a few moments before the truth sank in. Her cake had been a failure. Violet had still been alive when Annie put her in the car, albeit in something so close to a coma that Annie had been fooled into thinking she was dead. Somehow she had come back to consciousness, and escaped. Did she realise what had happened to her, or was she operating on instinct, just heading somewhere, anywhere, away from the unfamiliar confines of Annie's Volvo?

Did it matter? Annie had to find her again. Find her, and kill her for sure.

And whatever happened, she was never using meadow saffron again.

A faint trail of bent grass led away from the car and into the dank green depths of the forest. Annie checked the road, forward and back, once more, just in case someone was approaching. The road was clear. She set off in pursuit of Violet.

The floor of the forest was covered in twigs and low shrubs which Annie couldn't identify. The occasional fallen tree made barriers she had to manoeuvre around, but crushed flowers and disturbed patches of ground indicated to her where Violet had scrambled her way across the ground. Buttery light slanted down through the tops of the trees, and everywhere was hushed. Annie could hear her own footsteps shushing through the leaves, sounding almost as if she were making her way through thick snow. She could smell the deep, intoxicating scent of old wood and foliage, the world's oldest and most profound perfume. The occasional insect buzzed past her, and a sudden flurry of activity in a bush showed where a small animal had suddenly heard her approach and made its escape.

She wasn't looking for small animals. Her prey was much larger.

Annie stopped in a small clearing, listening. Somewhere across the other side she could hear a crashing sound, as if something was pushing its way heedless through bushes and shrubs.

Her breath was rasping in her throat now, and her legs were weak, but she kept on going. Low branches reached for her face, while roots clutched desperately at her ankles, trying to trip her up. Every so often she reached out to steady herself on a tree trunk, but the rough bark burned the palms of her hands.

Through a gap in the trees she caught sight of a flash of artificial colour, stark against the natural greens and browns of the forest. A bright red: the same colour as the cardigan that Violet had been wearing when she died. And when she came back to life again. Annie slowed down, taking her time as she approached, shielding herself behind a large bush.

Violet was bent on all fours by a large oak tree. A string of saliva dropped from her mouth. She was panting: a harsh, almost mechanical sound. The skin on her hands and knees was muddy with dirt and blood from the numerous small scratches she had sustained as she fled. But now she was here; out of breath, out of time, out of options.

Annie crouched and picked up a fallen branch from the forest floor. She hefted it in her hand: it felt almost industrial in its density, like a crowbar, or a tyre iron. Her hand fitted perfectly around it, and for a moment she wondered why she kept going back to poison when physical violence could be so seductive. And then she envisaged the dining room table, and the silent faces around it, and she remembered.

Violet reached out a hand towards the oak tree, supporting her weight so she could stand. Concerned that she might try to get away again, Annie took a step forward from behind the bush.

She must have made a noise, because Violet turned her head and caught her in a wild-eyed stare. Her teeth were bared wildly.

Annie took another step, and swung the branch loosely by her side, ready to use it.

'Why...?' Violet mouthed, her eyes seeming to lose focus and then regain it again. 'Why did you *do* this?'

'Because I could,' Annie said. 'Because I have before and will again. Because it gets me what I want. And, above all else, because I just got tired of your constant complaining, your continual sneering at your neighbours, your old friends and me.'

She took two steps forward and raised the branch up above her.

Violet turned away, ready to scuttle to safety, but Daisy brought the branch crashing down on the back of her head. She didn't know what she expected – a dramatic gout of blood perhaps, the skull crumbling beneath the branch like a snail stepped on in the garden, revealing the soft, grey, oozing flesh within, but there was none of that. Violet's head merely changed shape, a depression appearing beneath the sparse grey hair. Annie was reminded of the duck eggs she had eaten as a child, boiled hard, their shells crushed in by a spoon. And Violet slumped gracelessly to the floor of the forest with a soft sigh, the air leaving her lungs for the last time, free of that old body forever.

Annie sat down beside her for a moment and rested, letting the muted sounds of the forest – the soft susurration of the wind in the leaves and the calls of the birds – drain the tension and the tiredness from her bones. After a while, she reached across and checked Violet's pulse, both in her stick-thin wrist and also in the leathery wattles of her neck, but there was nothing. The blood was still within those prominent purple veins.

Annie walked unsteadily back to the car, partly to retrieve the plastic sheet that she had brought with her from the house

– the one she had laid Violet's body on when she cleaned it – and partly to check whether anyone had stopped for the car. The road was clear, and might have been that way ever since her burst tyre had occurred. She popped the boot of the car, and pulled out the grey plastic sheet, then paused. What was she going to do? Walk back into the forest, wrap Violet's body up and bury it as best she could? But the ground was hard, and difficult to dig without a shovel, and if she wanted to come back later to retrieve the body, how would she find it? At least the corner where she had stopped was reasonably memorable. Perhaps she could pull Violet's body most of the way back and bury her just off the road. That way, locating her again would be easier. It also meant that she would be able to hear if someone stopped to help her.

Looking around, Annie saw a rotted tree trunk, lying half-buried in the soil, victim of some long-passed storm. Walking over to it, she reached out and gave one of the branches an experimental tug. The trunk rolled over slightly, revealing moist ground, depressed where the trunk had lain, and pale white shoots beneath. She thought for a moment. If she could move this trunk out of the way then it would leave behind something similar to a half-dug grave. She could wrap Violet's body in the plastic sheet, drag it back, lay it in the grave, then cover it over with leaves and earth. It would do, until she could come back again for it. It would do.

It took her ten minutes to move the rotten trunk out of the way and make it look as if it had always been where she put it. Rolling Violet's body in the sheet, dragging her back to the side of the road and laying her in the scar took another five, as did the task of kicking twigs and loam and leaves over the top of the sheet.

Half way through, when the plastic-wrapped corpse was lying in the depression in the forest floor, but before she could cover it over, Annie heard the sound of a car engine, far away. She stopped. Of all the times to be offered help, this was the worst. Quickly she stepped back into the darkness of the forest. The car drew closer. She glanced out at her Volvo, checking that the doors were closed and the emergency lights were not flashing. Reassured, she moved further back into the forest, trying to become as one with the trees. The sound of the car engine changed as it approached the bend. For a moment she was terrified that it was about to stop, that the driver had seen her car and was going to park and see if anyone needed help, but whoever was in the car was just changing down gears as they approached the bend. The car swept past, the driver just a blurred figure, then the engine noise changed again and the car accelerated away.

When she was sure that Violet's body was completely covered, Annie stepped back to examine her handiwork. Apart from a bump in the forest floor, no different from so many others she could see around her, there was no sign that a human being rested there. No sign at all.

Annie returned to her car and sat quietly in the driver's seat, letting the world pass her by. She kept casting glances over at the mound where Violet lay, half wondering whether she might see the ground move slightly, or a hand push itself out of the earth like a fat pink spider, but there was nothing. Nothing at all.

After a while she reached out and switched on the emergency lights. The clicking seemed incredibly loud to her, after so long sitting in the quiet. Perhaps someone would stop for her now.

Rooting around in her handbag, she brought out a mobile phone. She had bought it some years back from a branch of W. H. Smith in Brent Cross, having carefully established from the sales assistant that it worked on a 'pre-pay' basis, and she could charge it up with credit at most supermarkets or petrol stations. She had forgotten which of her many identities had bought it, but as far as she knew there was no way it could be traced back to her. And she only used it sparingly.

She dialled a number for Directory Inquiries.

'Good morning,' Annie – Violet – said primly, 'I would like

a garage somewhere near the Thetford Forest. I've broken down, you see.'

'I have three garages nearby,' the voice on the other end of the phone said, 'or I could put you through to the AA or the RAC.'

'Could you put me through to the first local garage you have?' Violet said.

Within a minute she had talked to a mechanic, told him where she was, told him what had happened and arranged for him to come and get her back on the road.

The mechanic turned up half an hour later in a big truck. He was a rather common man, of the kind that Violet had always preferred not to deal with, and he kept up a constant stream of chatter whilst he changed her tyre for her. Noticing the dirt on her hands, he asked her jokingly what she'd been doing. 'I fell over,' she said sharply.

She paid by cheque – using the chequebook and cheque card that she had found in the handbag, of course, and signing with Violet Chambers' rather flowery signature. He waited until she had got in her car and driven off, just to check that the tyre held up, and she had to decide whether to keep on going to where she had originally been heading – her special place, where all her friends waited for her – or to start the long drive back. She wasn't going to disinter the body – the nameless body, as she was already thinking of it – while the mechanic was watching her, and she didn't want to drive off, turn around, come back and do it all then. And without the body there was precious little point in heading to her special place. Reluctantly, she decided to go home. She could always come back another time for the body.

The journey took several hours, and although the tyre held up perfectly she was exhausted when she got back to the house. Violet's house. *Her* house. She toasted some bread, ate it without butter or margarine, and went to bed. She was asleep within moments, and her last thought was that the body was spoiled now. Broken. It would not fit with the others at the tea party. She would leave it where it was.

And as the night moved on, and the shadows crawled across the ceiling, Violet slept.

And Daisy woke up.

The smell of the seaside drifted in through her window: salt, candy floss and decay. The flat tyre, the burial in the forest, the drive back to Violet's house – that had all happened nearly a year ago now. She had been Violet for nine months, while she found and befriended Daisy Wilson. Now she was Daisy Wilson. Soon she would be Eunice Coleman.

And there were more people than ever at the tea party.

CHAPTER FOURTEEN

After four hours in the House of Death, as he had come to think of it, Mark Lapslie couldn't take any more. He walked outside, legs feeling as weak as if he'd run a cross-country race. He couldn't even think straight. Those faces – those ruined, rotted faces – would haunt his thoughts forever.

Four local police cars and a CSI van were parked outside the farmhouse. The van didn't belong to Sean Burrows' team; they were still working on the Volvo. Lapslie had, however, rung Burrows on his mobile to tell him that it wasn't just one murder they were working on now but thirteen, and the Volvo was now the most important evidence they had, as it may well have been used to move the bodies from wherever they had been killed to where they had been fated to spend the rest of their time. In the House of Death.

Looking back up at the red brick of the farmhouse, he could see a resemblance to a skull that he hadn't remarked on before. The upper windows were like dark, vacant sockets; the portico was the hollow nasal passage; the cracked steps were the top and bottom rows of teeth; and the crumbling brickwork was the bone itself, worn down by the passing of the years. It was pure fancy, of course – after four hours in that house, with the twelve bodies sat around the table, frozen into their perpetual tea party, everything he saw was going to remind him of skulls, skeletons and dry, rotting flesh.

Emma Bradbury was resting on the bonnet of his car, one booted foot up on the front bumper. She was smoking a ciga-rette.

'If I did that to your car,' he said, 'you'd deck me.'

'Sorry, boss.' She straightened up and threw her cigarette on the ground, stubbing it out with her toe. 'It's just—'

'Yeah. I know.'

The wind was cool on his face after the stuffiness of the house, and he breathed deeply, taking it into his lungs and flushing as much of the moribund air of the house as he could. That air had been laden with particles that had drifted from the corpses as they slowly slumped into deliquescence. Knowing that something of them remained within his mouth, his nose, his lungs, that it coated his suit as well, made Lapslie feel soiled.

'I need a shower,' Emma said, mirroring his thoughts.

'I feel the same way, but we've got to stay here and focus the investigation. The entire house needs to be examined. We're going to need to pull Sean Burrows' team in to cover it once they've finished with the Volvo. And frankly I don't see Jane Catherall managing all those autopsies this side of Christmas. She's going to need extra help.'

Emma turned to look at the house. 'I still can't believe it,' she said. 'From the outside there's no sign of what we found. With crack houses, or brothels, there's something about the outside that gives them away, if you know what you're looking for, but this ... You'd expect something that looked like a haunted house, all leaning sideways with stuff growing up the walls, but this place just looks old. It looks like my gran's place.'

'Still waters run deep,' Lapslie said, looking back at the house. Somehow the fresh air and the sunshine had blown away that resemblance to a skull that he had noticed. It was just a house again. Just an ordinary farmhouse.

'They're going to be like Violet Chambers, aren't they?' Emma asked. 'When we discover their identities we're going to find that they're not listed as being missing. As far as Social Services, and the Inland Revenue, and the Department of Health and everyone else is concerned, they're not dead.

Somewhere in England, they're still walking around, claiming benefits and taking the income from whatever properties they own. Someone out there is pretending to be them.'

'They're just puppets,' Lapslie agreed. 'Manipulated by their murderer. But isn't that the cleverest thing of all? If the thing that trips most murderers up is disposing of the body, then why increase the risk by scattering your bodies around? Why not keep them all together, somewhere isolated, where nobody will ever go, and then make sure that they won't be looked for by keeping their identities alive? Like Violet Chambers, I guarantee they'll all have no families and no close friends. They'll have been living solitary lives, alone and unremarked, until someone came along. Someone who befriended them and wriggled into their lives, then killed them and took on their identities.' He shook his head. 'So many identities, and whoever it is has to keep them all alive, because the income is still coming in. The pensions, the rents, the investments – everything. So much to juggle.'

'Where do we start?' Emma said simply.

Lapslie thought for a while. 'The Volvo will be a bust,' he said eventually. 'It led us here, and there may be evidence inside it linking it to some of the bodies, but it's still listed as being owned by Violet Chambers. I think our murderer just adopted it. Spoils of war. They probably do this with every victim: strip them of what's useful, then sell the rest. Unless there's some trace of the murderer in the car – and I think they're too clever for that – then it's a dead end.'

'The house?' Emma said, indicating it with her head.

'Similar. It will belong to one of those corpses. Probably the one that's been there the longest. What was the name – Rhona McIntyre? She'll be the one at the head of the table. The mortgage is paid off on the house, and our murderer makes sure the Council Tax is paid every year. Flawless.'

'Can't we trace the payment on the Council Tax?'

Lapslie shrugged. 'We can and we will, but I guarantee it'll have been paid from the account of one of the other women around that table. It's an unbreakable circle. The murderer is using each of the accounts to pay bills on the other ones, and taking cash out when they need it. They never pay for anything themself. There's no trail back to them.'

'Are you sure they're all women, boss? Some of those bodies are so decayed it's difficult to tell from just looking at them.'

'So far it's all to do with women: Violet Chambers, Rhona McIntyre, the woman who was seen leaving Violet's house, the more identifiable of those bodies.' He sighed. 'Don't you feel it? The poison, the precision, the planning ... and the choice of victims ... I guarantee the murderer's a woman as well.'

Emma gazed around. 'So what now?'

'Now we leave the CSIs to do their stuff here. I'll make some calls and arrange to get as many spare pathologists drafted in to help as we can.' He frowned. 'What *is* the collective noun for a group of pathologists, I wonder? We can't call them "a murder of pathologists". That's already been taken for crows. "An incision of pathologists"?' He shook his head. 'Never mind. I want you to check into the background of this house. Find out when Rhona McIntyre was last seen, what her background was, what happened to her and especially whether anyone else was seen with her just before she was last seen. Talk to anyone who lives nearby. Go into the nearest village and talk to the publicans. Local stores. Anyone. Just get me some background on Rhona McIntyre.'

'And when I've finished with that, some time next week?'

'Then you can have a rest.'

Emma looked around. 'I haven't got a car.'

'Get one of the local constables to drive you around. It'll make them feel useful, and who knows? They may have some information about the house, or the owner.'

'Actually,' she said, 'I've got a friend in the area. I'll give him a ring.'

Emma walked off, pulling her mobile from her pocket, and

Lapslie just stood there for a while, looking away from the house. It was located in a valley: the ground rose gradually up, dark and imposing, on two sides, making the place feel claustrophobic. Behind him was the dirt track he had driven in on, and in front of him was … the garden.

He walked over to the gap in the fence that gave access. The fence was well maintained, compared to the rest of the farm, and the plants, as far as he could see, weren't anywhere near as overgrown as the fields he had passed on the way. It looked as if whoever was visiting the house wasn't just planting corpses.

He walked through the gate, and it was as if he had walked through some kind of invisible curtain. The scents of the plants hit him like a rich and heady perfume. He felt giddy, but he breathed it in gladly, replacing the stench of old, dead flesh with the mixed aroma of pennyroyal, delphiniums, foxglove, corn cockle and countless others that he remembered from childhood, or from Sonia's attempts at growing borders in their back garden. Hydrangea and hyacinth, rhododendron and tansy: the garden was a riot of smells and colours. There were shrubs and trees as well: yew and peach, privet and eucalyptus. Small blue flowers hung beside large red ones, bell-shaped yellow flowers drooped over flat pink ones. It was chaos, and yet Lapslie could almost see some kind of plan to it. There was logic there, but not the kind of logic he could understand. Or wanted to.

He stood for a moment with his eyes closed, letting the scents rather than the sights guide him. For him it was the aromatic equivalent of standing in the middle of a factory, with the clashing of machines, and the shouting, and the tannoys and whatever else causing his olfactory senses to overload with synaesthesic signals. If he turned his head he could almost make out a pattern. The plants to the right of the gate were more floral; the plants to the left spicier, earthier, richer in tone. Ahead of him were more medicinal scents. It wasn't a random selection: these plants had been carefully chosen to tell some kind of story.

He opened his eyes and looked around. Selecting a low bush, he knelt and examined it. Some of the lower branches had been pruned back: the marks of the shears were still visible. The roots of the plants had been bedded in compost as well. Yes, the garden was maintained, looked after on a regular basis.

On a whim, he walked along the rows. When Dr Catherall had mentioned that Violet Chambers had been poisoned with colchicine, which was derived from a plant known as the meadow saffron, he had looked it up in a gardening book that Sonia had left behind when she moved out. A single stem splitting into three or four foot-long leaves that canted up at a sharp angle. Pink or white or purple flowers appearing in autumn. All parts of the plant poisonous. And there it was, nestled between two plants he couldn't identify: a whole row of meadow saffron.

He looked around with fresh eyes, and a cold feeling in his stomach. Twelve dead bodies in the house, plus one found in the woods, and at least one poisoning. Was it too much to suspect that they had *all* been poisoned? And what were the odds that they had all been poisoned with toxins extracted from plants in this garden?

The House of Death, and now the Garden of Death. What the hell was he up against here? What kind of person could take it upon themselves to cultivate an entire garden of poisonous plants? It had yet to be proved, of course, but Lapslie knew he was right.

' "The strongest poison ever known, came from Caesar's laurel crown",' he quoted softly, and shook his head.

Emerging from the garden and heading towards his car, he noticed that the vans had arrived to take the bodies away to the pathology lab. One of the bodies was being carried down the steps of the house as he watched, swathed in green polythene sheeting. Presumably it was so fragile that trying to get it into a body bag would have risked breaking it in half.

A red Jaguar was just pulling away from the house. From his

position Lapslie could see Emma Bradbury in the passenger seat, but he couldn't make out the driver's face. Maybe it was whoever she'd had in her car when they'd first found Violet Chambers' body in the forest.

Leaving the House of Death receding in his rear view mirror, Lapslie followed the pathology van along winding country roads until it joined the B101. Within half an hour they were on the motorway, heading for Jane Catherall's mortuary. The van drove sedately: not as slow as a funeral procession, but not pushing the speed limit either. It was as if the driver was acknowledging, even in passing, that death could not be hurried. Or perhaps he was frightened that the bodies might disintegrate if he hit a bump too fast.

Lapslie kept pace with the van for its entire journey. He could have accelerated past it and got to the mortuary with half an hour or more to spare, but it would have accomplished nothing, and he felt, as the driver presumably did, that the corpses in the back of the van deserved some kind of respect. Or an escort, at the very least.

Eventually they were driving along Braintree's familiar streets. Lapslie slowed as the van pulled off the road and into an unremarkable tarmac drive that led around the back of the mortuary. He parked in what he now thought of as his usual place.

Before he could buzz the door, his mobile rang: Bruch's 1st violin concerto.

'Lapslie.'

'Mr Lapslie! Nice to hear your voice!'

He tasted mustard and vinegar across the back of his tongue. 'McGinley? I was beginning to think you were never going to get back to me.'

He imagined Dom McGinley the way he'd last seen the man: sprawled behind a table in a pub, his stomach pushing his polo shirt out into a smooth curve, a pint of Guinness in front of him, and chuckling.

'You asked a favour, and then did me a favour in return before I could say anything. I owed you one, and I don't like owing people anything. I try and clear my debts as quickly as possible.'

'Very laudable,' Lapslie said. 'So what have you got for me?'

'You were asking about a man named Geherty, at the Department of Justice.'

'Yeah.' Lapslie thought back to the black Lexus that had turned up in the forest where Violet Chambers' body had been discovered, and again outside his police station. He thought back to the two men who had walked out of Chief Superintendent Rouse's office as he was walking in, and had glanced at him as if they recognised him. And he remembered the way that Jane Catherall's office had been searched, and files copied from her hard disk. 'Yeah,' he repeated, 'I was, wasn't I? What have you found?'

'I put out some feelers, and asked some friends of mine who work for the Department of Justice who he is. It wasn't easy – the bloke keeps his head down, but I eventually struck lucky. He's Assistant Director of the PRU.'

'I knew that. What else have you got?'

'PRU stands for Prisoner Rehabilitation Unit. It's a department that looks after long-term inmates in Her Majesty's prisons who, for whatever reason, need careful rehabilitation into society when they get released.'

'I've never heard of them.'

'I'm not surprised. They're a close-knit bunch. They don't advertise themselves. Myra Hindley was one of theirs, before she died of a chest infection. Apparently they were preparing her for release when she died, despite the number of legal appeals that she'd lost. Ian Huntley's on the list – the bloke who killed those two girls in Soham. So are Ian Brady and Rosemary West. All the jailbirds who keep getting mentioned in the papers are theirs. It's the PRU's job to make sure that when they eventually get out of jail they can reintegrate into society without having the *Sun* or the *Mirror* camped on their doorsteps within ten minutes of them getting out.'

'Lovely,' Lapslie said. 'I wonder if anyone ever leaves school thinking, "I know what I want to do – I want to prepare serial killers for release into a society that hates their guts".'

'Hey, we don't all end up doing what we wanted, you know? I was going to be a car mechanic.'

'I'm touched. I really am. What else did you find out about the PRU?'

'They also spend a year or so before the release training their "customers" up so they know who's Prime Minister and how much a loaf of bread costs. They were the ones who apparently found Maxine Carr a place to live and got her a new identity. And a new boyfriend, from what I hear. You remember her, she was Ian Huntley's girlfriend, but she got out way before he ever will. And Dennis Nilsen – he was the one who killed fifteen male lovers, boiled some of them up and then forced their remains down the drain. He's on their books. He'll be eligible for parole in a year or two: they must be getting him ready now, I would have thought.'

'I hate to say it, McGinley, but you've excelled yourself.'

'Yeah, but does it help?'

Lapslie thought for a moment. He couldn't see any connection with the case he was working on. 'I can't say it does,' he said.

'Then let me add something else. While I was asking around, I picked up a rumour or two. No corroboration, but it's whispered that Myra Hindley didn't die of a chest infection at all.'

'What, she killed herself? Not much of a story there, McGinley.'

'No, the rumour is that she's still alive, and she was released from prison under a false name. Rumour is that she's living somewhere in Wales, under constant observation. Costs the PRU a shed-load of money, but it was some kind of deal between the Home Secretary and the judiciary. There was no legal reason to keep her in jail any more, but the public outcry if she was released would have been immense.'

'The slate's clear, McGinley. I don't owe you anything and you don't owe me anything. Understand?'

'The ironic thing,' McGinley said, 'is that if things had gone slightly differently, if you had ever got the goods on me, then I might be a customer of the PRU myself.'

'A touching thought, and I suspect the closest thing to a confession I'll ever get.'

'Stay in touch, Mr Lapslie. There's precious few of us left, you know.'

And with that, the mobile went dead.

Lapslie stood for a moment, the mobile still in his hand. He knew more than he had before, but he didn't have a clue what it all meant. If the PRU were involved it meant that his case had something to do with a long-term prisoner who was either about to be released or, more probably, had already been released, but did that mean his murderer was their 'customer'? And if so, why were they allowing her to wander around committing murder?

'"Where is the wisdom we have lost in knowledge?"' he said softly, quoting T. S. Eliot. '"Where is the knowledge we have lost in information?"'

Jane Catherall was in the large autopsy room, supervising the placing of the corpses. One was being unwrapped on the furthest metal table. Three more were being lined up on gurneys on the far side of the room.

'How many more of these poor creatures can I expect?' Dr Catherall said, gazing at Lapslie from beneath lowered eyebrows.

'Another two vans' worth is my estimate,' he said. 'Assuming four bodies per vanload.'

'Twelve bodies? Apart from coach crashes and fires in night clubs, I can't think of many circumstances that produce so many bodies in here at the same time, and in both of those instances the cause of death is pretty well established before I start. I am going to have to conduct each autopsy here from first principles.'

'I think I know what you're going to find.'

She raised an eyebrow. 'Please – no clues. It spoils the fun.'

Lapslie looked at the body on the metal table. Unlike poor Violet Chambers, whose body had been wrapped in plastic and had withered and dried rather than decayed, this one was mostly eaten away by bacteria and by bugs, leaving behind a stained skeleton to which leathery flesh still adhered. The eyes had vanished, and the skull was covered by a thin, dry coating of skin that had drawn back from the discoloured teeth, making the corpse look as though it was perpetually screaming.

'Are they all like this?' Dr Catherall asked.

'If you lined them up in the right order,' Lapslie told her, 'you could take a photograph and use it to illustrate the process of decomposition from beginning to end.'

'The deaths occurred at different times then? Over the course of several years, perhaps?' Her faced creased into a smile. 'I'm actually looking forward to this.'

Lapslie looked at her diminutive, twisted frame. 'Can you cope?'

She looked perversely mutinous for a moment. 'I'm going to have to, aren't I?'

Lapslie frowned. 'I tried to get some of the bodies diverted to other mortuaries, but I was told nobody else was available.'

Dr Catherall smiled, and turned away. For the next few hours she examined the arriving bodies, one after the other, with the same concentration and dedication that she had displayed when she examined that of Violet Chambers. Samples from the bodies were placed in plastic jars, sealed into transparent envelopes and sent away for testing. Photographs were taken, sketches made and notes dictated. It all began to feel like a dream to

Lapslie as he sat, watching her work; a never-ending, recurring dream in which the same words were spoken, the same incisions made and the same samples taken, with only the state of decomposition of the body changing. There were moments when Lapslie's concentration slipped, or he fell asleep for a while, that made him think that Dr Catherall was carrying out the same long autopsy but that the body on the table was more and more decayed each time he looked.

Eventually she consigned the last body to be taken away, and walked slowly across to Lapslie. She looked exhausted. No, he thought; she actually looked ill.

'I find that my body tires so much quicker than my mind, these days,' she said, weariness evident in her voice. 'So many autopsies on the trot has not been a pleasant experience.'

'"Ah, but a man's reach should exceed his grasp, or what's a heaven for?"' Lapslie asked.

Dr Catherall smiled through her tiredness. 'Robert Browning. How nice.'

'Is there anything you can tell me?'

'There is much I can tell you, most of which you won't be interested in. The key things you want to hear about are approximate time of death and likely cause of death, and on both of those issues I am sadly bereft of much useful information. The approximate time of death will be plus or minus several months in each case. I will need to make some calculations. What I can tell you, however, is that the deaths were not equally spaced apart.'

He frowned. 'What do you mean?'

'I mean that there appears to be over a year between the times of death of the oldest bodies, but there's only a few months between the times of death of the freshest ones. Your killer, whoever it is, is striking more and more frequently. Whatever their reason is for killing, it's not giving them the same satisfaction now that it used to. They're speeding up.'

'Satisfaction?' Lapslie asked.

Dr Catherall looked up at him. 'Oh yes. You don't kill twelve women over the course of many years in a fit of rage. You do it because you want to. Because it fills some sick need.' She looked back at the bodies. 'The cause of death in each case is not immediately obvious, although I have sent samples away for toxicological testing, for obvious reasons.'

'Obvious reasons?' Lapslie asked.

She looked askance at him. 'You failed to mention it, but these deaths are connected to that of Violet Chambers, are they not?'

'I believe so,' he said. 'What makes you think so?'

'They are all elderly women, for a start, and the lack of a distinguishing cause of death suggests that poisoning is a possibility worth investigating. And, of course, there's the fingers.'

'The fingers?'

'You didn't see?' Dr Catherall shook her head. 'How careless of you. As with poor Violet Chambers, the fingers on the right hand of each of the victims had been cut off, all the way down to the knuckles.'

CHAPTER FIFTEEN

Daisy spent most of every day for the next five days with Eunice at the Arts and Crafts Centre, helping get the meagre accounts in order, and in all that time she could only remember a handful of people actually coming inside. One of them had been a local artist, thin and grey-haired, clad in black corduroy, hoping to have his wares exhibited by Eunice. He was doomed to disappointment: Eunice held one of his paintings in front of her, turning it this way and that, squinting as if the sunset over seascape that the artist had tried so hard to emulate was actually putting out fierce rays of light.

'Oh no,' she had said. 'Oh no, no, no. These waves are all too similar. Waves should be majestically chaotic. No two alike, you see? And they should blend together indiscernibly. These ones look like you've painted them separately, cut them out and stuck them over one another.' She paused, making a gradual left-hand turn with the painting. 'The framing is quite good though.'

Two of the remaining visitors had been local people who had been sorting through the effects of recently deceased loved ones and found what looked to Daisy like a piece of gimcrack china and a dusty and over-varnished painting. Eunice had surprised Daisy by buying both pieces; one for fifteen pounds, the other for thirty-five. After they had left, clutching their cash, Daisy had quietly asked Eunice what she had seen in the pieces. The replies had surprised her.

Of the china piece, which resembled nothing so much as a seagull with an unnaturally large and removable head, the whole thing coloured with a lurid yellow wash, Eunice had said: 'This is a Martin Brothers bird, I believe. Made around 1901 in Southall. The Martin brothers were well known for their grotesque animals and fish. This base is ebony, if I'm not mistaken.'

'And you intend exhibiting it?'

'No, I intend selling it.' Eunice sniffed. 'At auction, this little piece will fetch over five thousand pounds.'

'And that woman who sold it to you – she had no idea?'

'Caveat emptor works both ways, my dear. If they don't do their research, I cannot be held responsible. Not in law.'

Concerning the painting – a hunting scene with fat horses tottering on matchstick legs across a brook, the whole thing browned and glossy with old varnish – Eunice had told the seller that it was a mass-produced Victorian item of little or no value. When the man had gone, she had placed it reverentially on the counter in front of her and sat, head in hands, gazing at it.

'It's very badly done,' Daisy had said. 'Those horses are exceedingly top-heavy.'

'It was the style of the time,' Eunice had sighed. 'Don't let the varnish deceive you: underneath the surface is something rather surprising. This is an original Henry Alkin. I've seen prints taken from it, but I never thought I would see the original.'

'And you intend selling it at auction?'

'After a while,' Eunice had said dreamily. 'After a while.'

'For how much?'

'In excess of ten thousand pounds, I would imagine.' Eunice had glanced up at Daisy, who had put what she had hoped was a disapproving expression on her face. 'You don't imagine I earn enough from *this* place to make a living, do you?'

Eunice was proving shrewder than her blowsy, artsy exterior had led Daisy to believe.

The remaining visitors had been holidaymakers, breaking their car journeys for a cup of tea and a slice of cake, or sheltering from the rain when they were out walking. They had spent an hour or so in the barn, looking around in a desultory manner, and then vanished, taking with them a few token postcards and leaving behind a faint smell of damp clothes and cigarette smoke.

And each of the five days that Daisy had spent at the Arts and Crafts Centre had seen her hating Jasper more than the last.

Jasper was Eunice's pride and joy. He was a small, snappy dog of indeterminate breed, and he hated Daisy. He growled at her constantly and followed her around the barn, his overly large black eyes glinting malevolently at her; and he smelled like old washing. His expression seemed to say: 'I know who you are, old woman. You can fool her, but you can't fool me.'

Daisy determined to do away with Jasper as soon as she possibly could. Eunice could wait – Daisy needed to squeeze her of as much information about her past life as possible – but the dog had to go. Regard it as a dry run, she told herself. A chance to test out a poison she had never used before, but had been meaning to for some time.

Every day that week that she had spent at the Arts and Crafts Centre, Daisy had brought in a bag of apricots for her and Eunice to eat. With the excuse of tidying up, she had collected all the apricot stones once the fruit had been eaten and taken them home with her each night, drying them out on her kitchen windowsill. On the fifth evening, using a cheese grater bought on the way home from a small kitchen store in Leyston, she had carefully rasped at the kernel of the stones until she had a pile of grey powder on a piece of kitchen towel. If she was right then the grey powder contained a lethal dose of hydrocyanic acid, but she had never used apricot kernels before, and she was worried that she might have misjudged the dose. Perhaps the apricots needed to have achieved a certain ripeness before the poison could be extracted. Or maybe the kernels needed to be heated first before being grated.

Fortunately, Jasper would act as her test case. She could sprinkle a little on his food every day and monitor what his reaction was. And when he died, *if* he died, then all Daisy had to do was to multiply up the amount she had used to take Eunice's weight into account, and then bake it into a shepherd's pie or something similar. Perhaps an apricot crumble. After all, it seemed a shame to waste the fruit she would be buying.

On the sixth day, Daisy rested. She needed to give some thought to her next steps, but more than that, she needed Eunice to realise how empty her life was when Daisy wasn't there. Using the excuse that she needed to do some work on the designs for the Arts and Crafts Centre leaflets, she stayed at home. But before she left the barn, she turned the ringer volume on Eunice's telephone down to zero. Eunice would be able to make outgoing calls with no problems, but if anyone tried to ring in then Eunice wouldn't be able to hear the phone. It was crude, but it would help to make her feel even more isolated from her few remaining contacts. And after a couple of weeks of Eunice failing to answer her phone, people would stop calling. It was so simple, it was perfect.

The next day, Daisy returned to the barn. Eunice was pathetically glad to see her.

'My dear,' she said, 'you have no idea how boring it is here. I've been going gaga. Thank heavens I've had Jasper to keep me company.'

'Actually,' Daisy said, 'I brought some food in for Jasper. I cooked some chicken yesterday for my dinner, and I thought he might fancy the leftovers. Would that be all right?'

'You are so very thoughtful,' Eunice said. Jasper just eyed her warily from his position by his mistress's side. 'Jasper really appreciates the way you look after him.'

Daisy took her bag into the kitchen area at the back of the barn and put the chicken on a saucer. A translucent jelly had congealed around the pieces, making them glossy and brown. Looking around to check that Eunice wasn't watching, she took a tupperware container from her bag and, pulling the lid off, sprinkled a teaspoon of the grey powder on top and then mixed it in with the jelly. With luck, Jasper would not suspect a thing.

Returning to the barn, she set the saucer down by the side of the counter. The dog trotted across to sniff at it. He looked up at Daisy, then back at the food. He sniffed again. Bending his head, he snuffled the chunks of meat and jelly and poison up into his wrinkled little mouth.

'There's a good dog,' said Daisy.

At lunchtime, Daisy made a cup of tea. Eunice took a packet of pills from her bag and, as she had done every lunchtime that Daisy had been there, pushed a small blue and red torpedo-shaped pill from its blister pack and popped it in her mouth, swigging it down with a mouthful of tea. The blister pack looked like it was mostly used up.

'I hope you don't mind me asking,' Daisy said, 'but are they vitamin pills?'

'I'm afraid not,' Eunice said. 'Atorvastatin, I think it's called. It lowers cholesterol. Prescription drug, from my doctor.'

'It must be awful, going into town all the time to get new prescriptions.'

'The damn surgery won't let me just phone up and order the tablets,' Eunice said with some bitterness. 'I have to drop the repeat prescription in to them with forty-eight hours' notice. Apparently it's all to do with that doctor who killed hundreds of his patients. The one with the beard and the glasses. Shipwell? Shipston? Can't remember his name. Anyway, it's such a pain.'

'Perhaps I could help,' Daisy said casually, as if she had not been planning this all the time. 'I have to go past the surgery and the chemists when I go home. Would you like me to drop your repeat prescription in and then pick the tablets up when they are ready?'

'I couldn't ask you to do that,' Eunice said.

'It's no trouble. It would make me happy if I could help in any way.'

Eunice gazed at Daisy for a few moments, then rummaged in her bag. 'I'm nearly out,' she said, pulling a green repeat prescription form out and ticking a box with a pen that lay beside the till. 'Would you be a dear, and drop this in for me?'

'Nothing would give me more pleasure,' said Daisy, and she meant it. Another small takeover of Eunice's life had occurred.

Jasper was wandering round the barn in some confusion. He was coughing, as if trying to retch something up, and going around in circles. Daisy made a mental note to double the amount of powder she used the next time she fed him. She wanted a quick reaction when she tried it on Eunice; not a slow, drawn-out death. She'd had enough of those. The last thing she wanted was Eunice waking up from a coma while Daisy was driving her to her last resting place. That would not only be embarrassing; it would be disastrous.

'Do you think he's all right?' Eunice asked, gazing at Jasper with some worry. 'He looks like he's swallowed something he shouldn't have.'

'Probably just a hairball,' Daisy said vaguely. 'He'll be all right in the morning.'

Eunice looked sorrowfully at the telephone beside the till. 'It's been very quiet,' she said. 'I can't remember any calls for an age. Should I get the engineers to take a look at the line?'

'Things go up and down,' Daisy said. 'There might be a glut of calls next week. Leave it until then: see what happens.'

'You're a brick,' Eunice said. 'I know I get paranoid some-times, but you're always there to bring me back to earth. I'm so glad you're here.'

'I'll always be here,' said Daisy. She gazed at the dog, who was still wandering around the barn as if he had lost some-thing. 'This place has become a second home to me. I feel as if I really belong.'

Daisy sipped her tea, and gazed at Eunice. She despised the

woman more now than she had when she first met her. The six days the two of them had spent together had been nothing but a long monologue from Eunice concerning her past life, her friends, her lovers, her various accidental pregnancies, which had either ended naturally or been terminated unnaturally, and her relationship with her family. Daisy had volunteered very little information about herself, and Eunice had hardly noticed. Even when she had asked Daisy a question about where she had lived and what she had done in her life, she invariably ended up talking about herself. The up side of this was that Daisy had quickly gained a solid appreciation of Eunice's life – the names, the dates, the significant moments. The down side was that, of all the women whose lives Daisy had taken over, Eunice's was the one furthest from her own experience. Becoming Eunice was going to take a major effort.

Ah, but when it happened … when Eunice was dead, and had taken her place in Daisy's tea party … that would be a moment to savour. Daisy let her mind wander, imagining Eunice's form not as it was now, fleshy and sagging, but sitting proudly at the table with the others, reduced down to its essentials; the skin removed by nature to reveal the purity of what lay beneath. That would be a sight for sore eyes.

A tiny moth of worry began to eat away at the fabric of Daisy's self-confidence. Violet Chambers' body had been found, in its unmarked grave out in the forest. Daisy had been on her way to the tea party with Violet when her tyre had burst and she had been forced to abandon the body. Especially after it had come back to life and Daisy had smashed its skull in order to stop it from escaping, rendering it spoiled and useless for the tea party. The thing that was bothering her was, did the police have any clever way of tracing her car, and working out where she had been going? She rarely watched television, and never watched crime dramas, but Daisy had some vague under-standing that the police had access to all kinds of scientific techniques that hadn't existed in the past. Things that seemed more fantasy than reality. Could they discover her little hideaway, her paradise, her refuge? The thought made her feel uncomfortable. She shivered and scratched herself.

'Are you okay?' Eunice asked. 'If you're not feeling well, you should go home. I don't want to catch anything!'

Forthright to the point of rudeness, that was Eunice. 'I suddenly felt as if someone had just walked over my graves,' Daisy murmured.

The thought nagged at her for the rest of the afternoon. Policemen, rummaging through everything that she held dear: the one thing that was constant through all the changing identities and the new homes. Her core. Her centre.

She couldn't remember where the house had originally come from. The identity of the owner was buried back in the mists of Daisy's past – and was, Daisy dimly recalled, still sitting at the head of the dinner table. All she knew was that she had inherited it from somewhere, and there was no mortgage outstanding on it. For as long as she paid the Council Tax on it – and she visited every month or so in order to pick up the letter from the local Council telling her how much to pay – she had assumed that it would remain safe. Undisturbed. She had deliberately switched the gas and electricity supplier several times, ensuring that the last time she closed the accounts without starting new ones up. That way there would be no reason for a computer glitch, or a gas leak, to start accruing costs on her account and eventually for bailiffs to get called in. That would have been a disaster. In fact, the last few times she had been at the house – the last time being six months before, with the body of the original Daisy Wilson – there had only been a few letters waiting for her. Long periods in which nothing happened at the house seemed to have caused the address to have dropped off even the most tenacious of postal marketing firms. Even the Reader's Digest didn't send letters there any more. Only that one occasion when she had, reluctantly, had to arrange for a mechanic to visit to start her Volvo had marred the isolation.

But now ... Daisy couldn't focus her thoughts on the accounts in front of her. The possibility that her guests might be disturbed, might even be *removed*, was making her tense and irritable. Twice she snapped at Jasper as he stopped near her and coughed.

Did she dare make a return visit? That was the question. When Eunice finally succumbed to the apricot kernels – assuming they worked their magic on Jasper first – then Daisy would have to dispose of the body somewhere. She quailed at the idea of just dumping it in a quarry or a wood, or throwing it off the Naze. That was not only clumsy and messy; it was also risky. Bodies disposed of like that were bound to surface, literally or metaphorically. A bad penny always turns up again; that was what they said. No, it was far safer to place bodies in a controlled environment, where the chances of passers-by finding them were so remote as to be discarded. And besides, Daisy had always taken great comfort in the notion that all of her victims – with the exception of poor Violet – were keeping each other company.

Despite her concerns, Daisy didn't want to risk making a visit now. Going to the house to see whether the police had found it was like wandering around with a lighted match looking for a gas leak: the consequences of discovering the worst were likely to be worse still. No, she would wait until Eunice was safely dead, and then make a decision based on what had appeared in the newspapers, and what her intuition was telling her.

'Do you want to go for a walk?' Eunice asked. 'Get some fresh air? You're looking a bit peaky.'

'That would be nice,' Daisy said. She had got about as far with the accounts as it was possible to go; not only sorting out for Eunice where all her money was going but also ensuring that Daisy herself had a list of account numbers and knew where all the relevant paperwork was kept. She would need that knowledge later.

'Jasper!' Eunice called. 'Come on, you slugabed. Walkies!'

Jasper had retired to a corner of the barn where, at some stage in the past, a tartan blanket had been thrown down for him. Now it was matted and twisted into a mirror image of his shape, and he was nestled into it, tongue hanging out, panting for breath.

'He's looking a bit peaky too,' Eunice said, concerned. 'I hope he's not coming down with something. He's quite delicate, you know. Quite artistic, in his personality.'

'I'm sure it's nothing,' Daisy said reassuringly. She thought she could see a trace of blue around the inside of the dog's mouth as it panted. Perhaps she had overestimated the amount of grated apricot kernel necessary to kill an elderly dog, in which case she probably had enough left to kill Eunice several times over. 'He's probably tired out from rushing around.' As if Jasper ever did anything as undignified as rushing around. 'We should leave him here and check on him later.'

Together they set out, walking first along the lane towards the road where the bus dropped Daisy off every morning and picked her up every night, and then striking out along an established track that ran between fields. The sky was bright blue, and what little cloud existed was being pulled in different directions, combining and drifting apart as it moved. Daisy could smell the pungent aroma of the flowers that lined the fields on either side of them; bright gold, spindly, and nodding in the same faint breeze that pushed the clouds around.

Eunice strode ahead, swinging a walking stick manfully. Daisy found it a chore to keep up, but the exercise cleared her mind of her worries concerning the house where her victims sat in their eternal tea party.

'I know all the walks around here,' Eunice confided over her shoulder. 'Some of them have remained unchanged for

229

centuries, perhaps millennia. They say that some of these tracks follow the paths of ley lines, you know? One can imagine Roman soldiers walking across these very fields. Or druids, perhaps.'

Daisy was spending more time imagining Eunice twisted in agony and turning blue as the hydrocyanic acid burned its way through her body, but she merely said, 'Yes, indeed,' as they walked. Her shoes weren't really ideal for this kind of thing.

They were walking up a slight incline, and at the top Eunice stopped and gazed, entranced, ahead. Daisy struggled to catch up. When she too crested the ridge at the top of the incline, she felt what little breath she had catch in her throat.

Ahead of them lay a church. An old church, made of grey stone, with a squat tower in its middle and an older structure, made of wood, attached to the end furthest from the large double doors that gave entry to the inside. It sat in the midst of a graveyard, separated from the surrounding fields by a dry-stone wall. A track led away towards some distant buildings.

'St Alkmund's Church,' Eunice said. 'No vicar, not since the 1970s. There's a padre who cycles round every four weeks, as part of a rota of local old churches without their own vicars, but the attendance is small and it's going down as people die off. Lovely architecture, though. Mainly Norman influence. Be a shame to lose it. Look at that wooden hut thing on the end: I remember reading somewhere that it dates from a previous church on the same site. Anglo-Saxon. Built without nails. Held together with wooden pegs, apparently. Let's go closer.'

'I'd rather not,' Daisy said, but Eunice was striding off ahead.

Daisy glanced again at the church. Something about the way it squatted, alone but unrepentant, in the middle of the fields made her uneasy. It was as if it had been waiting for her. Waiting all these years for her to return, with dark thoughts mouldering in its heart.

Eunice had reached the dry-stone wall now, and was walking

around to the lych gate entrance. Daisy followed, knowing that something was not right.

The graveyard was long overgrown with weeds and flowers. The gravestones had been eroded by the salt air and colonised by moss to the point where they were almost as rounded as boulders. Whatever writing had been carved onto them was nothing but depressions in the granite, like memories that had faded until there was nothing left but the faint recollection that something had once been there and was now lost forever.

Eunice ran her hands across a gravestone that was tilting at an angle. 'Imagine,' she said, 'the history of this place. The way it has stayed the same while everything around it – the countryside, the country, the world – has changed.'

But Daisy wasn't listening. Around the corner of the church she had spotted a gravestone that had been set flat in the ground. She walked closer, feet unwilling to move but unable to stop. Protected, perhaps, by the bulk of the church, the letters carved into the slab were almost readable.

Madeline Poel, it said, but that was impossible.

Because before she had been Daisy Winters, before she had been Violet Chambers, before she had been anyone, she knew that she had been Madeline Poel.

CHAPTER SIXTEEN

Find one old lady dead, Mark Lapslie thought sourly, and you get a desk and a Detective Sergeant; find thirteen of them and you get an entire incident room and so many staff it's hard to remember their names. Even the DCS hadn't been able to stop the investigation from ramping up, although the rumour was that he had tried several times. Apparently Rouse had attempted to claim that until the deaths were attributable to foul play then he couldn't approve a murder investigation, but the fact that the Volvo 740 could now be used to link the corpse in the forest – which had undoubtedly been murdered – with the ones in the farmhouse meant that his objections were half-hearted and easily overcome by someone who still had a few friends at Scotland Yard.

Half of the room in the Chelmsford HQ was filled with desks, each loaded up with its own telephone and computer, each telephone connected to a headset with attached microphone, each computer networked into the police system. The other half was dominated by two perspex boards. The first one had photographs of the victims blu-tacked all over it, along with notes written in wipeable pen. On any normal incident board there would be lines drawn between the photographs indicating connections: unbroken lines for the known connections and dotted lines for the ones where there was an indication but no corroborating evidence. On this board, there were no lines. Despite all of the constables manning the phones and the computers, nobody had yet established a connection between any of the victims. None of them had been to school together, none of them had lived in the same towns or villages, none of them had shared the same hobbies or subscribed to the same magazines. The only things they had in common were their sex – they were all female – their age – they were all over sixty – and their general geographical location – they all lived in the South or West of England. And, of course, the fact that they had all been murdered and mutilated.

Lapslie stood by the victims board, ignoring the flood of rust and salt and coconut that filled his mouth each time he came into the incident room and heard the chatter of people talking on telephones, talking to each other and typing away at keyboards. He kept shoving breath fresheners under his tongue to cover the melange of tastes, but it didn't work. The problem was psychological, not physical. He tried to spend as much time as he could in the Quiet Room, but he had to show his face to his staff, listen to their problems, brief them on new aspects of the case and generally be there as a figurehead. Emma Bradbury was doing the best she could to take the pressure off his shoulders, but he'd had a persistent headache for several days now and he was finding it difficult to eat. When he'd had a mouth full of conflicting flavours all day, the last thing he wanted was to add more to them.

It was driving him mad. This was why he'd taken leave of absence from the police in the first place; this, and having to split from Sonia and the kids.

He let his gaze scan across the photographs on the board. He'd never really thought about it before, but in the same way that all babies share similar features so all elderly people do as well. It was as if everyone is born the same and dies the same, and the bit in between is where we have the chance to distinguish ourselves from the rest. The correspondences were more marked than the differences: white hair, liver spots on the hands, skin that had sagged into set folds beneath the chin, eyebrows that had been pencilled in, bags beneath the eyes, faded, cloudy irises. Something told Lapslie that if he ever managed to catch his killer, he could put her photograph up there and it would just blend in with the rest.

Some of the photographs had names written in beneath them: Violet Chambers, of course; Daisy Winters; Deirdre Fincham; Alice Connell; Rhona McIntyre; Kim Stothard; Wendy Maltravers – identified by a combination of medical records, dental records and clues found about their bodies. Not missing persons records, of course – although that was a key factor in identifying most murder victims, it was no help here. Each of the dead women was actually still out there as far as the system was concerned. They were all still claiming benefits, paying their Council Tax, receiving rent from the properties they had moved out of, filling out their tax returns and sending the occasional postcard or Christmas card to the neighbours they had left behind.

'Everybody is dead who should be alive,' he murmured to himself.

Where the first perspex board had no lines linking the photographs, the second one had nothing but lines drawn all over it, with cryptic notes written alongside the lines. It was a map of the financial arrangements: direct debits and standing orders, payments in and out. Each node on the board was an account in a bank or a building society, and each line showed money being transferred. And there was nothing, in that complex web of finance, to identify the spider in the middle. There was no central account to which the others drained their money. Every so often there was a dotted line leading away from the web, like an anchor line, marking where cash had been taken out of one or other of the accounts – hundreds of pounds in most cases, sometimes thousands – but it was never in the same place.

On the other side of the board, a map of the Essex area had been blu-tacked in place. Red stickers marked where cash-points had been used to remove money from the accounts. There were clusters of stickers, but nothing that would indicate that their killer lived in a particular place.

Lapslie caught the eye of one of the passing constables. 'Who's responsible for updating this board?' he asked.

'PC Swinerd, sir,' the girl said in a smoke-filled voice.

'Can you send them over?' Lapslie asked. He wasn't entirely sure he could remember who PC Swinerd was.

He turned out to be a blond lad with a receding hairline. 'Sir?' he said as he approached. His voice was gooseberries and cream.

'These stickers – they're not ordered in any particular way?' He frowned. 'Sir?'

'There's no numbering on them to indicate which ones were the earliest transactions and which were the latest ones.'

'Trouble was, sir, I was putting the stickers on while the information was still trickling in. The banks haven't been very co-operative, and we're having to keep getting warrants signed off for each victim's accounts as they're identified. Until all the transactions are shown we don't know what the very first or very last transactions are, and so we can't number the ones in between.'

'And there are still six victims not identified?'

'That's right, sir.'

Lapslie thought for a moment. 'We might never identify them, that's the problem. Can you write numbers on these stickers – "1" for the first, and whatever the highest number is for the most recent. We can always change the numbers later, if more information comes in.'

'Sir,' the PC said. He looked sceptical, probably at the amount of work he was being asked to do, but he walked away without argument.

'One more thing,' Lapslie called after him. 'Put green stickers on to mark where the victims' houses were.'

'Yes, sir,' PC Swinerd called back.

Emma Bradbury walked in as PC Swinerd walked away. She caught Lapslie's eye, and came over.

'Boss, we've got preliminary autopsy results in from Doctor

Catherall. She's really pulled the stops out. Apart from the disfiguration on the right hand of all the victims, there's no signs of violence, but the toxicology reports suggest that poison was involved in at least five of the deaths.'

'Only five?'

'The other bodies are too decayed. The reports point out that some poisons degrade over time to the point where they can't be detected.'

'So – what poisons did they detect?' he asked.

Emma consulted her list. 'Pyrrolizidine alkaloid,' she read, stumbling over the words, 'andromedotoxin, taxine, cyanogenic glucoside, a complex terpene that can't be properly identified. And colchicine, of course, from Violet Chambers.'

'No strychnine? No cyanide? No warfarin?'

'Not so far. None of the classics.'

Lapslie thought for a moment, remembering back to the garden next to the house where all the bodies had been discovered. The Garden of Death, as he had thought of it.

'Get back to Doctor Catherall,' he said. 'I want to know if any of those toxins can be obtained from common or garden plants. Remember that colchicine comes from the meadow saffron.'

'Yes, boss. How could I forget?'

Lapslie looked around the incident room again as she walked off. Everyone seemed to be busily engaged in urgent activity. He left before the chatter and the clatter overcame him.

Sitting in the Quiet Room with the door closed, he gradually let himself relax. In his mind, a picture of the killer kept forming; vague, blurred, but definitely there. She was almost obsessively methodical, for instance. The way she had arranged the finances of her victims indicated that she could keep a complex series of facts in her head at one time, and the way she sent postcards and Christmas cards after the event suggested that she kept detailed records. She didn't just kill and move on.

No, she kept the plates spinning, kept all of her victims alive. Did she, in some sense, believe that if she kept them alive then they weren't really dead?

Bacon trickled across his tongue before he registered the knock on the door. He turned his head. Emma Bradbury was standing there. He gestured to her to enter.

'Doctor Catherall says that all of the poisons can be easily made up from sufficient quantities of plants. She kept talking, and I couldn't make notes fast enough, but I got the impression that some of the plants were common or garden – as it were – and others were rather more obscure. Specialist items, as it were.'

'That house where the bodies were found is our killer's base of operations, then,' Lapslie said grimly. 'She keeps going back there, not only to drop off fresh bodies but also to obtain her raw materials. I think that garden is our murder weapon.'

'The garden?'

'Get one of the constables to get in touch with a botanist. I want them to go through that garden and work out which plants are poisonous, which *part* is poisonous and what the poison is.'

Emma looked baffled. 'Where do we get a botanist from?'

Lapslie shrugged. 'A university or a garden centre, wherever. Get hold of Alan Titchmarsh, for all I care. Just get an expert in that garden. And make sure someone is keeping watch on that house. I want everyone who visits it checked out, postmen and door-to-door salesmen included.'

'Yes, boss. Oh, and PC Swinerd was looking for you. He says he's finished with the map.'

As Emma left, Lapslie took a deep breath and slipped another breath tablet into his mouth before leaving the Quiet Room and heading back to the incident room.

The perspex board with the financial spider's web was still rotated so that the map showed, but there were green stickers amongst the red ones now, and the red stickers had numbers on them. Lapslie stood a little way away and just tried to take the information in. It hadn't been obvious before, but now he could see there were clumps of red stickers around where the green ones were. It made sense: the killer got rid of a victim and moved into their house for a while, taking on their identity, and while she was there she had to take money out of whatever accounts she controlled. She may have used different cashpoints for safety, but she obviously didn't want to travel too far. Or perhaps she couldn't travel too far. Whatever the reason, she stayed within a few tens of miles of what was, for a while, home.

There was one cluster that didn't have a green sticker as its centre.

Lapslie moved closer, feeling excitement stirring within him. If the killer used her latest victim's house as a base, then a cluster of red stickers with no green sticker might indicate where the latest victim was.

Or would be.

Squinting, he checked the numbers written on the red stickers in that clump. They were all high numbers. Quickly, he scanned the rest of the board. There were no higher numbers anywhere else. Those transactions were the most recent ones.

She was there! He'd located his killer.

He focused on the map behind the dots. East and north of London. The area that used to be known as the Tendring Hundreds – a name that lingered on in the name of the local council and the local newspapers. Clustered around the coast: Clacton, Frinton, Walton and Leyston.

He had her. Or, at least, he knew where she was.

He turned around to face the incident room. 'All right – pay attention!' he yelled, cutting across the general commotion and, for the first time in a long time, causing a flare in his mouth that didn't correlate to any known fruit, vegetable or meat. The taste of his own voice, shouting. 'There's a good chance our killer is located on the east coast, somewhere in

Essex. That's where all the most recent financial transactions have taken place, but none of the victims so far identified have had houses there. I want a list of all hotels and guest houses along that stretch of coast, running back, oh, twenty miles inland, and I want to know if they have rented rooms for more than two weeks to a lone woman over sixty. I want every estate agent in that area contacted and I want a list of all flats or houses that have been rented out in the past six months to a lone woman over sixty. And I want it *now*. Remember, this woman is probably stalking her next victim while you're working. She's getting to know her, taking over her life, finding out everything she can before she poisons her. She might be slipping that poison into a cup of tea right now. We don't have any time to waste. Get on with it!'

Emma Bradbury had come in while he was shouting. Now, as the noise in the incident room suddenly ramped up, she crossed the room to where he was standing.

'There's always the chance that one of the unidentified victims has a house in that area,' she said. 'The murder might already have happened.'

'And a meteorite might suddenly wipe out this police station in a freak accident,' he riposted. 'But we still come in every day. We live our lives regardless. We can't plan for what might or might not happen. If we're lucky, we'll find her. If we're not, we won't. That's how it goes.'

She looked at him appraisingly. 'He said you never give up,' she said softly, as if vocalising some internal thought.

'Who said?'

Emma's face suddenly tightened. 'Nobody,' she said. 'Just a conversation I was having. Canteen talk.'

Lapslie stared at her for a few moments more, aware that something was going on but unsure what it was. 'Okay,' he said. 'Let's crack on. Keep the team on their toes – I want updates every hour on how that list is going.'

Emma nodded, and walked away. Before Lapslie could

move, one of the PCs in his team – Swinerd, he thought – approached.

'Message from the Chief Superintendent,' he said. 'Could you pop up to his office?'

Acting on a sudden impulse, Lapslie walked across to the window. The incident room was on the fifth floor, and he could see down into the car park. It was filled with the kinds of cars that police officers drove when they were off-duty; sporty cars: Ford Mondeos, Peugeot 406s and Saab 95s, all in nondescript colours. No Volkswagens, no Skodas, no Minis, and definitely no Volvos, which policemen generally referred to as Belgranos. It was similar to the auto factory car parks one could see from the train sometimes; row upon row of similar vehicles extending to the horizon.

And a black Lexus, parked at the end of one row. Its engine was idling; Lapslie could see vapour drifting up from the exhaust.

He looked around the incident room, feeling as if he was bidding it goodbye in some strange way. Everyone was working hard, heads down, headsets on, lips moving as they spoke into the microphones. Nobody was looking at him.

He walked out of the room, unnoticed.

The lift up to the floor where Rouse's office was located seemed to take an age to arrive. When the doors opened, it was empty. He was glad. The last thing he wanted was to make small talk when he was on his way to something that felt like it might be his execution.

Part of him wanted to press the button for the ground floor, walk out of the lift, through the security door that led into the car park and just keep on going, walking away, leaving it all behind, but he couldn't do that. He needed to know what was going on. As Emma had said, he never gave up.

Rouse's PA told him he could go straight in, but his gaze was fixed on the man who was standing by Rouse's desk. Alone. The DCS was notable by his absence.

'Detective Chief Inspector Lapslie?' said the man. 'Please come in.' His voice was like disturbed earth, or leaf mould. He was still wearing that black suit with the subtle pinstripe. His hair was sandy, brushed straight back off his forehead. The bare scalp that was revealed was covered with small freckles.

Lapslie leaned over the PA. 'Is there a key to this office?' he asked. 'We might need to leave some sensitive stuff on the desk and pop out for a while.'

'Er ... yes,' she said, reaching into a drawer and bringing out a Yale key. She held it out uncertainly towards him.

'Thanks.' He took the key from her. 'I'll bring it back later, I promise.' Turning to the office, he said: 'Mr Geherty, of the Department of Justice's Prisoner Rehabilitation Unit, I presume?'

Geherty had the grace to look a little abashed. 'You've been doing your homework.'

'I don't like being followed around. And I don't like thieves.'

'We haven't been following you, Mr Lapslie, we've been following your investigation. It's been an education for us all. Shame it's got to stop.'

'It stops when we catch the murderer,' Lapslie said.

'It stops when our Minister says it stops,' Geherty responded. 'And we're not thieves, by the way.'

'You broke into Doctor Catherall's mortuary and you took the information off her computer.'

'We're Civil Servants, and the mortuary belongs to the Civil Service. No problems there, surely? And I think you'll find that there's no information missing from Doctor Catherall's computer. We merely copied it and left. We just want to be kept apprised of your progress.'

'I'm intrigued. Your department deals with integrating serial killers and other undesirables into society when they've served their sentences. Does that mean the killer of these women is one of yours? Did you give her a new identity and a new place to live, only to find that she's returned to her old habits?'

'Old habits die hard, and you can't teach a dog new tricks. Clichés, all of them, but there's a grain of truth in there.' Geherty shrugged. 'These people spend most of their lives in prison, but when their time is up they have to be reintegrated. We prepare them. We teach them how to survive in a world that's moved on in the ten, or twenty, or thirty years that have passed since they were incarcerated. We get them houses and we get them jobs as waiters, or travel agents, or on the perfume counter in Debenhams. And we evaluate them, trying to determine whether they have actually changed, or whether there's still a core of evil within them. Sometimes we get it right and sometimes we get it wrong. That's the way it goes. When it goes wrong, we have to clear up the mess.'

'"A core of evil",' Lapslie said. 'You don't blame society or upbringing, then?'

Geherty shook his head. 'Oh, I've looked into the eyes of men who have killed more people than I've ever known. I've looked into the eyes of women who have banged nine-inch nails into the skulls of their victims with hammers. I have seen evil, Mr Lapslie. Society isn't blameless, and neither is upbringing, but in the end they are catalysts. If the evil isn't there to begin with, they have nothing to work with.'

'What I don't understand,' Lapslie said, 'is why you can't just arrest them, put them on trial and bang them up when they're found guilty. Why all the Secret Squirrel palaver?'

'Because some of them aren't even supposed to have been released,' Geherty said, checking his watch. 'You know what it's like in prison. They say we're almost up to capacity; in fact, we passed capacity years ago. For every person who's sent to jail, one has to be released. Sometimes we do it by commuting sentences, or arranging for criminals to get parole when they technically shouldn't, but that's only nibbling at the problem. The real issue is the lifers cluttering up the system. The

murderers who can't be released, either because there would be
a public outcry or because some judge somewhere has said that
life means life, and the Minister either can't or won't interfere.'

Something that Dom McGinley had told him suddenly
echoed in Lapslie's head. Something about the child-killer,
Myra Hindley, not having died of a chest infection at all, but
living her life under a new identity somewhere in Wales.

'So you release them anyway,' he said bitterly.

'We have to. We take all the precautions we can, but life is
life. Things go wrong.'

'And my killer?'

Geherty looked at his watch again. 'Time ticks away,' he said.

'Satisfy my curiosity. Who is she?'

'You've met her. Don't you remember? You were assigned to
ACPO, profiling major criminals. Actually, we were considering offering you a job, but that medical condition of yours
stopped us. You interviewed a number of lifers, looking to see
if there was any psychological test that could be applied to tell
whether someone was likely to become a killer or not. And you
interviewed her.'

The taste of lychees, almost impossibly sweet and decadent
in his mouth, like something rotting in treacle. 'Madeline ...
Poel?'

'Madeline Poel,' Geherty confirmed.

'Broadmoor. What – twenty years ago.' He remembered a
middle-aged woman, small and bird-like. She had been very
polite, very old-fashioned, and her voice had tasted of lychees.
'It was back towards the end of the Second World War. Her
grandmother had gone mad and killed all of Madeline's sisters
and brothers in the back garden of their house, snipping their
fingers off with a pair of garden secateurs and watching them
bleed to death. Madeline only survived because her mother
came back from the local factory where she was working. The
police were called, and while they were making their way over,
Madeline made a drink for her grandmother out of some of the

berries in the garden. She told her grandmother that it was sarsaparilla, but it was something toxic. Her grandmother died before the police could take her away. Everyone thought it was an accident, just Madeline trying to be helpful, but over the next few years Madeline started acting stranger and stranger and ten or twelve old ladies in the village died in exactly the same way. It was as if she'd decided that all old ladies were dangerous, and she had to get rid of them. The logic of a girl who'd been driven insane by watching her family killed in the most horrific way by the woman who was meant to be protecting them. After a while someone cottoned on, and she was sent away. Committed to Broadmoor.' His mouth was flooding with that dry, metallic taste as his voice got louder. 'She died fifteen years ago of a heart attack – at least, that's what the newspapers said – but she never died at all! Is that what you're telling me? You actually *released* her into society?'

'Because we didn't think she posed a threat any more. And because we needed the space.' Geherty suddenly looked tired. 'It was before my time.'

'That's no excuse.'

'That's not an excuse – that's an explanation. Her death was faked – we even made up a tombstone at a church near where she grew up – and a new identity was created for her. We got her a job waitressing in Ipswich, and a nice flat. And we watched her – extensively for three months, then intermittently after that. And then, when she thought we weren't watching carefully enough, she vanished. Turns out she'd spent several months crafting a new identity, and she just slipped out of the one we'd created for her and into the one she'd created for herself. We've been looking for her ever since.'

'And I'm looking for her now. We should work together.'

Geherty shook his head. 'The only reason you're looking for her is because we asked Chief Superintendent Rouse to bring you in on the case. You'd known her. You'd talked to her. If anyone had an insight into how her mind worked, it was you.'

'So let me catch her.'

'You've located her. That's all we need. If you arrest her now, she goes to court and it all spills out. If we catch her, she vanishes. Forever.'

'That's not justice.'

'No, but it's *just.*'

Lapslie gazed at Geherty. 'I can't let that happen,' he said.

Geherty nodded. 'I'm not asking you to,' he said. 'I'm telling you. Or rather, Detective Chief Inspector Rouse is currently taking a call from my Minister telling him to put a stop to this case. It's over. We'll take it from here.'

'Over my dead body,' Lapslie snapped.

'No – over your dead career,' Geherty said, and smiled.

CHAPTER SEVENTEEN

'Are you feeling better?' Eunice's voice boomed from the kitchen.

Sitting in Eunice's sparse front room with a cup of tea clutched in her hands, Daisy's stomach was churning. All she could see in her mind was the graveyard.

The churchyard and the gravestone.

The gravestone with the name on it: Madeline Poel.

'I'm ... not sure,' Daisy said. It sounded to her as if her voice was coming from a long way away. Or perhaps a long time ago. Something was wrong with her ears: everything sounded muffled, distant, unimportant. Her hands were trembling.

'Perhaps I should call the doctor?'

'No.' She swallowed, trying to ease the feeling in her ears, but it would not shift. 'No, I'll be fine. I think it was just the sun.'

Daisy did not want to think about Madeline Poel, but now that she had seen the name on the gravestone she found that she could not stop. She felt dizzy and breathless, the way she imagined Eunice's dog, Jasper, was feeling now, with his food dosed with poison. Unbidden, unwelcome, faces were appearing in her mind. Faces and names.

So many names.

Before Daisy Wilson there had been Violet Chambers, and before Violet Chambers there had been Annie Moberley, and before Annie Moberley there had been Alice Connell, and before Alice Connell there had been Jane Winterbottom, and before Jane Winterbottom there had been Deirdre Fincham, and before

Deirdre Fincham there had been Elise Wildersten, and before Elise Wildersten there had been Rhona McIntyre, and before Rhona McIntyre there had been someone whose name was now lost to the past, and another before her, and another before her, all just shadows in the darkness now, but before all of them, at the very beginning of it all, there had been Madeline Poel.

Daisy sat in the chair in Eunice's front room, rocking gently to and fro. Tea slopped from the cup into the saucer, and from the saucer onto the floor, but she didn't notice. The past, long denied, had her in its grip.

'Daisy?' Eunice was standing beside her. 'Daisy, my dear, whatever is wrong?' She took the cup and saucer from Daisy's hands and placed them on a nearby table.

'I used to live here,' Daisy said quietly. 'I had quite forgotten, but I used to live here when I was a child. My father had a house near the Naze, and I used to go to school in the town. I thought there was something strange when I came back. I still recognised some of the buildings, and the streets, and the pier, and the church. But a lot of things have changed. It is as if I can see the town the way it was, and the way it is, both at the same time. If I tilt my head, or narrow my eyes, I can even see them both at once. Isn't that strange?'

'Daisy, I think you need to lie down. Come on, let's take you up to the spare room. You can stay here tonight.'

Eunice led Daisy upstairs and eased her down on a single bed with white sheets and a pale blue duvet. Daisy was disoriented enough that she failed to take in anything of what she saw. Eunice took Daisy's shoes off and swung her legs onto the bed. 'Sleep for a while,' she said. 'You'll feel better when you wake up.'

'My handbag …' Daisy murmured.

'I'll get it.' Eunice went downstairs and returned, a few moments later, with Daisy's bag. She put it on a chair beside the bed, closed the curtains and left.

Daisy reached out and grabbed the handbag from the chair. Opening it up, she fished around inside until she found what she was looking for. And then, holding the secateurs close to her chest, she laid her head back on the pillow and slept.

And she dreamed about Madeline Poel and a garden in summertime, long, long ago ...

The green lawn was still dappled with shadows of rust-coloured blood, although Madeline's brothers and sisters had been taken away some time before. Carried away, limp and helpless, hands trailing down. Hands that seemed strangely deformed.

She knew that she wouldn't be seeing them again. Even though they had looked like they were sleeping, their eyes were open, staring up at the bright, bright sun. And their eyes were dry. Dry and wide.

The blades of grass were stuck together in clumps by the blood. It reminded Madeline of the way her hair went sometimes when she'd got sap in it from the trees in the garden: matted and gummy and impossible to brush out. She didn't know how they were going to clear up the garden. Perhaps they were going to wait until the rain came. Nobody seemed worried about the garden. Instead they were clustering around her mother and her grandmother, or just standing around saying nothing.

Madeline stood in the shade of a bush, fingering the ripe red berries. The poisonous berries. Every so often she glanced over at where her mother was sobbing in the arms of a neighbour. People were standing around the garden as if they didn't quite know what they were doing there. And none of them were paying any attention to her.

Off to one side her grandmother was sitting in a cane chair by the table. A policeman was sitting with her and another one was standing behind her. The policeman sitting with her was asking her questions, but she wasn't replying. She was just twisting her fingers in the material of her cardigan, making tight little spirals of cloth, her face an impassive mask hiding something feral underneath.

Her grandmother had done something bad. Madeline knew that, although she didn't understand exactly what the bad thing was. Her grandmother often did bad things. She hit Madeline and her brothers and sisters when her mother was working. She pretended to Madeline's mother that she didn't, but she lied. Sometimes she twisted their arms behind their backs, or hit them with branches, and then screamed at them that if they told their mother she would hurt them even more. And now she had, even though they never told a living soul.

Madeline took a handful of berries from the bush and crushed them slowly in her hand. The juice ran out between her fingers, red and slow, falling to the ground where it stuck the blades of grass together.

Madeline glanced over to where the tea party had been set up and then forgotten. The cups sat, ignored and forlorn, on the crisp white tablecloth.

She glanced down at her stained hands.

Perhaps her grandmother would like a drink, she thought.

Day turned into night, and dreams slipped past each other like deep-sea fish, stirring up sediment from the bottom of the ocean as they went. But as the night wore on the sediment settled and the fish hid themselves amongst rocks and strands of seaweed. By the time the sun rose and poked intrusive fingers through the gap between the curtains, Daisy Wilson had forgotten who she had been, and remembered only who she was now.

Eunice brought her a cup of tea while she was still in bed.

'How are you feeling?' she asked.

'I'm as weak as a kitten. What happened?'

'You had some kind of a fit. I think it must have been the exertion of the walk to the church, and the sun. You overdid it. Poor thing.'

'I suppose you must be right.' Daisy tried to remember what had happened the day before, but the attempt made her uneasy.

'Could you manage some breakfast?' Eunice asked.

'Feed a cold and starve a fever,' Daisy replied. 'Perhaps just a cup of tea and a slice of dry toast. I'm sorry to be a burden.'

'No burden,' Eunice said, as she headed for the door. 'It's nice to have someone around the place. I do get lonely.' She stopped and looked back. 'I'll leave the Arts and Crafts Centre closed today. I think you need to rest.'

'Nonsense,' Daisy said. 'God tempers the wind to the shorn lamb. I'm sure it will be a quiet day, and pottering around will give me time to recover.' She paused momentarily. 'Perhaps I could lie here for a while this morning and then join you later in the barn. I am still feeling a little unsteady.'

After breakfast, Eunice opened up the Arts and Crafts Centre and Daisy, having first made sure that Eunice was out of the way, spent her time making an inventory of the items in Eunice's bedroom and the spare room. She had long suspected that Eunice was a diary keeper – all artistic people kept diaries, in her experience – and she found it within a few minutes, in a drawer of the bedside cabinet. Found *them*, in fact, for there were multiple volumes going back years. Flicking through the most recent one, Daisy realised that this was all she really needed, apart from the financial records in the barn. Everything Eunice thought, believed or experienced was in there. Every memory was preserved like a flower pressed between the pages of a book. She didn't need to spend time pumping Eunice for information now – she had it all. Everything that was Eunice was now accessible to Daisy.

Which meant that there was really no reason to keep Eunice alive any more.

Determinedly, Daisy set out from Eunice's house – soon to be her house – for the barn which housed the Arts and Crafts Centre just across the way. She still felt light-headed, but she had work to do and there was no point moping around in bed. She had to up the dose of grated apricot kernels that she was putting in Jasper's food and see how long it took him to die.

That way, she could calculate the precise dose needed to kill Eunice.

In fact, Jasper died three days later.

He had been breathless and twitchy for two of those days, during which Daisy progressively increased the dose of grated apricot kernels that she was sprinkling over his food. On the morning of the third day he lay in his basket in the back of the barn, unwilling or unable to move his hind legs.

'Poor angel,' Eunice murmured, bending down to stroke his head. 'Poor, poor angel. We shall call the vet, yes we shall.'

'Let me,' Daisy said. She went to the phone and made a great play of pressing the buttons with one hand whilst her other hand unplugged the cable from beneath the phone. 'Hello?' she said to dead air. 'Is that the Tendring Veterinary Surgery? I need an urgent appointment for a dog that's having difficulty breathing.' She paused for effect. 'It *is* an emergency, yes. Nothing until tomorrow? Nothing at all?' She sighed. 'Very well. We'll bring him then. The name is Jasper. Sorry – yes, I see. The owner's name is Eunice Coleman. C-O-L-E-M-A-N. Yes, thank you.' She turned to Eunice with a mournful face as she put the phone down. 'They don't have any appointments until tomorrow afternoon. They suggest keeping Jasper warm and letting him have plenty of fluids.'

Eunice's eyes were heavy with tears. 'I don't know what I would do without Jasper. He's my constant companion. He's everything to me.'

'There is a time for every purpose under heaven,' Daisy said. 'If it is Jasper's time, then we can do nothing but make him comfortable, and be with him. And when he is gone, then *I* will be your constant companion.' *Until you in turn die, breathless and paralysed*, thought Daisy, but she kept the thought to herself.

Jasper's breath came slower and slower. At some stage during the morning, while Eunice was fussing about, finding blankets to put over him, he breathed no more.

Daisy, in contrast, breathed a sigh of relief. She had hated that little monster. Every dog had its day, that's what they said, and this particular dog's day had passed. And now Daisy had a good idea how much of the grated apricot kernels she needed in order to kill Eunice. It also looked as if the death would be mess-free, based on the way that Jasper had just slipped away. No vomiting, no diarrhoea, nothing to clean up. After the problems she'd had last time, Daisy was grateful.

Eunice sobbed inconsolably over Jasper's body. As Daisy had hoped, the dog's death had sent her into a spiral of grief which, if Daisy was any judge, would leave her even more dependent on the only person she had left.

Daisy took Jasper's body outside in a wooden box left over from a delivery some time in the past. She promised Eunice that she would take the body to the vets, and ensure that he had a decent burial. In fact, Daisy intended only to throw the box over the nearest wall when she left. She wanted as little to do with the dog now that it was dead as she had when it was alive.

Eunice spent the rest of the day lying down in her house, behind the barn. Daisy closed the Arts Centre down and joined Eunice in the house. While Eunice was sleeping, Daisy spent her time going through drawers and looking at photographs. All grist to the mill.

Later she checked in on Eunice. The woman was still asleep, snoring with a sound like bubbles forcing their way through mud. Daisy sat down on a chair beside the bed for a while, watching Eunice's face: absorbing every wrinkle and pore, every stray hair and mole. In sleep, Eunice's muscles slackened, gravity pulling the soft tissue downwards so that it seemed as if her flesh were slowly sliding off the skull beneath and pooling on the pillow. Her complexion was dry and over-powdered. The skin around her rouged lips was marked with thousands and thousands of hair-fine vertical chasms, like minuscule razor cuts. The signs of old age. The signs that the flesh was beginning to give way.

Daisy spent some time trying to twist her lips into the same shape as Eunice's; lower lip thrust forward, ends turned down, slightly parted. It wasn't that she had any delusion that she would gradually start looking like Eunice once she had taken on her identity; it was more that she wanted to fix the woman's face in her mind now, while she still could. When she was *being* Eunice, when she *was* Eunice, she wanted to be different from Daisy, from Violet and from all the ones that came before. And the best way to do that, she had found, was to hold the face in the memory, and never to look in mirrors.

Later, she rose from the chair and went downstairs to the kitchen. The percolator sitting fiercely on the marble surface frightened her, but she needed to master it. She suspected that the grated apricot kernels had a bitter taste, and she needed to mask it somehow. Strong coffee seemed like a good idea.

Girding her courage, she approached the device and tentatively pulled the glass jug out from where it sat on a circular metal hot plate. It came out surprisingly easily. Emboldened, Daisy examined the funnel-like arrangement that sat above where the jug went. There was a flap in the top which, when opened, revealed an opening where water probably went. Below that was a curved section that swung out when Daisy pulled on a projecting handle, revealing a plastic mesh filter, still damp from the last time Eunice had washed it. So – water in the top, coffee grounds in the filter, and jug underneath.

Chirpier, now she had worked out how the percolator functioned, Daisy filled the jug with water and poured it into the top of the machine. Opening a few cupboard doors, she eventually found a Portmeirion-design porcelain jar with a cork lid that proved to contain ground coffee and a plastic spoon. Before she put the coffee in the filter she reached into her handbag and retrieved the tupperware container she had brought with her. A spoonful of coffee, then a spoonful of ground apricot kernels, then a spoonful of coffee, then a spoonful of ground apricot kernels. The filter was half-full, and as Daisy was uncertain how much coffee to put in for a strong cup, she spooned in another measure of each, just for good luck. Pushing the filter holder back into the machine, she hunted around for a moment before finding a switch on the base of the percolator. When she pressed it, the switch lit up amber. Within moments she could hear the swooshing of steam from somewhere inside, followed by a reassuring *plup plup plup*. Coffee trickled into the jug in a thin stream. Coffee, and something else.

The kitchen began to fill with the rich, spiky aroma of fresh coffee, undercut with something drier and more bitter. Daisy sniffed, then quickly backed away. It hadn't occurred to her, but what if the fumes from the apricot kernels were fatal? That would be the ultimate irony – to be killed by her own poison!

Daisy stayed in the front room for ten minutes, until the sounds of coffee percolating had ceased. When she was sure that there was nothing else coming out of the machine she went back into the kitchen, holding her breath all the while, and opened the window behind the sink. A few minutes should blow any fumes safely away.

Daisy removed the jug from the hot plate, dislodging a final drip of coffee from the filter arrangement above. It fell onto the hot plate, hissing for a moment or two as it boiled away, leaving a faint trace of dry residue behind.

An oily film covered the surface of the coffee, reflecting the sunlight from the kitchen window in murky rainbows. Daisy swirled the jug around, hoping to mix it in, but the oil just circulated like something alive.

Daisy poured a mug of coffee for Eunice – a mug rather than a cup because she wanted the dose to be as high as possible. She debated putting milk in the mug, but she didn't want to dilute the poison any further. Eunice alternated in the way she took her coffee; sometimes with milk, sometimes without, depending on how she was feeling. She always took it with sugar, however, so Daisy carefully stirred two large spoonfuls into the drink.

Placing the mug of coffee on a tray, Daisy was just about to take it upstairs when a thought struck her. Biscuits! If Eunice had a biscuit with her coffee, it might mask whatever aftertaste was left by the apricot kernels.

When she got to the bedroom, Eunice was sitting upright. She was looking brighter than she had before.

'You're a marvel,' she said to Daisy. 'I really don't know what I would do without you. Now that poor Jasper is gone, I'm not sure how I'll survive. He gave me the strength to keep going.'

'Leave everything to me,' Daisy said. 'Let me be your strength. Now, drink your coffee and sleep for a while. I'll check on you later.'

Daisy watched for a while, but Eunice just rested her head back against the headboard and closed her eyes. Daisy didn't want to push her into drinking the coffee; knowing Eunice as she now did she knew that the woman just got more and more stubborn if she felt she was being ordered around. She had to want to drink the coffee herself.

Daisy left her alone, and wandered along to the back bedroom, where Eunice kept her clothes on a long metal rail that she had painted, at some earlier time, in a gypsy-like pattern of red and yellow flowers on a glossy black background. A full-length mirror had been propped against one wall. Daisy ran her hands along the clothes: frilled blouses, long skirts, kaftans and all kinds of what Daisy considered to be 'artistic' clothes. She would have to get used to them, though. When she became Eunice Coleman, she would have to wear clothes like that. Not because anyone would mistake her for Eunice, but because she was going to *become* Eunice and Eunice wore different clothes from Daisy, just as she moved differently and talked differently. It was as simple as that.

After half an hour, Daisy went to check on Eunice. The woman was asleep again, breathing heavily through her mouth. The coffee mug was empty.

On a whim, Daisy returned to the back bedroom. Selecting some clothes from the rack that she thought might just fit her, she held them up against her body and looked at herself in the mirror.

She glanced at the door. It was a risk, but she wanted to see what she looked like. She wanted to practise being Eunice.

She stripped quickly and dressed herself in the new clothes. They were on the large side, but she could take them in. And besides, artistic people wore baggy clothes, did they not?

Daisy felt edgy in Eunice's clothes while the woman was still in the house. She moved quietly along the landing and peered around the bedroom door, just to check on the progress of the poison.

The bed was empty.

Daisy rushed into the room, checking the other side of the bed just in case Eunice had fallen out and was lying hidden, but there was nobody there. Eunice had vanished.

Downstairs, the doorbell rang.

CHAPTER EIGHTEEN

Standing in Detective Chief Superintendent Rouse's office, Mark Lapslie gazed into the mild brown eyes of Martin Geherty. The expression on Geherty's face was calm, almost clinical, as he stared back at Lapslie.

Lapslie wondered where DCS Rouse had gone. Geherty was inhabiting Rouse's office as if he owned it. Perhaps, given his senior position in the Department of Justice, he did. But whatever the reason, Rouse wasn't around to support his subordinate. He'd obviously made his choice on how best to climb the slippery pole of promotion. And, not for the first time in his career, Lapslie was on his own.

'We're not giving you a choice, DCI Lapslie,' Geherty said with surprising gentleness. 'You can drop the investigation now, of your own volition, or you can have it dropped for you, but either way we are taking over, and we are going to recover Madeline Poel ourselves.'

'And what makes you think you can have my investigation dropped?' Lapslie said, although he already knew the answer.

'You've already got a reputation for instability, thanks to this neurological condition of yours. We can have you removed on medical grounds. Any evidence you've amassed will just ... go missing. Misfiled somewhere. It happens all the time.'

Lapslie walked across to the window and gazed out. Far below, the black Lexus was still idling impatiently. 'You arranged things that I'd get picked for this case from the start, didn't you?'

He saw Geherty nod, reflected in the glass of Rouse's office window. 'We did. Our psychologists put together a list of key elements of any crime that Madeline Poel was likely to commit. Based on her history and her mental state, they felt that she would be likely to murder elderly ladies who reminded her of her abusive grandmother, probably poisoning them using something natural, like berries or mushrooms, given that's the way she killed her grandmother in the first place. They also felt that she was likely to mutilate them in some way, probably by cutting their fingers off – visiting upon them the same mutilation her grandmother carried out on her brothers and sisters. There was a strong chance that she would keep changing identities – running further and further away from the child who had seen those terrible things, and running also from the knowledge that she was, in some horrible way, repeating the crimes of her grandmother. Based on that profile, we arranged for the police computer to throw your name up if any crime that met at least one of those criteria was reported. We wanted you to be put in charge of the investigation.'

'Why? Just so you could take it away from me at the last moment?'

'No – because you had the best chance of finding her for us. You had actually met Madeline Poel. You had talked to her.'

'So had your psychologists.'

Geherty shrugged. 'But they couldn't take part in an investigation without giving the game away. You were the only person who could look for Madeline Poel without *knowing* he was looking for her.'

'And yet you kept trying to stop me – taking away my resources, making things as difficult as you could. Either you wanted me to find her or you didn't.'

'We wanted you to find her, but only you. We didn't want the full force of the law descending on wherever she's hiding. You had to be made to walk a fine line – just enough resources to find her, but not to get to her before us.'

'That's madness,' Lapslie said levelly.

'Welcome to my world.'

Lapslie turned away from the window to face Geherty. 'It's a slippery slope, isn't it? You start off by covertly preparing murderers for release into an unsuspecting society, then you have to cover up their crimes when they fall back on their natures, and then ... what, exactly? You've already faked their deaths and constructed new identities for them, so you can't just rearrest them and try them again. That would give the whole game away. Do you end up having to kill *them* as well, just so the knowledge about this whole prisoner rehabilitation programme doesn't get out? Is that *right*? Is that *just*?'

Geherty shrugged. 'Fortunately it's never gone that far. There are places we can put them, if they slip back to their old ways. The US Government are happy to let us add one or two people to the roster at one of the para-legal detention centres they run, for instance, so long as we turn a blind eye to whatever extraordinary rendition flights touch down for refuelling at our airports. It's ... convenient.'

'And it's evil.'

'No,' he said patiently. 'What *they* do is evil. What *we* do is pragmatic. If it becomes known that we deliberately release murderers into society under new identities having faked their deaths, it would bring the Government down. The Minister now, and Home Secretaries for the past twenty years, would be called to account for their actions in the Old Bailey. You cannot imagine the fallout, both politically and socially. It must not be allowed to happen.'

' "Let justice prevail, though the heavens fall",' Lapslie quoted softly.

Geherty's lips pursed: the first sign of strong emotion that Lapslie had noticed. 'I studied Classics at Oxford, DCI Lapslie. I can find a quote to match any occasion or opinion as well. And you're wasting time that I could be spending recovering Madeline Poel.'

'What about the thirteen women she's already killed? And

what about the woman she's probably stalking now? Don't they deserve anything?'

Geherty flicked his head, as though dislodging a fly. 'They are dead, and they had no family or close friends. There's nobody left to get closure, and Madeline Poel will be punished by us for what she has done. What else is there?'

'The fact that you're even asking the question is proof that you're not qualified to answer it,' Lapslie said.

Geherty slipped his hand in his jacket pocket and removed a sheet of paper which had been folded, twice, into a long rectangle. 'This is a letter from DCS Rouse to you, relieving you of your responsibility for this case.' He held it out to Lapslie.

'It doesn't take force until I read it,' Lapslie said, and turned to walk out of the office.

'Don't be stupid,' Geherty snapped. 'If I have to follow you out there are a dozen witnesses out there who will see me handing this letter over.'

'The first step is always the hardest,' Lapslie said, and shut the door behind him as he exited the office. Turning, he quickly locked the door using the key he had taken from Rouse's PA earlier.

The door handle twisted as Geherty tried to open the door, then twisted again, more violently. Lapslie could hear the lock straining as Geherty threw his weight against it. He wasn't cursing or shouting, just calmly putting all his energy into trying to break the lock.

DCS Rouse's PA was watching, open-mouthed, from her desk.

'I don't know how he got into the building,' Lapslie said to her earnestly, 'but we need to keep him there until the psychiatric nurses arrive.' He leant across, lifted the receiver from her phone and pressed the button that he knew would connect it to the one in Rouse's office. Behind the locked door, which was shaking furiously, a phone began to ring. 'Keep it ringing until he answers,' Lapslie continued, 'and then leave the phone off the hook. I want to block the line.' Seeing the look in the PA's eyes, he added, 'He's known for making obscene calls from the phones of important people. Try not to listen – it'll just upset you. I'll go for help.'

He moved quickly away, taking the key with him.

As he got to the lobby, Emma Bradbury was emerging from a lift.

'Boss, I was just looking for you.'

'What's up?'

'The lists of lone elderly women in the Essex coast area that you requested have been coming in from all the hotels and estate agents and whatever that we've been calling. They're arriving by fax and email and just dictated over the phone. I've had one of the constables cross-check the list as it's been growing with the names of the dead bodies. One of them sprung straight out – Daisy Wilson. She apparently rented a flat in Leyston-by-Naze two months ago, even though she's lying dead on a slab in Doctor Catherall's mortuary.'

Lapslie nodded. 'It's where she was brought up. It's where all this started. What drove her to go back?'

Emma looked like he'd just pulled a rabbit out of a hat. 'How do you know that's where she was brought up?'

'No time to explain. I'll drive down there now. Text me the address, then clear up the loose ends here and meet me in Leyston-by-Naze. And don't tell anyone else where I'm going, or why.'

As Emma Bradbury walked away Lapslie headed out of the building and straight for his car. He reckoned he had no more than five minutes to get out of the car park before Geherty managed to get out of Rouse's office or Rouse returned and ordered the door broken down. Reaching his car, he tossed the key to Rouse's office away, gunned the engine to life and swept out of the car park, programming the satnav for Leyston-by-Naze with one hand as he steered with the other. His mobile rang eight or nine times in the next fifteen minutes, but he ignored it. Eventually, when he was on the A12 and heading east, it bleeped to indicate an incoming text message, and he tasted bitter chocolate. That would be Emma Bradbury texting Daisy Wilson's address through to him. Or DCS Rouse suspending him. Either way, he kept driving. Time to check the message later, when he was closer to his goal. While he still thought he had a career, he needed to find Madeline Poel.

He kept checking his rear view mirror as he drove, half-expecting to see a black Lexus keeping pace with him, but the cars behind him were anonymous and amorphous, blurred together into a general haze. His mind kept skipping between two poles; the one being Martin Geherty, hopefully still locked in DCS Rouse's office, the other being the one interview he'd had with Madeline Poel long ago.

He could hardly remember her now. He'd been working on his Masters Degree in Criminal Psychology, having been given time off from the police. His thesis was that there were certain key traits of a criminal personality that could be detected by a simple questionnaire, and he was talking to as many criminals as he could in order to try and determine what they were. His synaesthesia was helping, although he would never admit that in his final dissertation; there were certain key flavours that kept coming up when he heard criminals' voices, like base notes in perfume.

Madeline Poel had been small and polite, he remembered, but she hadn't liked to talk about what had happened that day at the tea party. She had been diagnosed as borderline psycho-pathic, with a score of thirty-two on the revised Hare's Psychopathy Checklist. She had actually offered him tea, he remembered, although there was nothing on the table in the interview room. When he said yes, just to see what happened, she poured him an invisible cup of tea from an invisible pot, then added invisible milk and invisible sugar. All the time he watched her, waiting for her to realise what she was doing, but she continued the charade, even asking him why he wasn't drinking.

When he had read in the newspapers that she had died of a heart attack he had felt relieved and sad at the same time. Relieved, because he had felt when he talked to her that she would never be able to function normally in society. Sad, because underneath it all she had been friendly and talkative. And because she had offered him tea.

'Everybody is dead who should be alive,' he whispered, 'and those who are alive *should* be dead.'

Colchester came and went, and the car drove on. Signs for Clacton and Frinton passed by. The car screamed across roundabouts with as minimal deviation from a straight line as Lapslie could manage. The landscape was flat and coloured in great swathes: the brown of ploughed earth, the green of fields that had been left to recover naturally and the eye-aching yellow of flowering rape plants. The sky near the horizon was a deeper blue, reflecting the unseen ocean. He passed tractors, overtaking them on straight stretches of road when there was nothing ahead. Signs for Walton-on-the-Naze flashed past, advertising the sports centre, the pier, the sea front. And then there was only Leyston ahead: the end of the land, the end of the trail.

Lapslie stopped in a lay-by and checked his mobile. There were several voicemails waiting for him, but he ignored them in favour of the one text, from Emma. It was an address in Leyston-by-Naze, followed by a simple message: *World is ending here – don't answer phone.*

The satnav guided him past the station and down a hill towards the centre of town. Suddenly there was nothing on his right apart from a low stone wall and the implacable sea, but then houses intervened again and he was dropping down into the town, past a tea room, a bingo hall and a seafood restaurant, and along the High Street with its collection of butchers and bakers and newsagents alternating with tattoo parlours and shops selling inflatable rings, beach balls and candy floss. He braked to a halt at a set of traffic lights, and heard sand crunch beneath his tyres.

The High Street petered out in a rash of fish-and-chip shops and pubs, and he found himself emerging into the other side of Leyston-by-Naze: past a long recreation ground and signs for the marina. The road was on a level with the esplanade now, running parallel to it and towards the looming mass of the Naze itself, the gnarled cliff face that towered above the town. This area, leading away from the town centre, was more residential, with detached and weather-beaten houses set back from the road in gardens filled with hardy, cactus-like plants that could stand the salt and the storms, and inhabited by retired and weather-beaten residents who revelled in their semi-isolation.

The satnav directed him to a road that lay in the shadow of the Naze, curled back on itself and felling gently back towards the town. A cool breeze blew off the sea, taking the edge off the warmth of the afternoon. He parked just down the street. The house was on a corner: a white-washed two-storey building with leaded glass windows and ivy trailing up the sides. He approached on foot, aware that he should be accompanied by Emma Bradbury at the very least, and a full Armed Response Team at best, but also aware that the option was no longer open to him. He was on his own, trying to resolve a situation despite the circumstances.

As far as he could tell from the two front doors, nestled side by side, the house had been divided into flats: one upstairs, one down. The bell for the upstairs flat was labelled with a name he didn't recognise. That left the downstairs flat as belonging to Madeline Poel, masquerading as Daisy Wilson.

He rang the bell, and waited.

When there was no response he took a small tool from his pocket, a kind of Swiss Army knife called a Leatherman that had been recommended to him years ago by Dom McGinley, looked around to check that nobody was watching from the street, and used its folding knife attachment to force his way into the downstairs flat. It was, he decided, just the icing on the cake as far as his career was concerned. And, if push came to shove, he could always claim that he thought a crime was in progress – which it probably was. Somewhere.

He could tell from the deadening silence in the hall that the flat was unoccupied. He walked into the front room. There were possessions scattered around – a cardigan, a bowl of petals, a pile of local papers – but something about it made him think of a theatrical stage set, waiting for the actors to arrive. Whatever was there was a prop, ready to support a performance. It wasn't real.

Having quickly checked the flat over to make sure that Madeline Poel wasn't asleep in the bedroom or out in the garden, Lapslie quickly searched the place without disturbing anything. Although he found some post addressed to Daisy Wilson he found nothing that mentioned Madeline Poel, and nothing that mentioned any of the previous victims. If Madeline – or Daisy, as she now was – kept trophies, or even just the kind of details she would need in order to keep twelve previous victims apparently alive, as far as the rest of the world was concerned, then she must have it all stashed away somewhere else. It certainly wasn't in the flat.

But he did find a pile of pamphlets advertising an arts and crafts centre on the outskirts of Leyston run by someone named Eunice Coleman. For some reason, Daisy Wilson was interested in it, and that gave him one more place to try if he wanted to locate her. Perhaps Eunice Coleman was her next victim. Perhaps, by now, Eunice Coleman was her.

The arts and crafts centre was probably twenty minutes away, according to the satnav in his car. He pulled away from his parking spot and accelerated on down the road, back towards Leyston town centre.

He found it along a muddy track. There were two buildings

in sight: a sad, barn-like structure that was probably the centre itself and an impressive farmhouse built of red brick sat a hundred yards or so beyond.

Lapslie turned his ignition off and got out of the car. The fan in the engine ran on for a few seconds, disturbing the silence of the countryside, then it fell silent. The only sounds were the ticks of his cooling engine and the singing of the birds.

Eunice Coleman deserved to know that she was in danger, and she might know where Madeline Poel – now calling herself Daisy Wilson, of course – could be found. Daisy might even be there, and Lapslie was unable to think of any circumstances in which he couldn't manage to arrest her without help. She was only an old woman, when all was said and done.

He walked over to the barn. Mid-afternoon, and the arts and crafts centre should have been open, according to the times displayed on the door, but it was locked. He banged on the door, just in case, and peered through the smeared glass, but there was nobody about. He headed across to the house.

Lapslie rang the doorbell, and waited. Just as he was about to ring it again, the door opened. A woman looked at him enquiringly. She was wearing a velvet waistcoat over a frilled blouse, and a purple skirt with a fringed hem that brushed the floor.

'Mrs Coleman? Mrs Eunice Coleman?'

She nodded. 'None other,' she said. 'Can I help you?'

He waited for the taste of lychees, but there was nothing save a hint, perhaps just his imagination at work. Was this the same woman who had poured an invisible cup of tea for him in an interview room in Broadmoor? She had aged, and her hair was different. It might have been her, but it might also have been Eunice Coleman. He wasn't sure.

'Detective Chief Inspector Mark Lapslie,' he said. 'I need to talk to you. I'm looking for a woman named Daisy Wilson.'

She smiled. 'Daisy's not here right now,' she said. 'I suppose you'd better come in. I've made a pot of coffee – would you like some?'

Lapslie stepped inside the house. Shadows enfolded him. There was a smell of sickness wafting through the hall, but he didn't know where it emanated from. Perhaps Eunice was lying upstairs, dying. Perhaps this was Eunice walking down the hall in front of him. He just didn't know.

She led him into a cluttered room in which sofas and armchairs fought for space with low tables and potted plants. 'Make yourself comfortable,' she said. 'I'll just be a minute. Sorry if I'm a bit dozy, by the way – I had a strange nap this afternoon.'

She vanished off towards what he assumed was the kitchen. He listened out for movements elsewhere in the house, but there was nothing. He still wasn't sure, and he couldn't afford to get this wrong.

The woman calling herself Eunice Coleman came back into the room with a coffee jug and two cups on a tray. She seemed surprised to find him still standing. 'You're making me nervous,' she said, putting the tray onto a side table and gesturing towards the sofa. He sat, and while she poured two cups of coffee he looked around the room. There were paintings of various kinds on the walls – some landscapes, some portraits and some abstracts – and all of the chairs were covered with embroidered throws. Obviously Eunice Coleman brought her work home with her.

'Milk?' Still, that maddening uncertainty. Did her voice taste of lychees, or was he hoping too hard that it would?

'Please.'

'Help yourself to sugar.' She put the cup on another table within his reach, then sat down in one of the armchairs holding her own cup. 'So, what can I do for you, Detective Chief Inspector Lapslie?' she asked.

'About Daisy Wilson ...' he said, watching the cup in her hands. It didn't tremble.

'Mad as a box of frogs, the dear thing,' she said. 'Yes, she's been helping me out at the crafts centre. I think she's gone to the pharmacy. What did you want her for?'

'I need to ask her some questions.' He raised his cup to his lips, then paused as he watched her face.

'What kinds of questions?'

'Questions about some women she might know.'

'Perhaps I could help. Daisy doesn't talk about her friends much, but she might have mentioned their names.'

'Has she ever referred to Wendy Maltravers?'

'No.'

'Violet Chambers?'

'I don't think so. Don't let your coffee get cold, by the way.'

'Alice Connell, Rhona McIntyre, Deirdre Fincham, Kim Stothard...?'

'I'm sure I would have remembered. They are very distinctive names.'

He raised the cup to his mouth. The steam prickled against his skin. There was something spicy about it. His lips felt hot and swollen.

Eunice Coleman was watching him intently. She hadn't drunk any of her own coffee either.

'And what about Madeline Poel?' he said carefully, and watched as her hand twitched, sending coffee splashing across her lap.

CHAPTER NINETEEN

The sudden flush of heat on Daisy's leg shocked her, making her twitch again. The cup clattered in the saucer. 'Oh dear,' she said automatically, 'Many a slip 'twixt cup and lip, as they say. I'll just go and get a tea towel. I won't be a moment.'

She stood up, hesitating for a moment, then placed her cup and saucer down on the tray and walked off into the kitchen. 'I don't believe Daisy ever mentioned Madeline Poel,' she called back to the police officer who was sitting in Eunice's living room. 'No, I don't believe she mentioned her at all. Were they friends?'

Once in the kitchen she leaned on one of the work surfaces for a few moments, trying to regain her composure. Whoever this policeman was – and he looked strangely familiar to her, as if they had met before under different circumstances – he knew too much. He knew names that Daisy herself thought she had forgotten.

Including that of Madeline Poel.

Patting herself down with a cloth, Daisy's mind was frantically going over what he had said, looking for some explanation of how he had found her. The only possible way was if he'd discovered the pamphlets advertising the Arts and Crafts Centre in her flat, and that meant she had nowhere to retreat to. Her safe haven was compromised, contaminated. She could never go back there again. The only thing that was saving her from arrest now was that the policeman thought she was Eunice Coleman. Or perhaps he wasn't sure whether she was Eunice or not and was trying to find out. Either way, she had to play along, and get out of Eunice's house as soon as she possibly could.

But where would she go? Even her special place was lost to her now; her garden, with its beautiful scents and flowers. She had to assume the police knew about it, although she couldn't think of any way they could have found out. And that meant they had also found her little tea party.

All lost. All gone.

Black despair threatened to engulf her. She leaned against the refrigerator as her legs threatened to give way. Her heart was racing, and she could feel her breath rasping in her chest. The complex web of bank accounts and building society accounts was of no use to her any more. All that money, all that security, all those identities were lost now, washed away by the tide of circumstance.

She had to be strong. She had to move forward. She couldn't have expected her luck to last forever: the pitcher goes so often to the well that it is broken at last, wasn't that what they said? She'd started with nothing before; she could do it again. She would have to cut her coat according to her cloth; things would be hard for a while, but she would survive. After all, after a storm comes a calm.

Concentrating on those old, familiar proverbs, Daisy felt her heart slow and her breathing return to something approaching normal. The policeman wouldn't be a problem for long: the moment he had mentioned her name – well, Daisy Wilson's name – she knew that she had to get him inside the house and get him to drink some of the coffee that she had so carefully prepared for Eunice. With luck, he would be comatose before he finished the cup and dead within the hour.

Which reminded her – where was Eunice? Despite the way Daisy had dosed her with cyanide she wasn't in the bedroom upstairs any more. When Daisy heard the doorbell ring she had been terrified that Eunice had staggered downstairs and was going to open the door in some kind of delirium, but there was no sign of her. Where could she have got to?

That could wait. First things first: she had to rid herself of this policeman.

Pulling open the cutlery drawer, she retrieved a butcher's knife from the plastic tray where it sat: a grey triangle of metal that came to a razor-sharp point. She didn't like the idea of using a knife, but it was a useful backup. Just in case.

She emerged from the kitchen holding a tea towel behind which the knife sat, comfortable in her hand. 'Clumsy of me,' she said. 'I do apologise.'

The policeman was holding an empty cup. He looked at her with a slight frown, twin wrinkles forming between his eyebrows.

'Oh, my dear,' she said with exaggerated concern, 'you do drink quickly. Would you like another cup?'

'No ... no thank you,' he said. She noticed with pleasure that his hand was trembling slightly, and there was a mist of perspiration across his forehead. 'The coffee's a little ... a little strong for me. I'm fine with just the one cup.'

'As you wish,' she said, sitting. One cup should be enough. She had proved that with Jasper the dog, and then again with Eunice – wherever she was. A man was a slightly unknown quantity – she had never poisoned anyone apart from women before – but she didn't think the difference in size or sex would delay things by more than a few minutes. And if it did, well, there was always the knife.

The policeman put his cup down on the table beside him. He misjudged the distance and fumbled slightly, banging the saucer hard on the varnished surface. 'I think I should be ... going ...' he said. 'Perhaps I could come back when Daisy Wilson is here.' He tried to stand, but he couldn't seem to co-ordinate his movements. His hands slipped off the arms of the chair, pitching him sideways, and he straightened up slowly. 'What's happening?' he said vaguely.

'You are probably feeling your stomach twisting,' Daisy

said. She leaned back in her chair, resting the towel-wrapped knife on her lap. 'That will be your digestive system hydrolysing the cyanogenic glycosides from the apricot kernels into hydrocyanic acid. Or cyanide, if you prefer. You will start to feel increasingly tired as the cyanide is carried through your body, and you may start to vomit, although I really hope not. It's such a tedious business, clearing it up. That's the trouble with poison, though – the body always seems to want to expel it, although it's usually too late.'

'Apricots?' the policeman said.

'Apricot *kernels*,' she corrected. 'I grated them up and mixed the powder with the ground coffee. I hoped that the bitterness of the coffee would cover any taste. *Could* you taste anything? I really would like to know. I may want to use this method again, at some stage. On another old woman.'

He lurched forward in his chair, and Daisy allowed the tea towel to drop away to let the policeman see that she was holding the knife. The blade gleamed in the light. 'I suggest you stay where you are while the poison gets to work. If you try to get up, I will have to stab you, and that would be a shame.'

'Madeline,' he said. 'Madeline Poel.'

'No.' She shook her head firmly. 'There is no Madeline Poel. I am Daisy Wilson now, just as I was Violet Chambers before and I will be Eunice Coleman next. Madeline is long gone.'

'You become these people. You take on their identities.'

'I have always had a knack for imitation. I enjoy watching people, working out their little foibles and habits. And it has paid me dividends over the years.'

'But you don't do it for the money, do you?'

'The money helps,' she said, almost unwillingly. 'It makes me comfortable.' She leaned forward. 'How are you feeling, by the way? Are your joints tingling yet? Can you feel the dryness in your mouth?'

'But you aren't rich, and you never will be. You choose old

ladies who won't be missed, but you also choose ones who have a small amount of money. Nothing too obvious.'

'I so dislike ostentation,' she said. 'You must be feeling the discomfort in your bowels now. That will get worse. Much worse. Again, the clearing up will be wearisome, but it will be worth it for the effect.'

'But the money isn't that important,' he pressed. 'You do it for the comfort, of course, but you could have stopped at any stage. You could have stopped when you were Rhona, or Deirdre, or Kim, or Violet, or Daisy. What was it that kept you moving?'

Daisy glanced away from him. His questions were disturbing her. She would much rather he died in silence, or at most with some groaning and gasping.

'Habit, I suppose,' she said eventually. 'Your head will be throbbing, I think. I will enjoy watching you die.'

'What were you running from?'

'Nothing. I just wanted to be safe.' She raised the knife and pointed it at him. 'We have met before, haven't we? A long time ago. I offered you tea then, as well.'

'*What were you running from?*'

She suddenly flung her arm out, knocking the small table over with the knife and sending her forgotten coffee splashing across the room. 'My *grandmother*!' she screamed, the words tumbling out of her in a rush, almost colliding with each other. 'I was running from my *grandmother*, and what she did to me, and what she did to my sisters and my brothers, but she kept following me. Whenever I thought I'd got away from her I would turn around and see her reflection, or catch sight of her from the corner of my eye. I had to keep on running. I had to get away from her and what she did!'

'And what you did,' the policeman said. 'You killed her. You poisoned her.'

'She deserved it. She kept hurting us. And then ... and then ...' Tears were suddenly coursing down her cheeks as

273

she remembered back to the garden, and the heat, and the way little Kate screamed and screamed as the blades of the secateurs came together and her thumb fell away, trailing a ribbon of blood behind it.

'And you ended up here. In Leyston, where it all started. Where Madeline was born.'

'What goes around, comes around,' she said slowly. 'That's what they say, isn't it? I never really understood that before, but it's true.'

'And Eunice? The real Eunice Coleman? Did you kill her as well? Did you take out on her this bizarre retribution you've been carrying out on your dead grandmother for all these years?'

'She is upstairs somewhere: comatose, as you will be. She managed to stagger out of the bedroom. I assume she is in the bathroom, or the spare room. When I have finished with you I will go and check on her.'

The policeman straightened in his chair. His face lost its slackness, its vacancy. 'We found your house,' he said. 'We're digging up your garden. The people at your tea party have all gone home, I'm afraid. It's over, Madeline. And you are under arrest for the murders of Daisy Wilson, Wendy Maltravers, Rhona McIntyre, Violet Chambers, Alice Connell, Kim Stothard, Deirdre Fincham and six other as yet unidentified women, as well as the attempted murder of Eunice Coleman.'

Daisy just gaped at the policeman. 'But – the coffee? You drank it!'

'I poured it away,' he said impatiently, 'into one of your potted plants. One of *Eunice*'s potted plants.'

'No!' she screamed, and leaped at him, knife raised. He caught her arm as her body crashed against him and pushed her backwards, holding onto the knife. She staggered back, the seat of the armchair catching her beneath her knees and forcing her to sit down suddenly. 'No!' she said again, the anger replaced with denial.

'We're going upstairs,' he said. 'Eunice Coleman might still be alive up there.'

Grabbing her wrists, he hauled her up from the chair and pushed her ahead of him up the stairs to the first floor. She squirmed in his grip, but she had no strength left. She could feel her bones grinding together beneath his fingers. His rough masculinity overpowered her, rendering her helpless as he took the knife away from her and threw it across the hall. Everything she had, she had invested in other identities. There was nothing left to fight with.

The policeman moved towards the front of the house, to the master bedroom where Daisy had left Eunice, dying. He pulled Daisy along behind him. Pushing open the door, he glanced around the room, but she already knew that he would find nothing.

He pulled her after him to the next room, the spare bedroom, but it was empty as well. The bathroom was at the end of the hall, and he pushed the door open with one hand while keeping Daisy's wrist pinioned with the other. The moment the door opened, Daisy could smell the sour smell of fresh vomit.

Eunice was lying twisted in the bath. Her face was glossy with sweat. Blood was trickling from her lips where she had bitten through them. Daisy could almost see the miasma of decay and death rising up from every pore and every orifice of her body.

'Stay here,' the policeman ordered, and pushed Daisy down on the toilet seat. He moved across to Eunice to check her pulse, then quickly turned her into the recovery position so that if she threw up again she wouldn't choke. Not that it would do any good. Daisy had watched enough old women die to know that Eunice was beyond all help now. Like a barnacle-encrusted lifeboat heading down a slipway into a cold, dark ocean, there was no calling her back. The journey into death, once begun, could not be reversed.

The policeman had taken a mobile phone out of his jacket and was calling for an ambulance, and for extra police. While he was distracted, Daisy slipped quietly out of the bathroom and into the hall.

There was no escape for her now.

No, she was wrong. There was one avenue left, if she dared take it.

Moving quietly but rapidly, Daisy descended the stairs to the hall. She cast a longing glance at the front door, but where would she go? She had no car, and the police would hardly have to exert themselves to find her waiting for the bus at the bottom of the road. No, she would not demean herself by running away like that.

Instead, Daisy turned and headed toward the kitchen.

The coffee pot was still where she had left it, sitting on the hot plate, half-full of black and steaming liquid. She reached out for it and picked it up by the handle. The weight of the jug almost overbalanced her, and she had to put out her other hand and hold the worktop to prevent herself falling.

For a moment she debated pouring the coffee into a cup, placing a splash of milk and a spoonful of sugar in it, just the way she liked it, and then drinking it slowly, in a civilised manner, but she thought she could hear the sound of footsteps pounding on the stairs, so she brought the glass jug to her lips and gulped the coffee down, tipping the jug further and further back. Steam wreathed her head, bringing beads of perspiration out on her forehead. The glass burned her lips and the liquid scalded her throat, but she kept on going. She could feel a growing heat in her stomach, spreading through her abdomen. Her mouth was raw, blistered, the coffee searing her throat like acid as it poured into her body.

Someone knocked the jug from her hands, and somewhere in the distance Daisy heard it smash against the wall, but her world was consumed by the fire in her stomach now. She fell forward, trying to stop herself from retching, but the heat of the coffee had made her throat close up and she could hardly take a breath.

Hands caught her from behind and lowered her to the kitchen floor. Tears blurred her eyes. Someone was talking urgently but the words slipped past her.

She seemed to have been lying down for a long time, although she had little sense of time passing. Pain creased across her stomach and sent tendrils along her arms and legs. Shivers racked her body. Snatches of meaningless conversation drifted past her – 'The woman upstairs is dead, boss', 'Where the hell's that ambulance?', 'DCS Rouse is having kittens back at the HQ!' – but it was all remote, abstract.

What was real was the gateway ahead of her. A hedge led off to either side, but through the gap she could see flowers of every hue. Entranced, she moved towards the gateway, and was not surprised when it swung open at her approach.

A path led through the garden, and she followed it eagerly. On her left was a bed of bright blue Cuban lilies virtually dripping with poisonous glycosides; on her right a clutch of Star-of-Bethlehem plants reached their little white hands up to heaven, filled with lethal convallatoxin and convalloside. Beyond them, on both sides of the path, Daisy could make out a profusion of water arum, with its bright red berries and its roots laden with deadly calcium oxalate raphides. And around them all, the oval green leaves of ipecacuanha plants, source of the drug emetine which could take weeks to kill if enough was given, and years to recover from if too little was used.

'I *will* escape her,' she said firmly. 'I *will*,' and as her legs gave way, dropping her to the floor amongst the plants, the beautiful, beautiful plants, they reached out to enfold her with their tender stems and cover her mortal body with their eternal leaves and petals. And finally, nestled in the bosom of her beloved plants, she found the peace she had craved all those long years.